Ordinary EVIL

BOOK FIVE OF THE SYDNEY LEGAL SERIES

CHRIS TAYLOR

LCT Productions Pty Ltd
18364 Kamilaroi Highway, Narrabri NSW 2390

ISBN. 978-1-925119-54-1 (Paperback)

Ordinary Evil is a work of fiction. Names, characters, places, brands, media and incidents either are the product of the author's imagination or are used fictitiously. Any resemblance to actual persons, living or dead, events, or locales, is entirely coincidental.

Published in the United States of America.

BOOKS BY CHRIS TAYLOR

THE MUNRO FAMILY SERIES

The Profiler
The Investigator
The Predator
The Betrayal
The Deception
The Negotiator
The Christmas Vigil
The Ransom
The Defendant
The Shooting
The Maker
(Available in Audio)

THE SYDNEY HARBOUR HOSPITAL SERIES

The Perfect Husband
The Body Thief
The Baby Snatchers
The Final Bullet
The Debt Collector
The Lab Test
The Stolen Identity
The Cliff-top Killer
The Likeable Fraudster

THE SYDNEY LEGAL SERIES

An Accidental Murderer
At the Hand of Her Father
A Woman Scorned
Lies and Deception
Ordinary Evil
The Ties That Bind
The Perfect Crime
Malicious Love
Toxic Inheritance

THIS IS WHERE IT ENDS SERIES

Jessie's story

Ryan's story
Holly's story
Sarah's story
Veronica's story

THE CRAIGDON FAMILY SERIES
Callum
Joel
Isabella
Nicholas
Sophia
Flynn
Noah
Logan
Elizabeth

THE BARRINGTON FAMILY SERIES
Broken Lives
Broken Promises
Broken Bonds
Broken Spirits
Broken Vows
Broken Minds
Broken Dreams
Broken Hearts
Broken Homes

Get a FREE book when you sign up for Chris Taylor's newsletter at: www.christaylorauthor.com.au

Love Audiobooks? Check out Chris Taylor Books on audio on Audible.com, Amazon.com and the iBooks store.

Join Chris Taylor's Facebook reader group/fan page and be among the first to receive news of book releases, read and review books prior to release and other amazing offers. Join Now at: www.facebook.com/groups/1758023621144744/

Find out more about all of Chris Taylor's books, by visiting her website at: www.christaylorauthor.com.au/about/books

DEDICATION

This book is dedicated to Angus, Imogen, Rory, Millie and Madeleine for all the hours, days, weeks, years you have travelled on the school bus and lived to tell the tale!

And as always, to my very own sexy hero: my husband, Linden. I love you to the moon and back.

Acknowledgments

As usual, no book comes into being without a lot of help and support by my friends and family. A world of thanks must go to my wonderful editor, Pat Thomas. Thank you for everything that you do to make my stories even more amazing than I could ever dare to dream. To former Detective Superintendent Michael Kilfoyle, thank you for lending my story credibility. Any mistakes are wholly my own.

To Damon Freeman, Alisha Moore and all of the staff at damonza.com, thank you for yet another fantastic cover. To my sister, Nicole Guihot and to my friend, Ally Thomson, thank you for your excellent editorial comments, proof reading skills and suggestions. I hope you like the final result.

To Amy Atwell and her dedicated staff at Author EMS who are so much more than book formatters. Amy, once again, thank you for your magic.

To the fantastic writer organizations such as Romance Writers of Australia, Romance Writers of America and Romance Writers of New Zealand for all the help, support and encouragement they offer new and aspiring writers, including me.

To my readers, thank you for your support and love for my stories. Your encouragement and enjoyment make this journey all worthwhile.

And lastly, to my friends and family, especially my husband and children. Thank you for putting up with late dinners and even later conversations as I've emerged day after day from the sometimes scary but always enthralling world I've created on my computer.

PROLOGUE

The squeals of laughter from the little children sent a rush of excitement through his veins. Hidden as he was behind an ancient fig tree, he was not only shaded by the huge branches, he had a perfect view of the school yard. It was playtime and the children had been freed by the bell.

A group of boys shouted and tussled over a football. Three girls played with a skipping rope. A little further over, a solitary child sat on a bench, reading a book. He couldn't see the title, but he bet it was one of the Harry Potter books. The kids couldn't get enough of those. He ought to know. He spent enough time watching them, cataloguing their habits, knowing who needed a friend. And it wasn't only their friends he noticed.

He paid particular attention to those kids who headed for home alone. They were his favorites, the ones he fantasized over when he was back in the privacy of his bedroom, alone and in the dark. As he watched them play, the beast inside him urged him to snatch one there and then, but he resisted, just as he'd resisted similar predilections for so many long months.

He was ashamed of his need to be close to little children—as close as two people could get. And yet, the beast was getting restless. He could feel it way down deep inside. It refused to be silenced. Sooner or later, it would force him to act. It was best that he be prepared.

Keeping careful note of the special ones was the least of what he had to do. When the beast demanded appeasement, he needed to be ready. The more preparation he made beforehand, the less likely he was to be found out. That was part of the game. The secrecy. Getting away with something so hideously wonderful. He smiled at the thought.

Chuckling quietly to himself, he undid the button on his jeans and slid down his zipper. Concealed behind the fig tree, he slipped his hand into his pants. His cock was hard and throbbing, like it always was right before he made his move. Soon, he'd bring an offering to the beast and the animal inside him would be satisfied.

Until next time. Oh yes, there was always a next time...

CHAPTER 1

Daisy Green pulled her cell phone from the pocket of her suit jacket and checked the time. She grimaced. If she didn't get a move on, she'd be late collecting her daughter from the bus stop. Again.

Emma had barely spoken to her during the short walk to their house the last time she'd been late and Daisy didn't blame her. It seemed more and more often, Daisy was held up at work and her nine-year-old was forced to walk the two hundred yards from the bus stop to their home on her own.

It wasn't like Daisy planned it that way. She tried really hard to leave work in time to meet Emma's bus. It was just that her job as a lawyer at the prestigious Sydney Legal didn't always run on time parameters that made sense and it seemed like the day was barely beginning when half-past three rolled around. Often she was meeting with clients or on the phone and it was difficult to cut either activity short, particularly when the client was a juvenile in trouble with the law.

As a child advocate, Daisy loved her work, but it was often quite stressful and upsetting and she found it hard to leave her young clients in the middle of a serious conversation. In those moments, doing the best she could for them was the only thing on her mind. Collecting her daughter from the bus stop slipped from her awareness. Not for the first time she wished she had someone she could rely on to meet Emma every day. The fact was, there was no one.

Daisy thought of her husband and closed her eyes on a quiet sigh. Pete had been gone five years. It should have been long enough for her to adjust to living life on her own. Even before his death, he'd barely spent more than a month or two at a time at home. As an officer in the Australian Army, he'd often been sent on deployment. Over the course of their marriage, he'd done three tours of Afghanistan before he was killed by an improvised explosive device. The vehicle he'd been traveling in had run right over the IED. The driver and two of Pete's colleagues had also been killed.

It saddened her that Emma would never really know her father. Their daughter had been four when Pete died. All of her memories of the man who'd adored her were those of a young child and what Daisy had relayed to her through stories of the past and the photos and pictures that filled nearly every room in their house. Some days, Daisy wondered if it was healthy to have so many reminders of Pete, but she couldn't bring herself to remove any of them.

The sound of the phone ringing at her elbow interrupted her morose thoughts. She leaned over to answer it and then paused. If she didn't leave now, she'd be late and Emma would give her the silent treatment again. It wasn't that her daughter meant to be rude. That was just how she expressed her disappointment that her mother hadn't made it to the bus stop in time.

Daisy understood Emma's insecurity and tried hard not to exacerbate it by being late. Still, work had a way of turning her best intentions on their head. But it wouldn't happen today.

Resolutely, she ignored the phone and pushed away from her desk. She gathered her handbag and coat from the wooden locker that stood in one corner of the room. The phone continued to ring, but she forced the guilt aside and strode to the door. With a brief wave of farewell to her secretary on her way past the reception desk, she headed toward the elevators.

A gust of wind blew up the street and lifted strands of Daisy's hair. The ends of her long coat flapped and she shivered and pulled it closer. Winter was well upon them and with it the chilly air. To top it off, the clouds overhead were dark and heavy. A storm was on the way. She only hoped the rain held off until she and Emma made it home. Spying the familiar yellow school bus just up ahead, she sighed in relief.

"Momma! Momma! You made it!"

The bus pulled away from the curb and Emma came running toward her. Daisy smiled when her daughter threw herself at her. Daisy laughed and hugged Emma close, pressing a kiss against her blond curls.

"Of course I made it, honey!"

"Last Friday you were late and I had to walk most of the way alone," her daughter muttered, her tone faintly accusatory.

Daisy nodded. "You're right and I'm still sorry about that. Sometimes things come up at work and it's hard to get away. I—"

"I know. You're a very important person with a very important job," Emma interrupted.

Daisy frowned and wondered where Emma had gained her insight. *Had she been talking to some of her friends, the daughters of two other lawyers Daisy worked with?* The three of them often bemoaned their workload and the difficulty they had leaving the office on time. At least the other two had husbands to help share the burden at home. Daisy didn't have anyone; even her parents had passed away.

"We got to do art today at school, Momma. I painted a picture of my dad."

Daisy's heart skipped a beat and she swallowed past the lump that formed in her throat. "Did you, honey? That's nice."

"Yes, he was tall and strong with big muscles. And he had curly blond hair and blue eyes, just like mine. And the nicest smile you'd ever seen. You always tell me how much you loved his smile."

Daisy stared at her daughter in shock, a little taken aback. Emma looked at her mom, her face a picture of innocence. Yes, she looked like her father, a father she'd never know... Daisy blinked back tears and pulled her daughter close.

"You're right, honey. Your daddy did have a lovely smile."

Emma pulled back and regarded her mother intently. "Do you still miss him?"

A surge of emotion tightened Daisy's chest, blocking off her air supply. She forced herself to reply: "Yes, sweetheart. I miss him very much." It wasn't a lie. After all, they'd had a lot of happy times together. It was only later near the end that things went off course...

"Do you think I'll ever have another daddy?"

Daisy started in surprise. "Why would you ask something like that?"

Emma shrugged and stared at the ground. "I don't know. Annie Walker said she's getting a new daddy. Her momma met him at the hardware store a few months ago. He's moving in with them over the weekend."

Daisy's mind spun as she tried to think of something to say. The thought of dating again filled her with panic. Despite the gentle urging of her colleagues and the recent marriage of her best friend, Sally-Ann Li, she'd resisted their attempts at matchmaking. She was happy on her own. She didn't need the complications of a man in her life...

Most of the time, she even believed that.

Giving Emma another quick hug, she took the

coward's way out and avoided the question. Opening the front gate to their modest bungalow, she gently pushed her little girl forward. "Let's go inside. It's getting cold out."

As if on cue, another gust of wind blew across the path in front of them and sent dry leaves and grass clippings dancing in the air. Together they climbed the wide front steps to the porch. After sharing a pitcher of hot chocolate and a plate of cookies, Daisy urged her daughter to attend to her homework. Emma pulled a face and sighed.

"But, Momma!"

"No 'buts,' Emma. You know the drill. We always do our homework after school. Now, it's been more than thirty minutes since we arrived home. Go and get your reader and I'll join you on the couch."

With exaggerated reluctance, Emma slid off the stool near the kitchen counter and dragged her feet toward her school bag. The sound of Daisy's phone ringing broke the silence. Tugging it out of her pocket, she glanced at the screen and answered it.

"Hi, Marcie. How are you?"

"Daisy! Thank goodness you answered! Did you meet Emma today at the bus stop?"

Daisy frowned at the fear in the woman's voice. "Yes, of course. She's here with me now. Is there something wrong?"

"Did you happen to notice if Lila-Jane was still on the bus?"

"Um, no. I'm sorry. I wasn't looking for her. Why? Is something wrong?"

"Lila-Jane hasn't made it home. I called the bus

driver and he said he dropped her on time at her usual stop. She's the last one to get off. She should have been here by now. I got caught up in traffic and arrived home a little late. I've already walked her bus route. She's nowhere to be found. Can you ask Emma if she talked to Lila-Jane on the bus? Perhaps she said something to her about her plans?"

Concern swirled in Daisy's stomach. "Of course. Hang on." Covering the mouthpiece, Daisy waved toward her daughter to gain her attention.

"Honey, did you see Lila-Jane Morrissey on the bus this afternoon?"

"Yes. She was sitting a few rows behind me."

"Did you speak with her?"

"No, but she was still on the bus when I climbed off."

Daisy nodded and returned her attention to the phone. "I'm sorry, Marcie. Emma didn't speak with Lila-Jane this afternoon."

The woman on the other end of the phone cried out in a voice that was now tinged with panic. "Oh, my heavens! Where *is* she? She knows better than to go wandering off. She knows the rules. She's to come straight home after she gets off the bus. No detours. I knew I shouldn't have started letting her walk home by herself. It's only that, she's just turned ten and she kept bugging me, telling me she was old enough to come home from the bus herself. After all, it's only half a block. *Oh, God!* What if something's happened to her? What if someone saw her get off the bus and kidnapped her?"

Marcie's tone rose to a strident cry filled with fear and panic, and as a mother, Daisy immediately understood. At the same time, she made an effort to comfort and calm the woman.

"I'm sure she'll turn up, Marcie. It's only been about twenty minutes, right? Perhaps she got distracted on the way home. There's a park right by your place. Did you check there?"

"Yes! I've checked everywhere! I can't find her!"

"Are you sure she got off the bus?"

"Yes! I already told you. I called Larry Grayson. He said he dropped her at her usual stop."

Daisy fell silent and tried to ignore the increasing dread that trickled into her veins. Unconsciously, she moved closer to Emma. "Is there anything I can do? Perhaps I can come over and help look for her with you?"

"*Would you?* All I want to do is call the police, but when I start to dial the number I feel foolish. She hasn't been gone long. I don't want to waste their time."

"I understand and of course I'm happy to help, and Emma can help, too. We'll come right away."

The woman's relief was palpable. "Thank you, Daisy! I really appreciate it. I'm sure I'm overreacting, but she's my baby and she's never been late before. I just want her home."

"We'll find her, I'm certain." Daisy reassured the woman and prayed silently that her words would prove true.

Ending the call, she tossed her phone into her handbag and once again took Emma's hand.

Walking quickly, she headed back down the steps.

"Where are we going?" Emma asked.

"Lila-Jane hasn't come home from school. Her mother's a little concerned. We're going over to her place to help look for her."

Emma frowned. "Did she miss her stop?"

"No. Lila-Jane's mom called the bus driver. He said he dropped her off not long after you."

"Maybe one of her neighbors has puppies, like the Owens family do. I love stopping by their place to pat the puppies."

Daisy stared down at her daughter in surprise. "Do you stop there on the days when I've been late meeting you at the bus stop?"

Emma kept her gaze focused on her feet. She scuffed the pavement with her shoe. "Yes. Sometimes. But I never stay more than a few minutes."

Daisy opened her mouth to reprimand her daughter and then closed it again. It wasn't Emma's fault that sometimes her mother was late meeting her off the bus. Coming to a halt, she bent down until she and her daughter were on eye level.

"I know how much you love puppies, Em, but it's important you listen to me. I don't want you stopping on your way home for anything. I'll try even harder to make sure I'm here on time, but if I'm not and you start walking home, I want you to promise me you'll go *straight* home. No stopping for puppies, or anything else. Do you understand?"

"But, Mom—"

"No 'buts,' Emma." Taking her daughter by the arms, Daisy maintained stern eye contact. "This is important. I need to know that you'll do as I say."

A stubborn expression crossed her young daughter's face and Daisy's heart clenched at the sight. She looked so much like her father... Still, this was important and Daisy wasn't about to give in.

"Emma..." Her voice held a warning.

The little girl's shoulders slumped on a sigh and she slowly lowered her gaze. "It's not like I go into their yard. Mom. It's only if the puppies are close enough to the fence. I—"

"If you want to pat the puppies, honey, we can do it when I get home. Even on the few occasions I haven't been here to meet you off the bus, I haven't been far away. Now, I need you to tell me you're on board with this and that you'll do as I say."

The girl remained silent. "Emma? Look at me." Daisy's tone brooked no argument. With another sigh, Emma looked up at her.

"No stopping for the puppies, okay?"

"Okay." The words came reluctantly, but were issued just the same.

"Promise?"

"Promise."

Daisy hugged her daughter close and then, just as swiftly, set her away. "We need to hurry. I promised Lila-Jane's mom we'd help look for her daughter. Come on."

"Do you think Lila-Jane ran away?" Emma asked.

Daisy frowned. "No, honey. Why would you say that? Did Lila-Jane mention something to you?"

"No, but I'm reading a book about a boy who lives with his evil step-mother and he decides to run away."

"Lila-Jane's mom is lovely. I'm sure her daughter hasn't run away."

Emma shrugged as if the issue was of no real concern. "Whatever."

At the thought of Marcie's desperation, Daisy took hold of Emma's hand and together they picked up their pace. In no time at all, the two of them had climbed the steps to Marcie's house. Only a couple of blocks away, the brick bungalow was similar in style, age and size to the one Daisy owned, except Marcie's garden beds were filled with flowers. Even in the middle of winter, Marcie had managed to make things grow. Daisy could only dream of the day she'd have the time to put into a garden...

Pushing that thought aside, she pressed the doorbell. Almost instantly, the door was opened and Marcie appeared. Her mouth was pinched with worry, her face was pale and drawn.

"Oh, thank goodness you're here! Just knowing I have someone else looking for her is such a relief."

Daisy offered a smile of reassurance. "We'll find her, Marcie."

Ignoring her comment, Marcie bent low and spoke urgently to Emma. "Are you *sure* you didn't talk to Lila-Jane on the bus?"

"Yes, I'm sure. She was behind me, sitting

opposite Jonathon Cleaver. He's in her class. He gets off a couple of stops before her. Maybe you should ask him."

Marcie immediately stood and looked hopefully at Daisy. "Do you have Mary Cleaver's number? Perhaps Lila-Jane said something to him about where she was going?"

Daisy shook her head. "I'm sorry, I don't. Why don't you call the school? They probably won't give you her number, but they might call her for you."

"Yes, yes. That's a good idea." Marcie patted her pockets in search of her phone. "Oh, dear! Where did I leave my phone? I thought I put it in my pocket. I must have left it inside. I—"

"Here. Use mine." Daisy unlocked her phone and handed it to Lila-Jane's mom. She moved a short distance away to give Marcie some privacy while she made the call. A few moments later, Marcie was finished.

"What did they say?" Daisy asked.

"I spoke to the lady in the office. It's lucky I caught her. She was about to leave for the day. Anyway, she's going to call Mary Cleaver and get back to me."

Her voice faded away and she stared off in the distance. The trees stood stark and naked in the winter breeze. All of a sudden, she shivered and rubbed her hands up and down her arms. Daisy moved closer. She didn't know the woman well, but no one should be forced to endure such a thing alone. She was sure the little girl would turn up sooner or later, but still... She imagined it was Emma who was missing and her heart clenched.

Words of reassurance formed in her mind. They seemed so ineffectual, but she said them just the same. "It's going to be all right, Marcie."

Marcie merely offered her a quick nod, as if it were all she could manage. Daisy understood how words could be beyond her at that time. The two of them stood there in silence. Emma scuffed the toe of her shoe along the edge of the porch. A blue wren darted among the bushes that formed a hedge along the front fence.

The momentary stillness was broken by the sound of Daisy's phone. Both women sighed in relief.

Daisy checked the screen. "It's the school."

CHAPTER 2

Christian Grayson reached for a Coke from the door of his Uncle Larry's fridge. Kicking it closed with his foot, he twisted the top off the bottle and tilted it to his lips. Swallowing greedily, he relished the cold sweetness. Thank God the day was over. It had been longer than he could imagine.

A meow came from the other side of the kitchen and a moment later, a warm body brushed against his leg. Bending down, he picked up his cat.

"Hey there! Sooty! Did you have a good day?" The cat answered him with another meow and, with a scratch between his ears, Christian set him back down.

Padding in his socks across the living room, he called out to his uncle before pushing open the sliding doors that led out to the back deck. There was no response. His uncle usually beat him home from work, although Christian hadn't seen any sign of the school bus out the front. He might have taken the bus in for servicing, or maybe he was parked out back.

Dismissing his idle thoughts, he made himself comfortable on one of the loungers that filled the small space and sighed quietly in relief. He'd survived another week.

Almost immediately, he was beset with a barrage of memories of his ex, Justine. Was she, even now, enjoying a glass of wine, relishing the idea of the evening that lay ahead? *Had she stopped by her new boyfriend's place for pizza on her way home from work, like she used to do when they'd been together?* Perhaps the new man in her life had other ideas? Was she even now making memories with someone else— memories that should have belonged to him?

Cursing under his breath, Christian took another gulp of his Coke. *What did he care what Justine was doing now?* She'd broken up with him more than four months ago and God knows she'd withdrawn from him emotionally weeks before that. He should have guessed there was something going on with her, but the truth was, he'd been so immersed in yet another court case, he hadn't realized anything was wrong. When she came to him with her suitcases in hand and told him she was leaving, he'd been taken completely by surprise. Which just went to show how out of touch he'd been with her, just like she'd accused.

She told him she needed to be with someone who appreciated her. Someone who'd be there for her. *Really* there, not just a man who made all the right noises, but who spent more time with his clients or buried knee deep in cases than he did with his long-term girlfriend. For goodness sake, he didn't even have his own place! Thirty-three years old and he still lived with his uncle! And that was another thing. She wanted a man who made her heart sing, who was prepared to put her first.

Christian had been neither. It wasn't his fault, it was just the way he was, but things between them had been getting serious. Both of them were past the age of playing around. They were in their thirties. They didn't have time to waste. She'd decided he wasn't the man for her and she was leaving before it was too late. 'Why couldn't he understand?' she'd told him.

The accusations had been tossed at him one after the other until he felt battered from all sides. Shocked that the woman he thought he would marry one day was walking out on him, Christian made a desperate plea to keep her. He promised to be more attentive, to make time for just the two of them. He told her he'd take the next weekend off. They could go to dinner, take in a live show, visit the markets, wander along the beach. All the things they didn't normally get to do while he was busy with work. He'd even promised to go house hunting. She was right. It was way past time. And then he got down on one knee and proposed to her in an effort to get her to stay. But despite his efforts, she remained adamant.

"It's too late, Christian. I've found someone else." And with those words, she tore his heart in two.

The creak from the door that led to the

basement snagged his attention. His uncle must have been downstairs. He sat forward in anticipation. "I'm out back, Uncle Larry. Grab a drink and join me."

A few moments later, the sliding door opened and Larry Grayson stepped out. He was still dressed in his bus driver's uniform. Christian smiled at him in greeting and saluted him with his drink.

"Good afternoon, Uncle Larry. I bet you're just as glad as I am to see the end of the working week."

His uncle grimaced. "Yes. I just wish it hadn't ended in such a distressing way."

Christian's smile faded. "What do you mean?"

"A little girl from my bus run hasn't arrived home. Her mother's frantic."

Christian sat up in the lounger and leaned forward. "What do you mean, she hasn't arrived home?"

"Just what I said. I dropped her off at her usual stop and continued on my way. Her mother called me a short time later to say she didn't arrive home." Larry shook his head. "I don't know where she went."

"Did any of the other kids see anything?"

"She's the last child on the bus. There was no one else. I was already home when I took the call from her mother."

Christian shook his head. He didn't have any children, but he could imagine how concerned the mother of the missing child must be. "Did you see anyone strange hanging around the bus stop? Anyone you don't normally see?"

"No. The police have already asked me that question. There was no one. At least, not that I saw. I only pulled up for a moment. Just long enough to let her off the bus." Larry ran a hand through his thick white hair and dropped into the nearest chair with a heavy sigh.

"It's not your fault, Uncle Larry. Besides, kids go missing all the time. You and I know that better than anyone. Remember that kid back in Albury? And then there were a couple during the time we lived in Parramatta. And what about that girl who went missing in Wollongong?" He paused and took a swig from his Coke. "How old is she?"

"Nine or ten."

"So she's not a preschooler. She's probably gone to the shops or something and is taking longer than usual to get home. I'm sure she'll turn up."

His uncle looked at him, the lines on his weathered face creasing in concern. "She's been missing for more than two hours. Where could she be?"

"Did anyone try to call her?"

"She's a fourth grader, Christian. She doesn't have a phone."

He shrugged. He couldn't keep up with kids these days. It seemed everywhere he looked they were plugged into one device or another. He remembered the days when he was at school and all the entertainment to be had was a library book or a pack of playing cards. *How times had changed.*

His uncle stood and headed toward the door.

"Where are you going?"

"I'm going out to look for her. I can't sit here while a little girl is missing. I was the last person to see her. I have to find out if she's all right."

"It's not your fault she's gone missing," Christian reminded him.

His uncle regarded him grimly. "I know, but I feel responsible just the same. I shouldn't have let her off the bus without her mother being there."

"Does she normally get off the bus alone?"

"Yes, she has for a bit, but—"

"But, nothing. You weren't to know she was going to turn up missing, Uncle Larry. I think it's wonderful you care about the kids who ride your bus, but once they climb off it, they're no longer your responsibility, no matter how you feel."

"I get it, Christian. I do. But it doesn't change anything. I'm going out to help look for her. I'm not sure what time I'll be back."

His uncle disappeared the way he'd come and Christian didn't hold back a sigh. There was no way he was going to be able to enjoy his evening knowing a little girl in his neighborhood was missing. Finishing the last of his drink, he stood and followed his uncle back inside.

Larry was in the process of pulling on a coat. The sun had long since set and even though heavy clouds had gathered, the air held a distinct winter chill. Compared to many cities around the world, Sydney experienced a mild winter with temperatures rarely falling anywhere near freezing, but still, July wasn't the time to be outdoors without boots and a warm jacket. Stifling another sigh,

Christian followed suit and proceeded through the door behind his uncle.

"Do we have any idea where this child might have gone?" he asked as he climbed into the passenger seat of his uncle's pickup.

"No. The mother has spoken to some of her daughter's friends. No one has a clue where she might be."

"Have the police organized a search party?"

"I'm not sure. They hadn't at the time I spoke to them. That was about an hour ago. I'm guessing that they might have done something about it by now."

Christian's thoughts once again turned to the mother of the missing girl. A wave of sympathy swept over him and he sent a silent prayer heavenward that the child was found, unharmed. Night had well and truly settled in and with a drop in temperature there came the likelihood of rain.

"What was she wearing?" he asked.

"Her school uniform. A pinafore and blouse. She probably had on stockings."

"What's her name?"

"Lila-Jane Morrissey. She attends Chatswood Elementary. She's been catching my bus for the past year. Such a sweet thing. And so polite. She never fails to say hello and goodbye. Not like a lot of kids these days who walk past me like I don't exist."

Christian didn't respond. He knew exactly what his uncle meant. He came across kids every day in the course of his job as a defense lawyer. Many had failed to master the simple art of good manners. He didn't like to think he'd become immune to the rudeness. Rather, he chose to ignore it in the pursuit of gaining each young offender's trust and getting to the truth of what might have happened to bring them to his office in the first place.

His uncle continued to drive on in silence. A short time later, Larry pulled into the driveway of a well-maintained, single-story bungalow. The place was aglow with light. Several vehicles lined both sides of the street. Larry found an empty spot and brought the car to a halt.

"This is Lila-Jane's place. Her mom's been finding it hard since the divorce. I overheard Lila-Jane telling one of the kids only just the other day that she recently found her mom in tears over a pile of unpaid bills. I can't imagine how she feels right now."

Christian acknowledged his uncle's comments with a nod. Larry opened the door and climbed out of his truck. Christian followed suit. The number of cars surrounding them indicated a decent number of people had come out to show their support. He guessed that they were inside the house. Larry walked up the three steps that led to the front door and rapped sharply on the wooden panel.

Christian waited off to one side, not sure what he was doing there. Before he could formulate an answer to his unspoken question, the door opened. His breath caught in his throat at the sight of the woman who stood on the other side. Her dark hair gleamed like thick, rich chocolate in the golden glow of the porch light. The silken threads curled around her ears and kissed the very tops of her shoulders. Her eyes, large and round, matched almost exactly the color of her hair...

And then it hit him. He'd seen her before.

In fact, he'd seen her only a few hours earlier. Daisy Green. *What was she doing here?* She was a lawyer who worked on his floor. Or rather, *he* worked on hers. He was the newcomer, the one who'd only held a job down at the prestigious Sydney Legal for the past few months.

His rather depressing breakup from Justine hadn't just signaled the end of his relationship, it had also meant he was forced to look for another job. They had been coworkers. She was a paralegal who worked a couple of doors down from his office. Dating a coworker was all well and good while the relationship went well, but now that he and Justine had parted ways, the fact they worked in close quarters had proven more than awkward.

A week after the breakup, he'd been bemoaning that awkwardness in a bar to his friend and fellow lawyer, Colby Shearer. Colby suggested that he apply for a job at Sydney Legal. And the rest, as they say, was history.

He'd noticed Daisy Green on the second day of his new job. She'd been waiting for an elevator in the lobby. Her hair had been pulled back into a ponytail that brushed the top of her neck. Every now and then, she shifted her weight and he'd cop a waft of her perfume. Something sweet and spicy that tantalized his senses and everything in between.

They'd shared the ride up to the ninth floor and even though he hadn't spoken a word to her, when they'd alighted together, he paid attention to where she went. Her office was on the opposite side of the building to his. He guessed she had a nice view of Hyde Park. She might even have glimpses of Sydney Harbour. He, on the other hand, had a glorious view of the building next door and the busy six-lane street below. Not that it mattered. He was just happy there was no longer the possibility he'd run into his ex every day.

But what was Daisy doing at Marcie Morrissey's house? Did she live in the neighborhood? That meant she might even live close to him... The thought made his heart skip a beat. Daisy pulled the door open and he hurriedly thrust his musings aside. She frowned at his uncle. "Mr Grayson? What are you doing here?"

Uncle Larry nodded in greeting. "Hello, Mrs Green. I heard Lila-Jane was still missing. I guess you heard that, too. I stopped by to see if I can help. Is that why you're here?"

Christian swallowed his disappointment. He didn't even hear her reply.

Mrs Green.

She was married.

It was just his luck that the hottest female in his office was married. He forced himself to concentrate on the conversation taking place before him.

"The police have agreed to put together a search party," Daisy was saying. "Volunteers are gathering here. I'm sure Marcie will be grateful for any help you can give." She glanced at Christian.

"This is my nephew, Christian Grayson," Larry said, indicating Christian. "He's also here to help."

Daisy nodded in Christian's direction, but to his chagrin, didn't show any hint of recognition. He stuck out his hand.

"Nice to officially meet you. I believe we work together at Sydney Legal."

Her eyes widened in surprise and then slowly filled with recognition. "Oh, yes, now I remember you. You work on my floor."

"Yes. I've been there a little over three months."

She looked surprised at his announcement, but made no further comment. Christian hurried on.

"My uncle told me about the missing girl. I'd like to offer my help."

She threw him a distracted nod. "That's very kind of you. I'm sure Marcie will appreciate as much help as she can get. She's frantic, and understandably so." She moved backwards, out of the doorway, as if only now remembering she was blocking the way. "Please, come in."

They followed her down a narrow hallway that opened up into a crowded kitchen. The high ceilings made the room feel bigger, but it was still a compact space. People were gathered around the counter and perched on chairs around a four-seater dining table. The conversation was muted and tense, like the expression on most people's faces. Daisy walked over to a woman who sat huddled on the edge of a faux-leather couch. She looked like she was around Christian's age, but worry and stress had tightened her features and in that moment cast shadows in her eyes.

"Marcie, Mr Grayson has come over to offer his help. And this is his nephew, Christian."

The introductions were made. Christian shook Marcie Morrissey's limp hand. "I'm so sorry to hear about your daughter, Mrs Morrissey. We're here to do whatever we can to find her."

Marcie ignored his comment and looked past him to his uncle. "The police told me they'd spoken to you. Are you *sure* you didn't see anyone suspicious hanging around the bus stop?"

Larry shook his head. "I'm sorry, Mrs Morrissey. Like I told them, I saw no one."

"What about a strange car, someone parked close by?" she insisted.

"I didn't notice any," Larry replied. "Then again, I was concentrating on the traffic and getting Lila-Jane off safely. She was my priority."

Marcie lowered her gaze to her hands which were twisted in her lap. "Of course," she murmured.

"I'm really sorry, Mrs Morrissey," Larry mumbled. "I wish I'd noticed something. I feel so bad, knowing Lila-Jane is missing. I just hope she turns up soon."

Tears formed in Marcie's eyes and slowly rolled down her cheeks. Her hands tightened in her lap. "I hope so, too."

Her voice cracked with the strain of all that had gone on that afternoon. Burying her face in her hands, she sobbed. Daisy immediately stepped forward and sat beside the woman. Putting an arm around Marcie's shoulders, Daisy murmured words of comfort. Christian looked at his uncle and motioned that they should leave the women in private. Together, they moved away and found a spot in a corner of the room.

Christian blew out his breath on a heavy sigh. "*Phew.* That's difficult to take. I can't imagine what it must feel like."

"Yes," his uncle agreed, his expression troubled. "I feel responsible for the fact her daughter didn't come home. I dropped her off. I should have paid more attention to who was around."

"It isn't your fault, Uncle Larry. I've told you that already. And we don't know yet that she's been taken by anyone. She could have gone anywhere."

Larry stared out at the window. Darkness had settled in. Lightning flickered in the distance, followed by a rumble of thunder. The promised storm didn't seem very far away. Christian thought about the little girl who was out there, maybe scared and alone. He hoped she'd be found before the storm broke.

A knock at the door interrupted the muted conversations. Almost as one, the people in the room looked up toward the entrance where the sound of high heels clattered on the wooden floor. A moment later, someone announced, "The police are here."

CHAPTER 3

Daisy heard Marcie's quick indrawn breath and felt the tension in her friend's arm. A moment later, two police officers filled the open doorway and came toward them. The older officer, a man with sparse salt-and-pepper hair, who introduced himself as Detective Sergeant John McLennan, took the lead. He was followed by a much younger female officer who kneeled beside Marcie and took her hand.

"Mrs Morrissey, I'm Detective Carrie Westman. We wanted to let you know we've set up the search team. They're ready to head out." She looked around the room and then back at Marcie. "I see you've managed to gather a few volunteers of your own. That's good. The more people we have looking for Lila-Jane, the better."

Marcie managed the tiniest of nods. "Some of the neighbors have offered to help. Everyone's been so kind." Her bottom lip trembled and fresh tears crowded her eyes. "It's so dark outside. Lila-

Jane hates the dark. Please, officers! We need to find her! I need to find my baby!"

Detective Westman patted Marcie's hand. "We're doing all we can, Mrs Morrissey. You need to trust in our skills and accept that we know what we're doing. We've done this many times before."

Detective McLennan nodded. "She's right, Mrs Morrissey. We see kids go missing all the time. Most turn up within an hour or two after they disappear. A lot of them have been at a friend's place or were distracted by something on their way home. Just because your daughter didn't arrive home, doesn't mean someone has taken her. Of course we'll cover all bases and that's the reason for the search party," he added hurriedly as Marcie opened her mouth to protest.

"When are we heading out?" Daisy asked.

The female officer got to her feet and brushed off the knees of her pants. "As soon as everyone is ready. We have some volunteers from the State Emergency Services waiting outside. They are experienced in this kind of thing." She turned to Marcie. "Do you have a recent photograph of your daughter?"

Marcie nodded and struggled to her feet. "I have her school photograph. It was taken only a month ago."

Marcie moved slowly over to the sideboard and pulled a photo album out of the top drawer. She opened the cover and flipped through the pages. A moment later, she pulled out a photograph and turned back toward the officers.

"Here it is. She's wearing her winter uniform. The

same one she wore today. A light blue blouse and a navy and royal-blue tartan pinafore. She also wore navy-blue stockings and black leather school shoes, just like she has on in this picture."

"Thank you, that's very helpful," the female officer replied, taking the picture from Marcie. "I'll have it scanned ASAP and sent out to all officers and I'll get some copies made to pass around. That way everyone will know who we're looking for."

She handed the photograph to her partner. Detective McLennan studied the photograph and then looked back to Marcie.

"Does your daughter have the same haircut?"

Marcie nodded. "Yes. It might be slightly longer. She's trying to grow it. She wore her hair in pigtails this morning with two navy-blue ribbons."

"What about a jacket, or school blazer? Was she wearing one of those?"

"No," Marcie replied. "I told her to take her blazer, but she didn't want to. The sun was out earlier today. She was sure she wouldn't need it and she didn't want to have to carry it around all day." Her gaze went to the window and she sniffed. "Now it's about to rain." More tears gathered in her eyes and trickled down her cheeks. Her shoulders shook in silent distress.

Once again Daisy put her arm around her friend's shoulders to offer what little comfort she could. She looked up and noticed the bus driver and his nephew standing a little to one side. Both of them looked as somber as she felt.

Her gaze returned to Larry's nephew and she

realized he was looking at her. Her heart gave a little jolt. Now that he'd reminded her that he worked in her office, she remembered seeing him before. In fact, she thought they'd shared an elevator ride together. He'd worn a nice suit and his blue silk tie had matched the color of his eyes. They were as blue as the harbor.

She wasn't sure why she remembered that detail. She didn't pay attention to other men these days. Pete had been the love of her life. They'd met when she was fifteen. He was the only man she'd slept with. And despite everything, she was sure she'd never love again. Perhaps it had something to do with the air of quiet confidence that surrounded Christian Grayson. Maybe that was the reason her gaze was drawn to him more frequently than she liked.

From beneath her lashes, she glanced at him again and was unnerved to find his gaze still on her. She quickly turned her back to him and concentrated on Marcie.

"Do you have a scanner or printer we could use, or a copy machine?" Detective Westman asked, interrupting Daisy's thoughts.

Marcie nodded. "Yes, in the office. It's a scanner as well as a printer. It's two doors down on the left."

"I'll show you," Daisy offered. She headed out the doorway and down the hall. The older officer followed her.

Marcie had once given her a tour of the house Marcie had inherited from her grandmother. *Circa* 1950, it was a lovely example of a heritage-listed bungalow. The high white ceilings were decorated with elaborate cornices and the walls were painted in heritage green. Unlike Daisy's bungalow which was starting to show signs of wear, Marcie's was in pristine condition. Along with the house, her friend had confided that she'd also inherited a sizable amount of money, and that had gone a long way toward restoring their beautiful home.

Daisy sighed inwardly. What she'd give for a wealthy grandmother to leave her a nice inheritance... It would certainly make things a little easier for her and Emma. And then she remembered the reason why they were gathered in Marcie's beautiful home and was immediately flooded with guilt. Her friend's daughter had failed to come home and nobody knew where she was. A beautiful home paled to insignificance when compared to the fact the home owner's young daughter was missing.

"It's just through here," she said and pointed in the direction of the printer that sat on the corner of Marcie's desk.

The room was neat and tidy, as was the rest of the house. Not even a sheet of paper out of place. The officer moved inside the room and placed Lila-Jane's picture face down on the plate glass. He attached a flash drive, punched in a selection and pressed a button... The machine sprang into life. Daisy stood there in silence.

"That should do it for now at least," the detective murmured and gathered up the pile of papers that lay in the tray. He retrieved the small flash drive and handed it off to Detective Westman who appeared in the doorway and gave her directions to send the photo out on the airwaves.

Daisy caught a glimpse of Lila-Jane's smiling face on the top sheet and her belly clenched with dread. Once again, she was grateful it wasn't Emma who'd disappeared. *Speaking of Emma, where was she?* Daisy had lost track of her over the ensuing hours once more and more people had turned up. A wave of panic washed over her and, leaving the officers to find their own way back, she hurried from the room.

She didn't want to distress Marcie any further, so moved quietly around the room and asked some of the people if they'd seen Emma. As she was met with blank gazes and numerous shakes of the head she tried to stem her increasing panic. And then she came upon Larry Grayson and almost sighed with relief. At least he knew who she was talking about.

"Mr Grayson, you haven't seen Emma, have you?"

Larry frowned. "I think I saw her running through the kitchen a little while ago," he replied. "She was being chased by Jonathon Cleaver."

Daisy felt Christian's eyes upon her once again, but refused to look in his direction.

"Would you like me to help search for her?" he offered.

She forced herself to look at him and shook her head. "No, thanks. I-I'll go and look for her now."

She turned and started searching through the

rooms, calling out to Emma as she went. At the end of the hall was Lila-Jane's room. The door was half-open. Daisy put her shoulder to the panel and eased it wider. To her relief, Emma was perched on the edge of Lila-Jane's bed. A worried expression clouded her sweet face.

Daisy eased herself into the room and took a seat beside her daughter. She put her arm around her little girl's thin shoulders and drew her close. "What are you doing in here, honey?"

"I wanted to keep Lila-Jane's toys company. She used to take this teddy everywhere. I guess she's kind of too old to do that now, but I know she still loves him. Just like you still love Daddy." Emma turned her dark brown eyes up to her mother. "Where could she have gone, Momma?"

"I'm not sure, baby, but I'm certain the police will find her. That's what they do."

"Do you mean there have been other kids who have gone missing off the bus?"

Daisy stared down at her daughter and her heart clenched. The last thing she needed was to have her daughter think there was some boogeyman snatching children from the bus stop.

"No honey. At least, not around here. And we don't really know what happened to Lila-Jane. She might have been distracted by a litter of puppies or some kittens or something else, just like you told me you sometimes are, on your way home."

Emma scrunched up her nose. "Yes, but I never stop for more than a few minutes, Momma. And I'm never out after dark. At least, not without you."

Daisy hugged her closer. "Yes, baby. You're a good girl. Let's hope Lila-Jane will be home soon."

"Are the police going to go look for her?"

"Yes. In fact, we're about to head out now."

"Can I come?"

"No, honey. You can't. I need you to stay here."

"But, Mom—"

"No, Emma. I need to know where you are. Besides, Mrs Morrissey is going to wait here and see if Lila-Jane comes home. You could keep her company. There's a good chance Lila-Jane might even arrive home before we do."

"All right," Emma applied reluctantly. "I guess I could stay here. Do you think she'd mind if I had a little rest on her bed?"

Daisy hugged her daughter tight and then released her. "No, honey. I don't think she'd mind it all."

Emma turned to stare out the window. "It's dark outside, Momma." She shivered.

"Yes."

"Do you think Lila-Jane's scared?"

The question was asked so quietly, Daisy had to strain to hear it. Emma's face was pinched with worry. Once again, Daisy drew her daughter close.

"Yes, honey. I think she probably is scared. But let's hope she'll come home soon. I'm sure her momma can't wait to see her again."

Emma nodded solemnly and then curled up on Lila-Jane's bed. The room was painted in soft pastels with pale pink curtains and matching cushions lined up against the pillows on the bed. A large wooden dollhouse stood in one corner of the room. It was filled with miniature wooden furniture and tiny lifelike dolls. A small bookshelf stood against another wall. The books were lined up neatly with all the spines facing out. There were no clothes on the floor. No shoes scattered about. It was so unlike Emma's room, Daisy couldn't help but smile.

Then she thought about the little girl who lived there and sent up a silent prayer: *Please God, keep Lila-Jane safe. We need to have her back home. For all our sakes.*

———

From the corner of his eye, Christian saw Daisy re-enter the living room. The charcoal-gray pencil skirt she wore emphasized the slimness of her hips. Her black-and-white striped blouse was made out of some sort of soft material that fell gently over the curves of her breasts. She wore high heels, at least three or four inches high. Not that she needed the extra elevation. She was tall for a woman. Almost as tall as he was. She tucked a stray piece of dark hair behind her ear and looked around the room. Her gaze came to rest on Marcie.

Christian felt a stab of sympathy as he also looked at the poor mother. He'd overheard the police asking her to remain behind in the house while they conducted the search. She protested at first, but then reluctantly conceded when they explained that they needed someone there in case her daughter arrived home. Now she was huddled on the couch looking lost and forlorn, silent tears flowing down her cheeks.

"All right, everybody, listen up." It was Detective McLennan who spoke. The conversation in the room immediately came to an end and the people there gathered to listen.

"I have a few dozen copies of a recent photograph of Lila-Jane Morrissey. Anyone who isn't certain of what she looks like, please take a copy. I'll be distributing them amongst the police officers and the SES agents who are gathered outside. It's important to get this search underway as soon as possible. It's now been more than four hours since this little girl went missing. We need to find her and bring her home."

"What was she wearing?" someone asked.

"The same uniform that's in this picture," the same officer replied. "For anyone not familiar with it, it's the school uniform worn at Chatswood Elementary."

"Does she have any friends or family living close by?" The question came from across the room.

This time, the female officer answered. "No, and we've already knocked on some doors in the immediate neighborhood. No one has seen her."

"Does everyone have a flashlight?" the older officer asked. "It's dark out there and a storm is brewing. Make sure you have warm jackets and are well prepared. We don't want one of you stumbling in the dark and getting hurt."

He cleared his throat and held up a map. "We've marked nearby streets into sections. We're going door knocking, one by one. We've already checked the houses on either side of us and the one across the back fence. I want you to divide into three groups. Each group is asked to appoint a leader. The team leader can come to me and grab a map. Each team will search a different area. We're going to do this in a systematic manner. Take your time and check carefully. It's going to be more difficult in the dark, but we need to find out if anyone saw this little girl. Make a note of the houses where no one answers the door. My number is on the bottom of the map. If anyone finds her or finds anything connected with her, call me."

The officers stared solemnly at each of the volunteers, impressing on them the seriousness of the situation.

"Any questions?" the detective asked.

The room remained silent. Christian felt the weight of their concern and his gut tightened. The crowd of people began to move into roughly even groups. He was quietly pleased when Daisy moved into their group.

"Did you locate your daughter?" he asked.

She nodded. "Yes, thanks. She was in Lila-Jane's room. I told her to stay there while we go and look. Hopefully she'll fall asleep."

"Good. I'm glad you found her."

Up close, Daisy was just as beautiful as he remembered. It was a shame they'd met again in such strained circumstances. He hoped that Lila-

Jane would be found quickly and they could put this difficult moment in time behind them. He looked forward to seeing Daisy again under happier circumstances.

"I'll go team leader, if you like," his uncle offered.

Christian shrugged. "That's fine with me." He looked around him at the people who had gathered in their group. "Does anyone have a problem with Larry Grayson being the team leader?"

The group members shook their heads and murmured in the negative.

Larry nodded. "Okay, then. I'll go and get the map."

Christian watched his uncle head over in the direction of the police officers. He turned his attention back to Daisy. "Does Marcie Morrissey have anyone who can stay with her?"

Daisy's eyes widened. He guessed she was surprised by his thoughtfulness. Her next words confirmed it.

"That's very thoughtful of you, but, no. She divorced Lila-Jane's father a year ago. Her family all live in Queensland. There's no one here."

His gaze took in the room full of people and then he looked back at her. "I guess it's good that she has so many friends here then," he said.

Daisy nodded, her expression solemn. Worry still clouded the dark chocolate of her eyes. "Yes. I guess it is."

Uncle Larry returned, holding a piece of paper in his hand. He showed it to the group gathered around him.

"This is our section here," he said, and traced the highlighted route with his finger. "We have four blocks to cover. Let's hope we get it done before the storm hits."

The concern on Daisy's face deepened and Christian wished he could offer her some form of reassurance. The truth was, he barely knew her and he was in no position to offer anyone comfort.

The little girl was missing and nobody knew where she was. He didn't want to think that she might have been kidnapped by a child predator, but this was the twenty-first century. It wouldn't be the first time a child had been snatched. He knew better than most...

He pushed the dark thoughts aside. Grim determination flooded his veins. He didn't even know the little girl or her mother, but he'd been in this situation before. The image of Nikki Carlin filled his mind, a cloud of red hair and freckles. She'd only been ten when she disappeared. He'd only been a couple of years older, but he remembered it like it was yesterday. She'd been his best friend. To this day, no one had any idea what happened to her or where she was.

CHAPTER 4

Daisy laid her daughter gently down on the bed and covered her with the quilt. She stared down at the small form. She was growing so fast. She'd be ten next birthday. Almost too big to carry. If it hadn't been so late and if Emma hadn't been sound asleep when the neighbor who had offered them a ride home had pulled up outside their house, Daisy would have woken her. But it was a school night. Her baby needed her sleep. It wasn't Emma's fault a child had gone missing and they'd stayed out way past Emma's bedtime in an effort to find her.

The search for Lila-Jane Morrissey had been called off a couple of hours earlier, and despite them combing the surrounding streets for her, the only sign they'd found of the little girl was the navy-blue ribbon that could have fallen from her hair.

It had been found amongst the bare branches of a bush that grew on the nature strip about halfway along Lila-Jane's usual route home. It was the only evidence they had that she'd even passed by that way that day.

When the police had questioned Marcie about the ribbon, she positively identified it as belonging to her daughter and then was perplexed as to why she hadn't seen it on the trip she'd made earlier along that way. Still, they'd managed to establish that Lila-Jane Morrissey had alighted off the bus like her bus driver had said and had at least made it halfway home before she disappeared. It was a shame they hadn't found any clues about the little girl's whereabouts and Daisy was certain the discovery of the ribbon had done nothing to ease the torment and fear that must surely be consuming Marcie Morrissey's mind. Daisy smoothed the damp hair from Emma's forehead and sent a silent prayer of thanks heavenward that her daughter was safe and sound in bed, where she should be.

Against her will, Daisy's thoughts returned to the traumatic events of the afternoon. The fact they'd found little trace of Lila-Jane had left the search goers disheartened. The police urged them to keep their spirits up and had reassured them that it wasn't unusual for children to go missing overnight. But Daisy could tell from the expressions on the people around her that nobody believed their reassurances. Everyone present went home feeling that somehow they'd let the little girl down. Larry Grayson seemed to be taking it harder than most.

The bus driver had been relentless in his search efforts earlier in the night. Their team had covered their entire four-block section of the neighborhood in record time. They arrived back right before the storm struck. Fifty feet from Marcie's front door, the clouds that had threatened all afternoon opened up and drenched them with rain. They were soaked through by the time they reached the front porch, but the minor discomfort was nothing compared to the way Marcie was feeling and nobody uttered a word of complaint.

After regrouping in the kitchen and receiving a pep talk from the police officers, they'd been dismissed in a kindly manner and urged to return to their homes with a reassurance the police would resume the search in the morning.

From the top step of Marcie's front porch, Daisy watched Larry and his nephew depart, their shoulders slumped in defeat. They climbed into a white pickup and drove away, the rain lashing their windscreen. Christian Grayson gave her a half-hearted wave on his way past.

Christian Grayson. Tall and broad shouldered and athletic. His thick blond hair was plastered to his forehead by the rain. In another lifetime, she might've been attracted to the kindness in his clear blue eyes. But that was before Pete. Before the man who had broken her heart and left her with so many unresolved trust issues...

She'd kept up the façade of being a heartbroken wife for Emma's sake and there were times when she truly missed him, but more often, when she thought about Pete she got angry, just like she'd been the last time she'd seen him, before he'd walked out on her forever.

At the time, neither of them had known it would be forever, but Pete was fighting a war on foreign soil and death was a constant companion. He died before they'd settled their differences, before he'd apologized for destroying their love, before she could even begin to contemplate forgiveness…

It was like she was caught up in some kind of time warp nightmare where all the hurtful things never got resolved. No one got to fight and argue, to shout and express their hurt. No one got to say they were sorry, to beg forgiveness, to reaffirm their love. It wasn't right that Pete's life had been cut short so tragically with so much at home left unresolved. She'd been left to pick up the pieces, feeling rudderless and lost.

And yet, she'd been forced to put on a brave face for the sake of her daughter. Emma knew nothing of Pete's deceit and that's the way it was going to stay. There was no need to tarnish his memory. Emma thought her daddy hung the moon and stars and that's the way it would always be.

With a quiet sigh, Daisy pulled up the quilt to Emma's chin. It was too late in the evening and she was too tired to be thinking about such things. She'd had a big day at work and then the call from Marcie…and the search. Her shoulders slumped with fatigue. She thought longingly of climbing into her bed.

She leaned over to switch off the light and then spied the clothes Emma had discarded earlier that morning, lying on the floor. With another sigh, she hung them back in the closet. She collected the shoes that had been similarly tossed aside and stacked them neatly under the bed. Come morning, the room would be a shambles yet again, but for once the thought didn't irritate her. Her baby was home, asleep in her bed. Lila-Jane's neat-as-a-pin bedroom was empty.

The thought filled her with a sudden burst of pain. *How could Marcie even bear the thought of her daughter being gone? What if they never found her? What if she simply disappeared forever?* It was too much for Daisy to accept.

No, they'd find Marcie's daughter, just like the police promised. She'd turn up tomorrow, for sure. Everyone was counting on it.

———

The sun had barely poked its head above the horizon when Christian walked into the kitchen the following morning. His uncle was already at the table, his usual bowl of cornflakes and the morning paper in front of him. Christian popped two pieces of whole wheat bread in the toaster and then used the remote to switch on the television that stood on the counter. He was just in time for the six-thirty news.

The lead story was about an incident that had occurred in the inner west of the city the night before. Two men had gotten into an argument that had turned deadly when one of them produced a knife. The victim was in serious condition in hospital. The offender had yet to be apprehended by police.

The toast popped up and Christian spread it with butter. Cracking eggs into a pan, he waited a few moments before flipping them. From the corner of his eye, he saw a picture of Lila-Jane Morrissey flash up on the screen. It was the same photo that had been distributed among members of the search party last evening. He reached for the remote and turned up the volume.

"Uncle Larry, it's a story about that missing girl," he said.

Larry lifted his gaze from the newspaper and stared at the screen, his gaze solemn. The news story was brief. Nobody had many details, including the police. Just as they'd assured the group of volunteers the night before, they told the reporter that the search for Lila-Jane Morrissey would continue that morning. The police spokesman also urged members of the public to come forward with any information. The story finished with a tearful plea from the mother. She wore the same clothes Christian had seen her in the evening before.

Larry slowly shook his head, his expression filling with sadness. "I still can't believe it. I feel sick at the thought that someone might've taken her after I let her off. If only I'd waited around a little bit longer. If only I'd taken a bit more notice about who was around. Parked cars, strangers, someone who didn't belong..."

"Uncle Larry, how many times do I have to tell you? It's not your fault. The mother had given permission to allow her child to walk home. Your job was to collect her from school and drop her off at her stop. You did that. It's not your job to second-guess the mother's decision. You have nothing to feel guilty about."

Christian could see his words of reassurance had little impact on his uncle and he understood. If he were in his uncle's shoes, he'd be feeling the same way. It wouldn't matter if there was any real basis for the feelings of guilt. The fact was, his uncle let Lila-Jane Morrissey off the bus to walk home alone. Christian only hoped that she hadn't met with foul play. It was early days yet. There was still a chance she'd turn up, safe and sound. Not every missing child ended up like Nikki Carlin...

He set the fried eggs on his toast and took the chair across from his uncle. The reminder of Nikki brought with it a barrage of sad memories. She'd also disappeared on her way home from school. And then there were all the others. At least twenty-five over the years that he knew of. He was glad he'd never had to walk home from elementary school by himself.

Ever since the car accident that killed both his parents, he'd lived with his uncle. He was only nine when his mother and father died. Even then, his uncle had been a bus driver.

Christian would catch the bus first thing in the morning at the beginning of his uncle's bus run and after school he'd still be on it when the last child climbed off later that afternoon. He used to enjoy the times on the bus. Uncle Larry was the only family he had left. And though the man was often taciturn and quiet, Christian figured he was grieving, too.

Christian's father was Larry's younger brother. The accident had come as a shock to everyone. Christian was only grateful his uncle had been willing to take him in. God knows where he would have ended up otherwise. Probably not with a college education and a good job at a prestigious law firm. He had a lot to be grateful for.

"Do you remember Nikki?" he asked quietly.

His uncle started in surprise. "Yes, Of course I do. She was a beautiful girl."

"I wonder what happened to her," Christian murmured.

"I guess she's dead by now," his uncle mused. "That was more than twenty years ago."

Though he accepted his uncle's comment, the suggestion she was dead still had the power to hurt. The police had found no trace of Nikki, even though a comprehensive search of the entire area had been conducted over many weeks. She'd simply disappeared—never to be seen again.

"Few people realize how easy it is to take a child," his uncle murmured. "Kids are so predictable. They follow a strict routine. Just like bus drivers." Larry smiled briefly.

"Yes," Christian agreed. "I remember how we used to get up at the same time every morning and arrive back home again the same time every afternoon. Most of the kids I knew did the same. Even the ones who were collected by their parents from the school gate were picked up at the same time every day." He looked at his uncle and nodded. "You're right. It would be easy for someone with evil intentions to map out a child's routine. To know exactly where they'd be and when, and whether they'd be accompanied by anyone."

"Exactly. I could tell you the daily meeting time and place of every child on my bus. Morning and afternoon. When they get on, when they get off. Whether there is a parent waiting for them, or whether they walk home alone. It's scary how easy it could be to steal one of them away."

Christian looked at his uncle. "Do you think that's what's happened to Lila-Jane?"

His uncle's expression turned grave. "Yes, I do," he answered heavily.

Christian's spirits sank. Though in his heart, he already suspected the same thing, it was so much harder to hear it spoken aloud. The toast in his mouth turned to cardboard. He pushed his plate aside.

"I think this kind of thing happens more often than people realize," he said. "I remember a lot of other missing kids over the years. Some found, some not. I know we moved around a lot and lived in different places, but it still happened. It seems no place was immune."

His uncle nodded slowly. "Yes. It's a sad commentary on our society, isn't it? Evil lurks everywhere." He looked up at Christian and gave him a half-hearted smile. "I guess you're grateful you never had to walk home by yourself at that age!"

"Oh, I am—don't worry. I'm grateful for a lot of things." He gave his uncle a meaningful look, hoping to convey the depth of his gratitude for all his uncle had done. And just to make certain his uncle understood, he put his feelings very clearly into words.

"I don't know what I would've done if you hadn't taken me in after the accident," he said quietly. "I'm so grateful for everything you've done for me, Uncle Larry. Not the least is allowing me to ride on the bus all the way home."

His uncle's eyes welled up with tears. He smiled tenderly at Christian. "I can't say it was something I regret. You've been the best thing that happened to me. Besides, you had no one. What else was I supposed to do?"

"There was no one forcing you to do it, Uncle Larry. You could have just as easily turned your back. I want you to know I appreciate what you did, just the same. Plenty of other kids haven't been so lucky."

His uncle merely nodded and returned his attention to the paper. A faint blush stained his cheeks, turning them even redder. It endeared him even more to Christian that his uncle was embarrassed by his display of emotion. The old man had been a bachelor when Christian unceremoniously landed in his life. It couldn't have been easy for him to have a young child thrust upon him. And yet, he'd done it and though he wasn't one to show too much physical affection, Christian was sure his uncle cared. He'd never have taken him in otherwise.

Pushing away from the table, Christian patted his uncle's shoulder in a silent show of comfort and then dropped his plate in the sink.

He turned back. "I need to head into work early. I have a whole pile of files to get through before I'm due in court. And I have that hearing coming up in a couple of days. I might be back late."

"You work too hard, Christian."

Christian grinned. "I thought you told me there's no such thing as working too hard?"

His uncle chuckled. "Since when did you believe anything I said?"

Christian laughed and, with a fond wave of his hand, he left the room.

Larry brought the bus slowly to a halt as the stoplight changed from orange to red. He glanced at the rearview mirror and his gaze drifted across the rows of school children who had already boarded his bus. There were the usual bursts of laughter, chatter, and occasional shouts. Despite Lila-Jane's disappearance having made the morning news, he guessed that most of them hadn't heard about it yet. No doubt it would be discussed at school by the staff and perhaps even the children would be advised. There would be discussions about the need to keep safe, "stranger danger" talks and all that kind of stuff.

His thoughts shifted to Lila-Jane. She was such a

sweet little thing. He hoped she was okay. And then he wondered about all the other missing children, the children Christian had mentioned at breakfast that morning. He was surprised his nephew still remembered Nikki. That had been years ago. Christian couldn't have been more than eleven or twelve. Of course, Larry had known Nikki and his nephew had been close. In fact, if his memory served him right, the two of them had been best friends. It had been the exact opposite between Larry and his brother.

At the thought of Frank, an old and familiar pain tugged at his heart. Even after all these years, the knowledge that Frank had never liked him still had the power to hurt. They'd only been a year apart and yet, they couldn't have been more different. Frank knew all of his secrets, but his brother never repaid the compliment. In fact, Frank would laugh at Larry more than comfort him through the times he was distressed. It used to make Larry furious. Still, he had no one else.

Then Amanda had come into the picture and the little time Frank had for his brother dissolved into nothingness. Larry had been bitterly jealous of the attention Frank bestowed on the woman who would one day become Frank's wife. When the two of them got married, Larry had gotten so drunk he'd started a fight with one of the wedding guests and ended the night in a jail cell.

And then the car accident happened. One day Frank and Amanda were going about their business living their lives, raising their son. The next, they were dead. Everything moved by in such a blur, he could barely remember the details. What he did remember was hearing Frank's lawyer inform him that he was Christian's only next of kin and as such, the most obvious person to become the young boy's guardian.

Initially, the thought of taking on the responsibility of a young child irritated him, but almost immediately he'd seen the opportunities having a young ward in residence would afford him. With forced reluctance, he agreed to take his nephew in.

People accepted him as Christian's guardian. It gave him a veneer of civility and safety that a self-confessed bachelor had been lacking in some people's eyes. All of a sudden, he was just like them—going to work every day, doing his best to raise his nephew, getting on with the business of living. No one knew it was all a farce—that he couldn't give two figs about his nephew. And he had devised a backup plan if the worst happened and the things he got up to in his basement were one day discovered. It was funny how well he'd gotten at pretending. He'd even managed a tear or two at breakfast.

"Hey, Mister! Where's Lila-Jane?" The question was shouted by a boy seated toward the back. Jimmy Bennett was his name and he was more switched on than the average ten-year-old. He also lacked manners.

Larry contemplated his answer. He didn't feel up to conducting a discussion on whether or not Lila-Jane had been kidnapped. Leave that to the teachers and parents. It wasn't his job to fill them in on the details. Besides, no one knew what had happened to the kid. She could be anywhere.

"She's not on today," he replied and hoped that it would be enough.

"What about Emma Green? She's not on, either."

The comment had been made by the same boy and Larry couldn't help grimacing. Jimmy was right. Emma Green hadn't been waiting at her stop today. Larry could only assume her mother had kept her home after the late night she'd had. Either that, or Daisy had decided to drive her to school.

Knowing Jimmy would persist until he received an answer, Larry casually replied. "I don't know where she is. She might have caught a ride to school with her mother."

"She never gets a ride to school. Her mother's always too busy," Jimmy scoffed.

Larry didn't respond. He couldn't care less that Emma wasn't on the bus. At least he knew she wasn't missing. The light turned green and he accelerated. Traffic had been heavier than usual, and he was running a little behind time. Not that the children would complain. Nobody cared when they didn't get to school on time. Bella Rushby certainly didn't.

The little girl sat alone in her seat, day after day. As far as Larry could tell, she had no friends. It was a shame. Then there was Emma Green. With her curly blond hair and big blue eyes... She was a pretty little thing and always took the time to say hello to him. Not like some of the other kids.

The thought made him frown. Kids were different these days. Take Jimmy Bennett and any number of others. They had much less respect for people in authority. Hell, what was he thinking about? They didn't have respect for anything or anyone, it didn't matter who they were or what position they held.

He'd heard the teachers complaining about it in the bus line and parents saying much the same thing. He wondered how this generation of children had grown up with such a lack of manners and respect. When he was a boy, he wouldn't have dared answer back to a teacher, or any adult for that matter. If he'd dared, he would have been clipped under the ear by his father and told in no uncertain terms never to do it again.

That was the problem these days. There wasn't enough discipline in the homes. It had ruined a generation of kids—the same spoiled brats who would one day become spoiled adults. *Where would it all end?*

With a sigh of resignation, he pushed the depressing thoughts aside. All he had to do was get the children to and from school in a safe and effective manner. It wasn't up to him to change the world—or anyone in it. As for Lila-Jane, he was certain she'd be fine.

CHAPTER 5

Daisy tucked an errant strand of hair behind her ears and reached for her coffee cup. Keeping her eyes fixed to the witness statement she was reading, she absentmindedly drew the cup to her lips.

It was empty.

Darn it. She didn't even remember drinking it. She'd filled it in the staff tearoom on her way into the office earlier that morning and had been at her desk ever since. With a trial starting in less than a month and at least a dozen witnesses to interview for the purposes of going over their statements before the trial date, she'd been totally focused on her work.

Well, perhaps not totally focused.

Her gaze moved to the statements still piled on her desk. She'd barely made any headway. She'd arrived at work later than normal. It hadn't felt right to put Emma on the bus, like she usually did. Instead, she'd taken the time to drive her daughter to school. The change in routine had set her back nearly an hour. It was time she didn't have to spare, but there was nothing she could do about it.

Lila-Jane's disappearance spooked her. This morning had been too soon for her to contemplate putting her child on the school bus. Even though it would put her office in a spin, she'd do what needed to be done. On top of that, she'd promised Emma she'd be back to collect her when the bell rang that afternoon. She didn't know how she was going to manage it. Not only did she have a ton of work piled in front of her, she had back-to-back appointments until three. Having to collect Emma from school meant she'd need extra time to get there. She'd have to ask Rhonda to reschedule. Emma's safety was her priority. And right now, she needed more coffee.

With a sigh, she collected her cup and pushed back from her desk. She stopped in on her secretary. Rhonda reacted exactly like Daisy had predicted. She saw the confusion and questions in her eyes, but settled on giving the woman the barest of explanations. She didn't want to come over sounding all protective and panicky by telling her the truth.

Of course her decision had nothing to do with the fact she was a single mom and Emma was all she had. She was merely being cautious. There was nothing wrong with that. At least, that's what she told herself. Deep down, she knew that was all a load of baloney.

Rounding the corner, she bumped into one of her coworkers who'd come round the corner from the opposite direction at the same time. Black coffee sloshed out of the cup he held in his hand.

"Oh, I'm so sorry!" she exclaimed. Embarrassment heated her cheeks. She was even more mortified when she realized she'd collided with Christian Grayson.

He wiped at the coffee that had stained his pristine white shirt and then dismissed her embarrassment with a smile. "Don't worry about it. It's only a little coffee stain."

Despite his casual unconcern, her embarrassment continued to intensify. *Of all the people to run into...* And even worse, to spill coffee all over his expensive-looking shirt. The day had only just begun. Unless he had a spare one in his locker, he'd be forced to spend the rest of the day sporting a brown stain on his shirtfront, right where everyone could see it.

"Please, let me pay for the dry cleaning," she said.

Christian merely laughed. "Don't be silly. It's nothing."

"But it's only half-past nine in the morning! What will you do? You're probably due in court. Or at the very least, you'll have clients to see. With that stain, it looks like you're in yesterday's clothes. I'm so sorry. This is all my fault."

Christian chuckled and shook his head. "For goodness sake, lady, give yourself a break! It's only a little coffee stain. I'm sure it will wash out. Lucky for me, I keep a spare shirt in my office for just these occasions."

She looked at him, not sure whether he was joking. "Really?"

"No, not really. I was joking. But, today I'm in luck. I picked up a couple of shirts from the dry cleaner's this morning. They're hanging in my locker. I'll just go and change. It's no biggie."

Slightly reassured that he wouldn't be spending the rest of the day wearing a stained shirt, Daisy let her gaze drift over the rest of him. Once again, she noticed his broad chest and shoulders. He wore a charcoal-gray suit that looked like it had been custom made. His navy-and-green striped tie looked like it cost as much as a week's worth of her salary. The overall package spoke style and confidence.

Her gaze glided lower. His legs were long and lean. His belly, enviably flat. He had an air of authority, of understated confidence that was magnetic. She felt drawn to him. Thick blond hair that had been mussed by the storm the night before had now been brushed into a semblance of control. Blue eyes regarded her steadily. Her heart skipped the tiniest beat. In another lifetime, she might have been attracted to him.

He gave her a quick once over. She didn't miss the spark of interest in his eyes. She was flattered by his attention and then just as quickly reminded herself that she was not on the lookout for a man. In the five years since Pete's death, she hadn't even thought about finding someone else. She and Emma had done just fine on their own. Although she couldn't deny it would be nice to have someone close to confide in, someone to hold her when the going got tough. Like last night.

After tucking Emma into bed, Daisy had spent a

restless couple of hours trying to fall asleep. Images of Lila-Jane and a dark shadowy male figure—who might or might not have snatched the little girl from her bus stop—kept invading Daisy's dreams. She checked all the windows in the house three times and made sure the deadbolt on the front door was locked. She wasn't normally skittish at night, but something about Lila-Jane's disappearance and the storm that continued to rage outside her window had set her on edge. She was just grateful her daughter didn't seem to be affected.

"How did Emma do last night?" Christian asked, as if reading her mind.

She dragged her gaze up to his and steeled herself against the impact of his cobalt eyes. "She was fine. We talked a little about Lila-Jane and what had happened. Of course, it's entirely possible the child wandered off somewhere and got lost. We're all still hoping she's going to show up safe and sound."

"Of course. Nobody wants to think the worst. Do the police have any more leads?"

Daisy shook her head. "I'm not sure. I haven't spoken to Marcie this morning. I guess she's hoping like the rest of us that Lila-Jane shows up. After all, it's only been a little over fifteen hours. That's not so long when you think about it."

"You're right. Although I bet it feels like a lifetime to the little girl's mother."

Daisy looked at him. She was surprised that he was sensitive enough to put his mind to how Lila-Jane's mother might be feeling. She looked at him curiously. Before she could think about what she was about to say, she opened her mouth. "Do you have any kids, Christian?"

He shook his head. "No."

Without conscious thought, her gaze drifted to his left hand. His fingers were bare. A little spurt of excitement went through her at the thought he might be single and then she immediately told herself not to be silly. She wasn't looking for a life partner, or even a boyfriend, for that matter.

"No wife, either," Christian said. "Just in case you're wondering," he added with a cheeky grin.

Daisy's face flamed and she hurriedly lowered her gaze. The last thing she wanted was to have him think she was interested.

"What about you, Mrs Green? Is Emma your only child?"

"Y-yes," Daisy stammered, still unable to look him in the eye.

"And what about Mr Green? Does he work in the city?"

A shaft of emotion rushed through her. Most of the people on her floor knew about Pete's death. Christian had only been there a few months. It was obvious the news hadn't reached him.

"There is no Mr Green. He… He passed away."

Christian started in surprise and a faint hint of embarrassment stained his cheeks. "Oh, forgive me. I didn't know."

Daisy managed a shrug. "It's fine. Don't worry about it. He's been gone five years." She shook her head slowly back and forth. "Five years," she murmured. She could hardly believe it had been that long. The time had passed in an instant. Then again, there were nights when it felt like she'd been alone forever...

"Listen, do you want to go downstairs and grab a coffee? I could do with a refill," Christian chuckled, holding up his half-empty cup.

Daisy blinked in surprise. Her fingers tightened on her cup. *Was he asking her out?* It had been so long since she'd been in the singles game, she was a little rusty. *Did she want to go down that path again? Was she ready to start dating?*

"It's just coffee," Christian said evenly, as if privy to her wild thoughts.

She blushed furiously and was immediately angry at herself for letting her thoughts run away with her. "Of course it is," she answered hurriedly, "but I'm going to have to pass. I have a mountain of witness statements to read through before the day is over and I need to leave by three. But thank you, anyway," she added, and blushed again.

He inclined his head. "Some other time, then."

The grin he tossed her was sexy enough to curl her toes. Her nipples tightened involuntarily. Once again, she was annoyed by her body's instinctive reaction.

Not bothering to reply, she merely gave him a noncommittal nod and turned and escaped back in the direction she'd come. Fresh coffee would have to wait.

———————

Lila-Jane Morrissey pulled at her restraints, but they held firm. The leather bindings around her wrists were secured to the steel bed frame beneath her. She wasn't sure how long she'd been there, but it felt like hours.

The small room where she was held had only the smallest of windows. It was secured with bars and was so high up it was almost impossible to tell if it was day or night. A man wearing a rubber clown mask had come to her at least a couple of hours earlier and had offered her some food and drink. He'd sat on the bed beside her and had released one of the restraints so that she could eat. She'd strained to look through the eyeholes of the mask, trying to identify him, but it had been useless. The mask covered every inch of his face. He spoke in some kind of weird voice that freaked her out and was like nothing or no one she'd ever heard.

"What am I doing here?" she asked, hating that her voice trembled with fear.

"All in good time," the man crooned in his strange voice.

"Where's Mr Grayson?" she demanded, suddenly finding a burst of courage. He didn't respond. Instead, he merely sighed quietly and then secured her wrist once again.

He pushed her back down on the bed. She tensed in terror at what might follow. He reached out and took hold of a strand of hair between his fingers, rubbing it, as if enjoying the feel of it against his skin.

"You're such a pretty little thing, aren't you? I'm

so lucky your momma left you all alone. Pretty little girls like you should never be left alone."

A fresh wave of terror washed over her. She stared at the man in horror. She knew enough about creepy strangers and the talks she listened to in school to know she was in a whole lot of trouble. *He was one of those.* The man wearing the clown mask was one of those men the teachers talked about. One of those men her mother warned her about. She never believed she'd come into contact with one. That they were this real.

Of course, she'd been given all the lectures and her mother had often told her never to go near a stranger in a parked car and she'd listened every time. She hadn't done any of those things. She had climbed on the bus after school and had climbed off again, just like she always did.

Hang on a minute. She *hadn't* climbed off the bus. She remembered now. Mr Grayson had told her he'd received a call from her mother. Her mother was running late. She was worried Lila-Jane might get caught in the storm that had been brewing all afternoon. She wanted to know if Lila-Jane could wait for her at Mr Grayson's house.

At the time, Lila-Jane had thought the request a little odd. Her mother barely knew Mr Grayson. *Why would she want Lila-Jane to go home with him?* But in the end, she'd accepted his explanation and had stayed on the bus the few additional blocks after it passed her stop.

Mr Grayson... Could he have something to do with this? The very idea seemed ridiculous. Mr

Grayson was the bus driver. He'd been driving her bus for a year. He wasn't some strange man with a weird voice. He was nice and cheery and funny. He didn't even mind when the noise on the bus got too loud. Not like some of the other bus drivers.

Veronica Lake had told her all about *their* bus driver. He wouldn't even let them listen to their iPods. Dead silence was all they were allowed. *Dead silence. How awful was that?* Lila-Jane was glad she didn't travel on Veronica's bus.

Was she at Mr Grayson's house? This looked like no house she'd ever been in and the man who was with her didn't look anything like Mr Grayson. *What was going on?*

The man leaned even closer and through the gap in the mask, his lips grazed her forehead. She turned away, but not before she felt the cold rubbery feel against her skin.

"Such a sweet little thing," he murmured, slowly pulling back.

Then just as suddenly as he appeared, he stood and collected the plate and the cup and headed toward a door that she hadn't noticed until then. It was painted the same dark brown color as the walls and if she hadn't seen him push on the panel with his shoulder until it opened, she'd never have guessed it was there.

Just as quietly as he'd arrived, the doorway closed behind him and she was left alone once again. With a heavy sigh, she stared up at the ceiling. It was made of some kind of rough wood. It hadn't even been painted. The lack of adequate windows made the room dim and airless. The only substantial light came from a small lamp the man had left glowing dimly on the nightstand.

It felt like she was in a basement. *Maybe she was in a basement?*

Now that her eyes had adjusted to the dimness, she took the time to look closely at her surroundings. There were no pictures decorating the walls, no personal touches of any kind. The only furniture, apart from the bed, was a single wooden chair and an old couch. That was it. Even the floor was bare.

She wasn't sure where the bathroom was and she wished she'd thought to ask the man before he left. Her bladder was full to bursting. If she didn't go soon, she'd embarrass herself. She so much didn't want that to happen.

But what could she do? The man had gone and who knew how long it would be before he'd return. With a burst of determination, she knocked on the wall beside her as hard as she could.

"*Help! Help!* Can anyone hear me? Hey, mister? I need to use the bathroom! Can you hear me?"

The room remained silent. There was not even a hint of movement through the doorway. The man had just disappeared. She bit back a sob of helplessness and wished her mother was near.

"Please, Momma. Please come and get me. I'm scared, Momma. Please, I want to go home. Please, Momma. Please hurry."

Larry dropped the dirty dishes into the sink and turned on the hot water. Adding suds, he swished them until they turned into bubbles. Neither he nor Christian had the time to clean up after breakfast. Christian always left for the office early and Larry had to be on the road by seven-fifteen. It wasn't until after his bus run had finished that he returned and cleaned up the house.

The winter day was pleasant enough. The storm had cleaned the air and washed away the dust that gathered on the streets, in the gutters, on the cars. Of course, the oil from the asphalt had accumulated in a dark stain along the bottom of his bus and it would also have to be cleaned, but that was a small price to pay.

There was nothing like the smell of fresh air to stimulate the senses. He bet the kids he'd just dropped off at school were having fun in all the puddles. That was, if the teachers let them. These days, it seemed like the grown-ups did their best to take all the fun out of the simple things. It was a shame, really.

Collecting his cereal bowl from the table, he dumped them into the sink and rinsed them, along with Christian's coffee cup and plate. The window above the sink looked out on the back garden. Already the grass had turned from winter-yellow to pale green. The rain brought everything to life, him included.

Oh, yes, he was feeling better than he had in ages. On sudden impulse, he decided to put off weeding the garden and spending the time instead relaxing with the newspaper in his favorite room in the house. He'd had the basement fitted out just to his liking. A comfortable couch, a flat screen TV and a fridge. Oh, and of course, a soundproof wall. *What more could a man want?* He might even take a little nap before his afternoon bus run. *Why not?* No one was going to tell.

CHAPTER 6

Christian ran a hand through his hair and stifled a sigh of impatience. He'd been in court all morning dealing with one juvenile offender after another, when all he wanted to do was hide in his office and relive the few moments he'd spent with Daisy Green. She'd turned down his offer for coffee, but as far as he was concerned, that was a minor setback.

The discovery that she was a widow was the best news he'd heard all week and the knowledge that her husband had been dead five years...even better. Though she'd refused his invitation that morning, it was always possible, if he persisted—without becoming annoying—she might just give in and agree to spend time with him outside the office. It was what he hoped for. But first, he had to get through the day.

Swallowing another sigh, he gazed at the young boy who sat on the opposite side of the scarred wooden table. Most days he loved his job and worked hard to provide the best legal representation he could for his young clients, but every now and then the work got to him. Like at that moment.

He was in one of the interview rooms set aside for legal personnel, taking instructions from thirteen-year-old Marty Cooper. Christian had previously represented the boy in the capacity of duty lawyer. It was part of Sydney Legal's ethos that the firm's lawyers give something back to the community. For one week out of every month, a lawyer on Sydney Legal's payroll was put on the legal aid roster. This week, Christian had, once again, drawn the short straw. He gazed at his client.

"I've read the police facts, Marty. You were caught red-handed, stealing cigarettes. Not only did the security guard see you, you were caught on CCTV cameras. Do you have anything to say for yourself?"

The boy's sullen expression didn't change. He stared at the desk. His only response was the slightest of offhand shrugs.

Christian swallowed his impatience. "This is the first time your case has been listed. You can plead guilty today and get this over with, or you can enter a not guilty plea and we'll go to a hearing. From what I see of the police facts, you're going to be hard-pressed to defend yourself in this matter, but I'll do whatever you ask."

Marty's gaze met Christian's briefly before it returned to the desk. "What will the judge give me if I plead guilty today?"

Christian sighed. "Unfortunately, it's not as easy as that. You have a substantial record for someone so young and many incidents on record are for similar stealing offenses. To make things worse, you're also charged with one count of offensive conduct and one count of offensive language. According to the police facts, you spat at the arresting officer and told him to kiss your ass." Christian eyed his client steadily. "Do you have anything to say to that?"

"He roughed me up when he put the cuffs on. He deserved it."

"So you're not denying the offenses?"

Marty's eyes flared with anger. "I told him to kiss my ass. So what? Since when did that become offensive?"

Christian didn't bother to reply. If the boy truly didn't believe he'd acted offensively, there was nothing Christian could say to convince him otherwise. He'd leave that lecture up to the judge.

"Right, so we're pleading guilty to those two charges. Given your age and your criminal history, if you plead to the stealing offense as well, you might be looking at periodic detention."

Alarm filled the young boy's face. "You mean, they're gonna lock me up?"

Christian shrugged. "It's hard to tell. On their own, these offenses don't amount to more than a good behavior bond, but given that you've done this kind of thing countless times before and the court has already punished you with bonds and even a community service order, there isn't a lot left in their arsenal. To the judge, it looks like you don't give a toss about the legal system or the laws we as a society agree to abide by. You do something wrong, they punish you and a few weeks later, you do it all over again. There's a terrible pattern forming here, Marty, and for a kid your age, that's more than troubling. The judge is likely to see it the same way."

He sighed and pushed around the file that was spread open on his desk. "You'll get credit for your early guilty plea, but like I said, you could very well be facing some time in detention."

Marty's expression filled with resignation. "How much time?" he asked quietly.

"A month. Maybe two. If you're lucky, we might be able to get it reduced to periodic detention."

"What's that?"

"The term is likely to be longer than fulltime custody, but it means you get to stay with your family for some of the time. You usually go into detention over the weekend and then come out again during the week. It goes that way for as long as the judge orders."

Marty nodded and his expression turned thoughtful. "I could probably handle that."

Christian made a noise of exasperation. "The thing is, Marty, you're old enough to know right from wrong. There's no way you didn't know it was wrong to steal those cigarettes. You shouldn't have to choose between fulltime custody and periodic detention. You should be in school, getting an education, planning your future. Not wasting your time being an idiot like this!"

The young boy looked taken aback, as if surprised by his lawyer's outburst. Christian didn't blame him, but he couldn't help himself. There were too many Marty's in the world and if they didn't wake up to the reality soon, it would be too late. He'd seen it many times before and it always depressed him. It was one of the most difficult aspects of representing juveniles.

"It's not my fault the security guard just happened to come by. If he'd stayed where he usually is, I'd have been in and out before anyone even knew those smokes were gone."

Christian clenched his jaw tight, until it hurt. Sometimes he felt that nothing he said or did made a difference. Pushing aside his frustration, he drew in a deep breath and eased it out until some of his tension lessened.

"If you're going to plead guilty, I need to offer some kind of explanation for your behavior to the judge. Is there anything you can tell me that might be looked favorably upon and work to reduce your sentence?"

"My mother's dying with cancer. I'm her primary caregiver. If they send me away, she'll have no one."

Christian gazed at him with narrowed eyes. "You told me that last time. In fact, I seem to recall you told me your mother had less than a month to live. I remember telling the judge just that when I last represented you...two months ago. I take it her prognosis wasn't quite as dismal as you thought?"

His tone was drier than summer grasses in a forest fire, but his sarcasm seemed lost on the youth. The boy's expression grew belligerent.

"One month, six months, twelve. Who knows? It's none of your business."

Christian ground his teeth together and silently counted to ten. "You see, Marty, it *is* my business. I have an obligation to tell the court the truth. You told me your mother had less than a month to live and I passed that information on to the judge. If I recall, the judge took that information into account and reduced your sentence. If you're telling me now that what you told me before wasn't true, then we have a problem."

The calmness of his tone belied the anger that coursed through Christian's veins, but he refused to allow the boy the satisfaction of knowing he'd gotten to him. He wanted nothing more than to push away from the desk and storm out of there.

To hell with it and to hell with you. Go tell your sorry story to the judge yourself and see what result you get...

The words were on the tip of his tongue, but with a gargantuan effort, he managed to rein them in. He was the adult here. He needed to remember that. He was there to provide the best representation for his clients that he could and by God, he'd do that—even if it killed him.

Marty heaved an exaggerated sigh and held up his hands in a sign of surrender. "Okay, okay! Don't get your knickers in a knot. My mother has cancer, all right. That part is true. I made up the bit about her dying in less than a month. No one knows how long she has. She could live for years..."

He smirked and once again, Christian's anger rushed to the fore. Once again, he called on his self-control to remain seated behind the desk. That was no mean feat. Staring at the ceiling, he called on the heavens to give him the patience to get through this. The day couldn't end soon enough.

Daisy checked the time and hurried to the elevator. She had less than fifteen minutes to get to Emma's school or she'd arrive after the bell. She didn't want her little girl standing outside the school gate, wondering where her momma was, whether she'd been caught up at work again.

Impatiently, she waited for the elevator and watched the illuminated numbers move slowly up each floor. With a sigh of relief, it reached hers and the doors opened with a *ding*. Christian stepped out, carrying a briefcase, at the same moment she stepped in. She bumped into him and it was a case of déjà vu.

"Whoa!" he laughed, holding his briefcase up out of the way.

"I-I'm sorry," she stammered and cursed the heat that swept across her cheeks. *What was it about this guy that turned her into a stumbling, bumbling idiot? So unlike her.*

"It's fine. No harm done. I don't have coffee this time." He said it lightly and a smile played around his lips, but she was embarrassed just the same.

"I'm sorry," she said again and hurried inside the elevator.

"You're leaving early," he observed.

"Yes. I have to collect Emma from school."

He nodded. "I understand."

Daisy barely had time to acknowledge his comment before the doors slid closed. She leaned against the cool steel wall and breathed a sigh of relief. *Great.* Just what she needed. Another embarrassing encounter with the first man—since Pete—who made her heart beat faster. *Just great.* Still, there was nothing she could do about it now. She was just grateful the elevator made a speedy descent to the ground.

Stepping out, she waved to the doorman who sat behind a counter not far from the entrance doors, and hurried out of the building.

Emma's face lit up in a smile of excitement and relief when she spied her. Daisy's heart clenched with love at the sight of her daughter. She was reminded all over again just how much Emma looked like Pete. If her hair were shorter, she be a total mini-Pete. Children filed past them, shouting and chatting and calling out to their mothers. When Daisy spared a thought for Lila-Jane she immediately felt guilty. She hadn't thought about the little girl all day. She made a mental note to call Marcie and get an update. At the same time, she sent up a silent prayer that the child had been found.

"We had an important meeting today."

Emma's solemn announcement interrupted Daisy's thoughts. She switched her attention to her daughter. "Did you, honey?"

"Yes. We had to assemble in the hall. The whole school. Even Mrs Barber was there and you know how busy *she* is."

Daisy hid a smile at the way her daughter described the headmistress. "What was the meeting about?" she asked.

"Talking to strangers. It's because of Lila-Jane," Emma said matter-of-factly.

Daisy hid her surprise. "Did they mention her specifically?"

"No, but everyone knows she's still missing."

"Well, that was this morning. Maybe the police have found her now."

Emma's eyes widened with hope. "Do you think so?"

"I can call her mom and find out."

"Can you do it now, Momma? Please? I've been worried about Lila-Jane all day."

Daisy's heart clenched again. The look of earnestness on her daughter's face flooded her with emotion. It wasn't right that a nine-year-old should have to consider, for even a minute, the possibilities of what might have happened to a missing school friend. The fact that the worried nine-year-old was Daisy's daughter made it even worse.

She drew Emma close. "It's going to be all right, honey. I'm sure Lila-Jane's fine. The police might already have found her." She drew back a little and gazed at her little girl. "I'll call Mrs Morrissey right now, okay?"

Emma compressed her lips and nodded. Daisy stood and tugged out her phone. Scrolling through her contacts, she found Marcie's number. The phone dialed out in her ear. Once. Twice. Three times. Four times.

"H-hello?"

The hesitant, almost fearful murmur took her by surprise. "Marcie?"

"Yes."

"This is Daisy. I was... I was just wondering how you got on? Did you find Lila-Jane?"

A sob of distress sounded through the phone, followed by another and another. Daisy's chest tightened in response. Was Marcie sobbing from relief, or something else—something Daisy didn't want to contemplate?

"Marcie...are you all right?"

"*Noooo...*"

The howl of pain left Daisy in no doubt about Marcie's state of mind or the fact that Lila-Jane hadn't returned home. Daisy's fingers tightened on the phone. She glanced down at Emma. Her daughter was gazing up at her, watching, waiting. Daisy quickly turned away. She cupped a hand over her mouth and lowered her voice.

"Marcie, are you at home?"

"Y-yes."

"Is anyone there with you?"

"N-no."

"What about your sister? Have you called her?"

"N-no. She's out of t-town." Another round of sobs followed the announcement.

Daisy stared at the ground in dismay. Acutely

aware of Emma standing less than three feet away, she chose her words with care.

"Have you spoken to the police today?"

"Yes. They... They can't find any trace of her. No one knows where she is!"

The announcement was followed by another wail of anguish. Daisy closed her eyes briefly, in an effort to block out her friend's distress. A wave of helplessness surged through her, along with an overwhelming feeling of relief that *her* daughter wasn't missing. The feeling was immediately replaced by a rush of guilt.

"I'm so sorry, Marcie. I was hoping so hard that the police might have found her by now. Do you want me to come over?"

Marcie sniffed and hiccupped before replying. "W-would you mind?"

"No, of course not," Daisy responded.

"That would be nice."

"I'm just collecting Emma from school. We'll be there shortly."

Daisy ended the call and took a second or two to collect herself before turning back to her daughter.

"Honey, I just spoke to Mrs Morrissey. She—"

"Lila-Jane hasn't come home, has she?" Emma asked flatly.

Daisy opened her mouth to protest, but closed it again. Emma wasn't stupid. Besides, she deserved the truth. "No, she hasn't."

"Where is she?"

"I'm not sure. The police are still looking for her."

"I bet she's been taken by someone! A bad

man like what the teachers told us about."

Daisy took her daughter by the arms and held her gaze. "No one knows what happened to her, honey. It's no good making wild guesses. It doesn't help anyone, especially her poor mother. Now, I promised Mrs Morrissey we'd go over there right now. She doesn't have anyone to...talk to. You don't mind, do you?'

Emma shrugged and kicked at the ground with her shoe. Daisy saw the reluctance in every line of her daughter's body. She pulled her little girl close.

"Listen to me, honey. Mrs Morrissey's very upset. Her daughter's missing. I'd be very upset, too, if you were missing and I'd count on my friends to help me through it. Mrs Morrissey's sister is out of town. She has no one. She needs us."

"How long are we going to be there?" Emma asked, staring at the ground.

"I'm not sure," Daisy answered honestly.

"As long as we were last night?"

"No, honey. Not that long."

"Okay."

After another quick hug, Daisy took her daughter's small hand and headed toward her Honda.

Daisy added milk and sugar to Marcie's cup of tea and then pressed it into the woman's hand. Blindly, Marcie brought the cup up to her lips and took a sip.

"Th-thank you, Daisy. It's very good of you to come over."

Daisy patted her friend on the shoulder. "Of course. I can't imagine what you must be going through, waiting..." Her voice drifted off. She'd never felt so wholly and incredibly inadequate.

How did one act in such a situation? What could she say to make Marcie feel better?

There was nothing she could say. The only thing that would make this whole sad situation better was the arrival of Lila-Jane and that was totally out of Daisy's control.

Marcie looked at her with red-rimmed eyes. "Where's Emma?"

"She's in Lila-Jane's room. I hope you don't mind. She wanted to keep Lila-Jane's dolls company. She was sure they'd be missing your daughter, too."

Marcie nodded. Her lip trembled and her eyes filled with a fresh flood of tears. She set the tea cup aside and dabbed at her eyes with a tissue.

"Is there anything you need, Marcie? Anything I can do to help?"

"No. There's nothing. Except..." Marcie's voice drifted off.

Daisy sat forward on the couch where she sat opposite her friend. "Except what?"

"Some people have organized a prayer vigil tonight in the park down the street. Would you mind...?" She dragged her gaze up from where it had been fixed on the carpet and looked at Daisy. "Would you mind coming with me?"

Daisy stood and came closer. She reached out

and squeezed Marcie's hand. "Of course I will. And Emma will come, too. We'll go together. Would that be all right?"

Marcie gave her a grateful smile. "Thank you, Daisy. You're a good friend."

Daisy brushed her gratitude aside. "It's no trouble, Marcie. Emma and I are glad to go."

CHAPTER 7

Christian closed the front door behind him and sighed, thankful that his day was over. Tossing his briefcase on the couch as he walked through the living room, he wandered into the kitchen and found his uncle standing by the stove.

Larry glanced up at his entry and continued stirring something in a pot. The rich aroma of tomato and garlic reached Christian's nose.

"Smells good," he commented. "Spaghetti sauce?"

"Yes, I thought we might have an early dinner. A prayer vigil has been organized at the local park for Lila-Jane Morrissey. I'd like to go."

Christian frowned. "So they still haven't found that little girl?"

"No, they haven't."

Christian shook his head slowly. "That poor mother. She must be going out of her mind."

"Yes. I can't imagine how she must be feeling. I understand Lila-Jane is her only child."

Christian sighed and ran a hand tiredly through his hair. It had been a long day dealing with juvenile offenders and a host of other matters that had come before the court. Most days he loved his work as a juvenile defender, but today wasn't one of them.

His uncle shot him a concerned look. "Hard day?"

Christian nodded. "You can say that again."

"What happened?"

Christian laughed derisively. "Where do I start?"

"Like that, huh?"

Christian blew out his breath on another heavy sigh and pulled out a chair. Leaning his elbows on the kitchen table, he rested his chin in his hands.

"The day didn't start well. I collided with a colleague in the office and ended up wearing half a cup of coffee all over the front of my shirt only minutes before I was due in court. Thankfully, I'd stopped by the dry cleaner's on my way to work and picked up some shirts. I'd stored them in my locker. Then I spent the day dealing with one smart-ass juvenile offender after another. Marty Cooper was back before the courts today."

"Oh, Christian. Wasn't he the kid you told me about your first week at the new job? I thought he promised you last time he wouldn't be back again. How long ago was it? A couple of months?"

"Yeah, not long enough. He can't help himself. It's like he wants to get in trouble. Like he gets off on the attention, even though it's attention of the wrong kind."

"How did he do?"

Christian grimaced. "Not so good. We fronted up to Judge Stanley. He's not known for his leniency. Six weeks full-time custodial sentence. Marty was lucky it wasn't longer."

Uncle Larry moved closer and gave him a reassuring pat on the shoulder. "Don't take it to heart, Christian. I'm sure you're doing your best. They're lucky to have you on their side."

"Yeah, well, I didn't feel so lucky today. Three out of four of my clients were sent to juvie. Two more await sentencing and there's no guarantee they won't end up the same way. Some days I feel like I'm losing the battle."

Larry nodded sympathetically and moved back toward the stove. "I feel for you, Christian. I really do. I don't know how you do what you do every day."

Christian snorted. "Ha! I could say the same thing about you! There's no way I could handle driving a busload of school kids to and from school each day. You deserve a medal."

His uncle shrugged and smiled. "What can I say? I love it. I've been doing it for most of my life. I know each and every one of the kids on my school run. It's like they're my own. I couldn't imagine doing anything else."

Christian regarded his uncle in silence. "Do you ever wish you'd gotten married, had children?"

Larry pursed his lips and then nodded. "Yeah. I do. It would have been nice to have a family of my own." And then, as if becoming aware of what he'd said, he quickly added, "Not that I don't think of you as my family, Christian. You're as close as a son could be. I just meant—"

"It's fine, Uncle Larry," Christian replied, waving his uncle's explanation away. "I understand."

Silence fell between them. While Larry tended the food on the stove, Christian's thoughts returned to his day, including the run-in he had with Daisy Green. He wished he could get her out of his mind, but that was proving almost impossible.

"I don't suppose you want to accompany me to this prayer vigil?"

Uncle Larry's question broke into his thoughts. He looked up and nodded thoughtfully. "Yeah, I guess I could. I don't have anything else going on. Besides, it's good to show support for these things."

His uncle smiled. "Yes, you're right. And thanks for agreeing to come. It means a lot to me."

Christian gazed at his uncle. "This isn't your fault, Uncle Larry."

His uncle held his gaze for long moment and then looked away on a quiet sigh. "Yes, so you keep saying. I wish I could believe it."

"Uncle Larry, let's not start on this again." Christian's voice was firm, but he could tell from the look on his uncle's face that the man still wasn't convinced. "What time does the prayer vigil start?" he asked quietly.

"Seven. The sauce is done. The spaghetti will only take a few minutes. We should have plenty of time."

Christian nodded. "Anything I can do to help?"

———

Daisy crouched in front of her daughter on the sidewalk outside Marcie's house and made sure Emma's jacket was zippered. The sun had set hours earlier and there was a distinct chill in the night air. Normally Emma would be on her way to bed by now, but tonight they were showing their support by attending Lila-Jane's prayer vigil. One of Marcie's neighbors had arrived while they were waiting on Emma in the bathroom. She'd offered to walk with Marcie to the prayer vigil.

"Of course, Marcie," Daisy had responded. "You go ahead. We won't be far behind you. I'll make sure to pull the door shut behind us." Marcie had acknowledged the comments with a dull nod and had followed her neighbor outside.

The park was only a short walk away and in no time at all, she and Emma arrived at the meeting spot. Emma gasped at the sight of the crowd.

"Wow! There's so many people here, Momma! Have they all come to pray for Lila-Jane?"

"Yes, honey. And it's lovely to see. I'm sure Mrs Morrissey will be very grateful that so many are here. We're praying for Lila-Jane's speedy return."

Emma looked up at her with a curious expression. "What do you think has happened to her?"

Daisy's heart clenched at the concern in her daughter's eyes and took a moment to decide what to say. She didn't want to frighten the child, but on the other hand, she needed to instill enough caution in her little girl that the same thing didn't happen to her. Whatever that was. It was agonizing not knowing.

Had Lila-Jane been taken by a stranger? A pedophile who happened to be in the neighborhood at the exact time Marcie's daughter climbed off the bus? The very idea was unthinkable, but what else could have happened? Where else could she be?

Marcie's daughter was very familiar with the neighborhood. She'd lived there all her life. It was highly unlikely she'd wandered off and gotten lost. The only explanation was that she'd been snatched off the sidewalk and taken somewhere. The longer she remained missing, the more likely such a possibility became. Daisy was certain Marcie had already reached the very same conclusion. The thought made her heart ache.

"Look at all the candles, Momma! Don't they look beautiful? We should have brought some!"

Emma's comments interrupted Daisy's thoughts. She looked down at her daughter and nodded. "You're right, honey. They do look beautiful and we should have brought some. I didn't think about it. But we have our flashlights and we can still say some prayers for Lila-Jane."

Emma looked up at her with a solemn expression in her big blue eyes. "I've been praying for Lila-Jane ever since she went missing. I hope God brings her home soon. I'm sure she must be missing her Momma. I know I would be."

Tears stung Daisy's eyes and a lump filled her throat. Beyond words, she squeezed her daughter's hand in response. They joined the crowd of people who were softly singing *Amazing Grace*, surrounded by a circle of light. In the crowd, Daisy recognized faces from around her neighborhood. There were also many people she didn't recognize. Then one of the men standing close to her inclined his head in her direction and she realized it was Detective McLennan.

"Daisy, isn't it?" he asked.

She nodded. "Yes. It's nice to see you again, Detective McLennan."

He moved closer and lowered his voice. "Marcie Morrissey told me she's been divorced twelve months and the separation was anything but amicable. What can you tell me about Robert Morrissey?"

Daisy started in surprise. She'd never been close friends with the Morrissey family, but she knew them well enough. The thought that Bob might be behind Lila-Jane's disappearance was ludicrous.

"You're looking in the wrong direction there, Detective. There's no way Lila-Jane's father kidnapped her."

"You sound so certain, Daisy. Why is that?"

Daisy paused, unsure how much of Marcie's private life needed to be exposed. The detective must have read the indecision on her face.

"A little girl is missing, Daisy. We need to find her."

The graveness of his tone sent a shiver of apprehension flooding through her veins. She drew in a fortifying breath and slowly released it.

"Robert Morrissey didn't want children. That's the reason he and Marcie filed for divorce. There's no way he's taken Lila-Jane now. That wouldn't make an iota of sense."

The detective absorbed her words in silence and then nodded once. "That's what Marcie said, but she didn't know her ex-husband is now hooked up with some nasty guys. Drug dealers. The word on the street is that he owes them a lot of money and so far, he hasn't coughed up. That makes me think someone might be of the frame of mind to kidnap a child in order to increase the pressure to pay up. My guess is Mr Drug Dealer has no idea Bob isn't too fond of his kid. It's an easy enough mistake to make."

Daisy started in surprise. Bob had always been a bit of a loose character who found it difficult to hold down steady employment, but she'd never pegged him for a drug user. It was funny how she'd lived in the same neighborhood for almost as long as the Morrisseys and yet, she hadn't had a clue about Bob's less-than-savory past—and possibly his present. She wondered what else she didn't know...

The detective turned away and faced the enlarged photo of Lila-Jane that someone had placed against a centuries-old Moreton Bay fig tree. The exposed tree roots cradled the picture frame, like gnarled old fingers. Candles and bouquets of flowers surrounded the photo, reminding Daisy of a memorial—as if everyone present thought the child was already dead. A shiver of fear ran down her spine and she tightened her grip on Emma's hand. *Please, God, bring that little girl home. Bring her home to her momma, safe and sound.*

As her gaze moved around the people gathered

in the park, she snagged upon another familiar face. Her heart skipped a beat. Christian Grayson stood off to one side with his uncle. Emma spied them at the same time.

"Look, Momma! It's Mr Grayson! He must've come to pray for Lila-Jane."

Daisy nodded. "Yes, I guess so. It's nice of him to come."

"Who's that man beside him? I know! It's the man we met last night."

"You're right, honey. That's Mr Grayson's nephew. He's also Mr Grayson."

Emma's lips turned upwards in the briefest of smiles. "So they're both Mr Grayson..." She chuckled.

Daisy smiled back at her. "Yes, they are."

"Oh, look! They're coming over!"

Daisy glanced in the direction where the Grayson men stood and noticed Emma was right. Christian and his uncle were making their way toward them. Daisy's heart skipped a beat. She gave himself a stern talking to. *For goodness sake, he's only a man. He's no one to get excited about.* Who was she trying to kid?

"Mrs Green, it's nice to see you again."

Daisy acknowledged Christian's greeting with a nod. She wondered at his use of her married name. Though she hadn't given him permission to call her otherwise, it was still old-fashioned in this day and age. Most people, and especially work colleagues, referred to each other by their first names, like the detective had. She supposed it would only be polite to invite him to do the same.

"My name's Daisy. You can call me, Daisy," she added and then silently cursed the blush that stole across her cheeks.

His eyes glowed with pleasure and his gaze remained steady on hers. "Daisy, it is then," he said.

Daisy turned and acknowledged the bus driver. "Mr Grayson, you look well."

"Thank you, Daisy." He frowned momentarily. "You don't mind if I call you Daisy, do you? After all the time we spent together last night searching for Lila-Jane, I feel we've moved past the formalities. Please, call me Larry."

Daisy inclined her head. "Larry."

An awkward silence fell between them and Daisy sifted through her mind for something to say. "It's nice of you both to come out tonight." Her gaze fell on Christian. "You probably don't even know Lila-Jane."

"You're right," he replied. "I don't. But, of course, my uncle does. He wanted to come and show his support and he asked me to accompany him." Christian shrugged and then added, "I was happy to."

"Well, it's very neighborly of you," Daisy said. "I'm sure there are better ways you could be spending your time this chilly night."

"Oh, don't you worry, Christian loves little girls. I remember when he was younger he spent hours playing with the little girls in the neighborhood, didn't you, Christian?"

He directed the question toward his nephew who frowned and shook his head as if confused.

Larry seemed oblivious to his nephew's dark expression.

Daisy was equally confused. It was a strange thing to say about his nephew. *What was Larry getting at?*

"Remember Nikki?" Larry continued with a chuckle. "You two were inseparable." He turned back to Daisy. "Believe me, Daisy, this boy of mine was more than eager to come down here and show his support for Lila-Jane."

"Who's Nikki?" Emma's question surprised them both.

Daisy glanced down at her daughter and drew her close. She glanced back at Christian. "I'm sorry, she's just curious."

His answering smile looked forced. "Don't worry about it." He glanced at Emma. "Nikki was a friend. Someone I knew a long time ago."

"Are you still friends?"

Christian's lips tightened and Daisy thought she caught a flash of pain in his eyes. "No. She... she died."

"Oh." Emma fell silent and then quickly recovered her aplomb. "So, do you drive a school bus, too?"

This time, Christian's smile appeared more genuine. "No, I'm a lawyer. I work with your mom. Didn't she tell you?"

Emma shook her head and her golden curls bounced with the movement. "No, she didn't. Have you worked there long?"

"Not too long. A bit over three months."

"Where did you work before?"

Daisy squirmed. Her daughter's mind was way too curious. "Emma, honey, it's really none of our business where Mr—"

"It's fine," Christian interrupted. He glanced back at Emma. "I worked at another law firm in the city."

"Why did you leave there? Didn't you like it anymore?"

"Sure, I did. But, things got a little…complicated."

Emma stared at him with curiosity. "How?"

Daisy came alert, but refused to acknowledge even to herself that she was suddenly more than interested to hear what he had to say.

"Well, I was dating a paralegal from work and we were kind of serious, but then we broke up. It got a little difficult running into her in the corridors. I decided to get a job elsewhere."

"What was her name?"

"Justine."

"That's a nice name. Was she pretty?"

"Yes, she was very pretty."

"Were you going to marry her?"

Daisy's cheeks burned. She took Emma firmly by the arm. "All right, Emma. That's enough. Leave Mr Grayson alone. Come on, let's go and find Mrs Morrissey and let her know we're here."

Without even waiting to bid Christian or Larry farewell, Daisy hurried her daughter to the other side of the crowd where Marcie sat perched on a lawn chair.

Marcie's hair hung lank and messy and didn't look like it had been brushed since Lila-Jane's disappearance. She sat quietly, slumped in the chair, staring almost trance-like at the flickering candles that surrounded her daughter's picture. A pale-blue afghan was stretched over her lap.

Daisy approached slowly and reached out and gently rested a hand on her friend's shoulder. "Marcie?"

The woman jumped and turned wide, red-rimmed eyes in Daisy's direction. "Oh, Daisy. It's you. Thank you for coming. Have they found her? Have they found my baby?"

Daisy was filled with a rush of sadness and slowly shook her head. "No, I don't think so. I... I just wanted to let you know I was here and to tell you, if there's anything I can do, anything you need... You just call me, okay?"

"The only thing I need is Lila-Jane," Marcie whispered, her voice a mere croak of sound.

"I understand," Daisy replied softly. "The police are doing everything they can."

"Bah! The police! What do they know?"

Marcie's sudden show of spirit startled Daisy. "What do you mean?"

"They think Lila-Jane's disappearance has something to do with Bob! Can you believe it? Bob never wanted a baby. He fought harder over the furniture than he did over his child. It was one of the reasons we eventually separated. I lost count of the number of times he accused me of tricking him into conceiving our little girl."

Once again, Daisy was taken aback. For the second time that night, she realized she didn't know her neighbors as well as she thought. "D-did you trick him?" she stammered.

"Of course I did, but he left me with no other choice. He knew how much I wanted a baby. Right from the start, I made that very clear. Okay, so he also was just as adamant he didn't, but I thought I could change his mind. I thought once we were married and in our own home, he'd want a family. Only, he didn't."

Tears welled up in Marcie's eyes and her shoulders shook on a sob. She brought her hands up to cover her face and cried. "Even when little Lila-Jane was born, he didn't want her. He didn't even come to the hospital. I had to call a cab to get there and to get me home a few days later. And as my baby passed each milestone—her first smile, her first step, her first day of school—I was sure Bob would come around; that he'd look into the eyes of this perfect being we'd created and fall in love, just like I did. But it never happened."

She sniffed and wiped at her nose with the back of her hand. In silence, Daisy handed her a tissue. Marcie murmured her thanks.

"The police asked me if I thought Bob had something to do with Lila-Jane's disappearance. I nearly laughed in their faces. He hasn't seen her since the divorce. He's probably forgotten what she looks like. There's no way he's behind this."

"The detective mentioned something about drugs and money Bob might owe. Did you know he was involved in that kind of thing?"

"No, never! I would never have let him around Lila-Jane if I'd known that, but I haven't seen him for a year and a half. Who knows what's happened in that time?"

"Do you think Bob might have told these drug dealers about Lila-Jane?"

"No. I bet she hasn't once crossed his mind since I kicked him out."

"Perhaps they found out where you lived and watched the house for a while? It wouldn't take much to discover you had a child. Could they have taken Lila-Jane, thinking Bob would pay?"

Marcie groaned in frustration and tugged at her unkempt hair. "No! No! No! The police already asked me these questions. Bob isn't behind this. I just *know*."

Marcie broke into a fresh bout of sobbing and buried her face in her hands. The quiet tones of the crowd softly singing, filled the silence. Daisy looked around her, filled with despair. *Where are you, Lila-Jane? Please, Lila-Jane. Come home.*

Lila-Jane stuffed a fist in her mouth and tried to hold the tears at bay. Her captor had been down again earlier, but that was hours ago. Once again, she needed to use the bathroom and it was getting really hard to hold on. She prayed he might return soon so that she could relieve herself.

The sound of a kitten caught her attention and she stilled upon the bed. The room she was in only had one tiny barred window, so the fact she could hear it meant the cat must be in the house. A surge of longing went through her. She loved kittens. Now, more than ever, she wanted to feel its soft touch. The silky fur, the soft wet nose, the cute little pink tongue...

She sat up as far as her restraints allowed and called to it. "Here, kitty, kitty, kitty."

The meowing sound got louder and then she heard a scratching at the door. It was the same door the man had exited through earlier. Her heart pounded with excitement at the thought of having the kitten close. It couldn't open the door, but even knowing it was right outside brought her comfort.

"Here, kitty, kitty, kitty. Are you there?"

The meowing sound came again. Lila-Jane relaxed back against the musty pillow and managed a wobbly smile.

CHAPTER 8

The house was still and quiet. Christian had left for work. Larry had completed his bus run and had finished cleaning up the breakfast things. Now he was in Christian's office—the one his nephew had set up in one of the spare bedrooms. It seemed he was always working on some case or another. Really, the boy worked too hard.

A gentle smile played around Larry's lips and he whistled a long-forgotten tune. He snipped around the edges of the half-page newspaper story dedicated to the disappearance of Lila-Jane Morrissey. He pulled open the bottom drawer of Christian's desk and reached in for the scrapbook Larry kept there. Opening it to a blank page, he glued the story in. Idly, he flipped back through the pages. There were many such stories. Some of them dated back decades.

He especially loved the graphic close-up photos in the newspapers of the family members— in particular the parents. They always looked so...broken. It was wrong that their pain brought him so much pleasure, but he couldn't seem to help it.

The prayer vigil for Lila-Jane Morrissey had been well attended. It was obvious she and her mother were well known and well liked in the community. Marcie Morrissey looked as devastated as Larry expected, even worse than how she'd looked the night before. It was so very sad. She was lucky to have such a supportive network of friends and neighbors. Very lucky, indeed...

With a chuckle, he closed the scrapbook and tucked it away in its usual place in the bottom drawer, underneath a pile of old cases Christian had used in a trial more than three years earlier. Larry was almost certain the boy would never look at them again. It was the perfect place to plant his insurance, just in case.

———————

Christian stared at the legal form that filled his screen and tried to concentrate. He'd typed the same line three times already and still hadn't gotten it right. The truth was, he couldn't stop thinking about what his uncle had said at the prayer vigil. *Why would he talk about Nikki like that and make out that Christian had some kind of unhealthy fetish for young girls?* They were praying for the safe return of a child who just might have been kidnapped by a pedophile. At the very least, the comment was in bad taste. And then there was Daisy Green...

He'd noticed she'd spent much of her time by Marcie's side and it warmed him to know that Daisy was the kind of woman who put herself out for others and was there for a woman who must be going through hell. It told him a lot about Daisy's character and his admiration for her grew.

Images of her glossy dark hair and eyes that held so much mystery filled his mind. He didn't know what to make of her. Though she engaged in pleasant conversation with him and was polite to a fault, she sent out an aura of "don't touch" and had looked panicked at the thought of spending time with him over coffee.

Though a part of him was reluctant to begin a new relationship after his experience with Justine, he couldn't deny that he was restless to settle down and start a family of his own. Having lost his parents at a young age, he yearned to experience what it meant to be a family again.

Uncle Larry had done his best, but the man battled demons of his own. He'd made it clear the first night Christian moved in that he needed time to himself. He'd confessed he was a recovering alcoholic and needed alone time to rest and recover from the day's events.

There were many nights that Christian spent alone in front of the TV while his uncle watched old movies and listened to classical music in the basement. Though Christian never saw his uncle drink and out of respect, Christian kept no alcohol in the house, Uncle Larry had explained it was a constant battle and he needed to remain vigilant. It was for this reason, he took time out most days to recharge and relax alone, immersing himself in movies and music to ward off the beast.

It had resulted in a fairly lonely childhood for Christian, with his uncle often absent in his basement. He supposed that was one of the reasons why he yearned for a family of his own and for at least a handful of children. Somehow he thought having a wife and children of his own would alleviate the loneliness that had become like a second skin. And then in the harsh cold light of day, when he allowed himself to closely examine his reasons, he wondered if loneliness, on its own, was a good enough reason to settle down.

He would argue back and forth in his head, like any good lawyer would do, seeing the issue from all angles and examining every possibility. And then he'd come to the same conclusion that loneliness could be all-consuming and finding a life partner to spend time with was a natural urge for any person.

The fact was, humans weren't meant to live alone. Then again, he didn't want to become a statistic, either. The divorce rate around the world climbed higher every year. The thought of breaking up his family—ferrying kids between two parents who no longer loved each other, gutted him. That certainly wasn't a path he was prepared to walk.

He thought he'd chosen well with Justine and he turned out to be so wrong. He'd been sure she was the one and that she felt the same way about him. That mistake made him more cautious about his next choice, although he couldn't deny Daisy kept returning to the forefront of his mind.

It wasn't just that she came with a ready-made family—Emma Green was as cute as a button—it was more that she already seemed connected to him in some indefinable way. He was drawn to her without quite knowing why. It was more than her beautiful face and luscious figure. It was more than the keen intelligence in her eyes. It was something he couldn't define, something he'd never felt before, even with Justine.

The question was, could he trust the feeling, whatever it was? The answer was: He simply didn't know. He'd never been in this position before and it scared him half to death. With Justine, it had seemed easy. He thought that they loved each other enough to make it work. It hadn't turned out that way, and looking back, he realized he'd liked Justine more than he loved her and she probably hadn't loved him at all.

Even with that behind him, he wasn't against trying again and he was keen to see where this attraction to Daisy might go. He wondered whether his instinctive reaction to her would lead to something more permanent. More meaningful. And then there was the slight difficulty of overcoming her reluctance to get involved with him—or any man—if he'd read her signals right.

Even though her husband had been gone for half a decade, it was obvious she was still beholden to him. She'd only reluctantly provided Christian with the information that she was no longer married. And yet she blushed when he drew near and at times seemed awkward and nervous. Those reactions gave him hope that maybe she did feel something for him, something inside her that hadn't died along with her husband.

A knock on his office door interrupted his musings. He looked up and invited them to enter. He fully expected his secretary, Angela, to fill the opening and was surprised when Daisy stepped inside.

He immediately straightened in his seat. He adjusted his tie and tugged at his cuffs and tried to slow the sudden rush of nerves. Meanwhile, she looked fresh and beautiful in a pale-yellow linen suit. Her hair was swept back into a ponytail that made her look younger and emphasized the height of her cheekbones. He noticed that though she was well put together, dark shadows rested below her eyes and gave her an air of vulnerability... There was nothing vulnerable about the anger on her face.

"What did you say to Judge Stanley about Marty Cooper?"

Christian held up his hands and at the same time, leaned back in his chair. "*Whoa!* Where did that come from? I didn't even know you knew Marty Cooper."

"I represented him less than a year ago. I've just taken a call from his distraught mother. She told me he's been locked up for six weeks. How could you have allowed him to be put into detention? His mother relies on him for help! She's dying of cancer! Don't you know that? She has months to live. She needs him by her side!"

Christian eyed her steadily and waited for her burst of anger to subside. When she paused in her tirade, he calmly replied, "Marty Cooper has no one to blame but himself. If you'd taken the time to look through his file, you would have seen that he's been brought before the courts for one offense or another more than half a dozen times this year and it's only July."

She opened her mouth to respond, but he beat her to it. "As for his dying mother, he should have thought about that before he stole from his local supermarket or gave a mouthful of cheek to the police. It's not like he wasn't familiar with what happens when he flagrantly breaks the law."

She shook her head and glared at him, her eyes narrowed in disappointment. "Whose side are you on? You're meant to be *his* lawyer, not an assistant to the prosecutor. Did you even bother to tell the judge about his mother?"

Christian held her gaze, refusing to back down. He had nothing to be ashamed of in his conduct at his client's sentencing. "Of course I did, just like I did the time before. Only, this time, Marty conceded he hadn't been totally honest to me in the past."

Daisy frowned at him. "What do you mean?" Some of the anger had left her tone.

"The last time I represented Marty Cooper, which was a whole two months ago, he told me his mother was dying of cancer and had only a month to live. Naturally, I believed him and I advised the court of such. The judge took this into account and went leniently on him. Yesterday,

Marty said something that made me think he hadn't been completely truthful when it came to his mother. When I challenged him on it, he admitted she was dying of cancer, but no one knew how long she had to live. In fact, the way he understood it, she might yet outlive any of us."

Daisy's quiet gasp of surprise led Christian to believe this news was as unexpected for her as it had been for him. The tension left her body. With a sigh, she moved closer and plunked herself down in the seat that stood opposite his desk—the one usually reserved for clients.

"I can't believe he lied about a thing like that," she said morosely. Her gaze swept upwards and his gut clenched at the disappointment in her eyes. "I mean, *who does that*? Who makes up things about their mother's life expectancy for their own gain?"

Christian compressed his lips and shrugged. "I imagine you've been in this game for as long as I have. I'm sure this isn't the first client to lie to you."

"Yes, of course and with kids it happens more often than I like, but telling us his mother had a month to live! I mean, that really takes the cake! I can't believe I fell for it!"

"Don't be too hard on yourself. I fell for it the first time, too. No one's perfect. Not even you."

He lightened his comment with a chuckle so that she knew he was only teasing. To his relief, she answered with a reluctant grin and then sighed and absently brushed a strand of hair back off her face. Her skin gleamed like porcelain under the overhead lights. He wondered if it felt as soft as he imagined and fought against the urge to find out. His pulse skipped a beat at the thought of touching her and he was filled with an unexpected surge of need. His suit pants grew uncomfortably tight and he hunted around for another topic of conversation in an effort to distract himself.

"It was a nice prayer service last night," he murmured.

Her expression immediately sobered and he silently cursed himself for breaking the lighthearted mood.

"Yes, it was. Poor Marcie. She must be going out of her mind. The police are clutching at straws. They thought her ex-husband might be involved, but neither of us think so. Apart from him, the police don't seem to have anyone."

"It's not the first time a child has disappeared. A lot of them turn up," he said in an attempt to offer encouragement.

"Yes, you're right. Let's hope Lila-Jane is one of them."

"How is Emma handling it?"

"It's been a little tough," Daisy admitted. "She was so young when she lost her dad, but she can still remember what it felt like to have him around. At least, that's what she says. She understands how hard it must be for Marcie to have her daughter missing, to not know where she is. Emma's as concerned as the rest of us about where Lila-Jane might be."

Christian nodded sagely. "My uncle is taking it hard, too. He feels responsible for her disappearance. After all, he was the one who let her off the bus."

Daisy was shaking her head even before he finished. "It's not your uncle's fault. Everyone knows that. He was just doing his job. Marcie had given permission for Lila-Jane to get off the bus on her own. He wasn't to know there was someone in the vicinity with evil on their mind." She shuddered. "It frightens me how easily it happened. I've let Emma walk home alone. Not often, but sometimes I run late. You know how it is…and without any family close by… I don't know what I'd do if something happened to my little girl."

"Where are your parents?"

Daisy grimaced. "They died a couple years ago, not long after Pete." She shrugged. "I'm an only child. Everything stops with me. And Emma, of course," she added.

Christian regarded her steadily and had to ask, "Is there someone special in your life, a boyfriend?"

Her eyes flared wide in surprise and irritation. Christian wished he could take the question back, but it was too late. He only hoped she didn't take offense and break the fragile peace that had been created between them.

To his relief, she merely sighed again and turned her head to stare out the window. The day was bright and sunny. The expanse of clear blue sky stretched as far as the eye could see. There wasn't a cloud anywhere above the horizon. It was as if the storm a couple nights ago had never been. He hoped it was a good omen and the darkness surrounding the disappearance of Lila-Jane would soon be gone.

Daisy sighed quietly again and turned back to face him, her expression resigned. "In answer to your question, no, there isn't anyone special in my life. There hasn't been anyone since Pete."

He accepted her admission in silence, concealing his surprise. "You didn't die with him, you know."

And just like that, the anger was back and he knew he'd said the wrong thing.

Her lips tightened. "For your information, I haven't *wanted* to share my life with anyone else. I'm more than happy with the way things are. Just me and Emma." She shot him a look filled with defiance and once again, he read her signal to back off. He accepted her silent request with an inclination of his head and steered the conversation away to safer ground.

"So, how did you get into the legal business? What attracted you to becoming a lawyer?"

She acknowledged his change of subject with a brief nod and replied. "I guess I can blame TV for that."

He laughed. It was the last thing he expected her to say. "Really? How so?"

"I used to love watching crime shows and all things to do with the law. For a little while there, I even considered being a police officer. Then I fell in love with Bobby Donnell on the TV show *The Practice*. Do you know it?"

Christian grinned and shook his head. "You're kidding me?"

Crimson stained her cheeks. "Why? What do you mean? He's the hottest guy on TV. At least, he was back then." The blush on her cheeks deepened and she wouldn't meet his eyes.

He laughed outright. "Oh, my goodness! You mean to tell me you put yourself through the hell of law school because of a cute guy?"

She chuckled good-naturedly. "Hey, it wouldn't be the first time."

He acknowledged her comment with a nod. "You're right. But not many people go to that sort of trouble and expense. And did you forget, Bobby Donnell doesn't even exist? He's an actor on a TV show." He smiled and shook his head again. "What did your parents say?"

"They were as proud as punch I was going into law. I didn't tell them it was because of Bobby."

"Did they ever find out?"

She shot him a cheeky grin. "Of course not. What do you take me for? They paid for half of my tuition. I wanted them to think I was serious about my career in law. Which of course, I was."

He frowned. "Hang on a minute, there must be more to it than that. From what I've heard, you're a damn fine juvenile defense lawyer. No one goes into that kind of law without really wanting to make a difference."

"You're right," she murmured thoughtfully. "I guess somewhere along the way between lectures on torts and contracts, I discovered a passion for championing the cause of the more vulnerable in our society and that led me to the doors of the children's court. To tell you the truth, it's one of the reasons I chose Sydney Legal. Their Pro Bono Program is second to none."

"Why not go and work for the public defender's office? Their clients are probably among the neediest you'll find."

She nodded. "True. In fact, I worked there for the first few years of my career."

"What happened? It didn't live up to expectations?"

"No, nothing like that. Pete died, that's what happened. He had a small life insurance policy and an even smaller superannuation fund, but it wasn't enough for us to live on forever. I needed a better-paying job. So, I turned to the private sector. I'm embarrassed to admit I took this job for the money, but that's the truth. That's not to say I don't enjoy my work here. I absolutely do. In fact, I get paid double what I did in the public sector for doing something I enjoy. As far as I'm concerned, it's a win-win situation."

Christian regarded her steadily. The passion on her face and in her voice indicated just how deeply she felt about her chosen career. "You love it now, don't you?" he asked quietly.

She looked at him and nodded. "Yes, I do."

Their gazes locked and the silence drew out between them. Christian's heart thumped and the blood pounded in his ears. Her dark brown eyes widened, as if she could sense the turmoil inside him. Or perhaps it was her own turmoil that caused her disturbance? He could only hope.

And then, she looked away and cleared her throat and the moment was gone.

"I'm... I'm sorry to have barged in on you like that, Christian. I should have known you wouldn't have thrown a young client to the wolves. But I got off the phone to Marty's mother and I just couldn't believe what she'd said. I thought... I thought... I'm sorry. I should've come and asked you first before tearing a strip off you like that."

It's no problem," he replied. You're welcome to talk to me anytime."

She sent him a grateful glance. "Thank you. I appreciate that."

She pushed back her chair and stood, tugging at her short skirt to remove the creases. She turned and made her way to the exit. He stood too, and came around the other side of his desk. She had her hand on the doorknob before he found the courage to ask her the question he'd wanted to ask all along.

"Would you like to go for a drink after work?" He cursed the hesitancy in his voice and waited nervously for her answer.

She turned and looked at him for a long moment, as if debating what to say. Finally, she nodded and said, "Emma has a dance class straight after school. I can give you forty-five minutes. Don't be late."

Daisy pulled Christian's door closed behind her and on unsteady legs headed down the corridor toward her office. She still couldn't believe she'd agreed to see him outside of work. *What was she thinking?* She wasn't ready to date again. Not that this was a date. He was a work colleague. He'd merely asked her out to extend their conversation—their work conversation.

Yeah, right.

She winced at the voice in her head. There was no way this was merely an extension of their work conversation. He wanted to go out on a date. He wanted to spend time with her. There was no denying it. She'd seen it in his eyes and the way he watched her and in the way he'd been interested in what she said. It had been a long time since she'd paid any attention to a man's mannerisms, but it was clear Christian Grayson was interested. Period. That was it.

The very thought sent a shaft of terror surging through her veins. At the same time, she was filled with the thrill of unexpected surprise. *What would it be like to go out with a man like Christian Grayson?* A man attractive enough to grace the cover of glossy magazines, whose very presence spoke authority and confidence.

The initial attraction had been the same with Pete. In fact, it was Pete's confidence and air of authority that had attracted her in the first place. There were other similarities, too. Like the sun-bleached blond hair and golden tan, even in the middle of winter. Like the straight white teeth and the broad shoulders and strong arms that made a woman feel safe just looking at them.

But that's where the similarities ended. Pete had been introspective and often spent hours on his own. And that was while he was actually with them, at home on leave. His time with them, between deployments, happened so infrequently, she used to resent the time he spent on his own, but he'd tell her he needed the solitude to rest and sort out the thoughts in his head. She understood, with his challenging job defending the Afghans from ISIS attacks, that he lived in a constant state of hyper alertness and needed the time at home to wind down, but she still begrudged the times he chose to absent himself from his family.

Christian was different from Pete. Of course, Christian wasn't a high-ranking army officer facing constant attacks from enemy lines and with the responsibility of so many lives. The very notion that she'd tried to draw comparisons between the two men seemed ludicrous. Still…

She'd overheard two female colleagues talking about how Christian had lost his parents at a young age, so it wasn't as if he hadn't faced trauma. And yet, he seemed to have recovered from the experience. She couldn't imagine what it must've been like to grow up without a mother and a father, and to be thrust into the care of an uncle, even an uncle as kindly and generous as Larry Grayson. It had to be tough…

She had to admit the time she'd already spent in Christian's company had mostly been pleasant. The only time she'd been nervous or uptight was when she couldn't control her reactions to him. Long-denied feelings seemed drawn to the surface every time he was near. She couldn't deny he made her heart beat faster.

Was it only because it had been five years since she'd been with a man and her body was craving physical release? Was that all this was? She guessed there was only one way to find out.

With that, her heart lightened and for the first time in a long time she walked with a spring in her step. All of a sudden, she was filled with excitement at the thought of enjoying the company of a man and possibly exploring a new relationship with an eligible and very attractive man...

Christian Grayson. She couldn't do much better than that.

CHAPTER 9

Christian glanced nervously at his watch and drummed his fingers absently against the surface of the small wooden table. He'd found a seat in the quietest corner of the bar, but still the murmur of conversation filled the room. He looked around, scanning faces, but saw no sign of Daisy and he wondered if she'd changed her mind. They'd agreed to meet at five at a popular drinking establishment right down the street from where they worked. It was now already ten past.

He looked around the room again and tried to quell his disappointment. He'd been both surprised and pleased when she'd accepted his spontaneous invitation. It had been so nice talking with her about work and other things that he'd wanted the conversation to continue. It was the reason he'd invited her out again, in the hope that this time she'd say yes. And she had.

Except, the meeting time had come and gone and it looked like she wasn't going to show.

And then the door to the bar opened and let in

a gust of cold, wintry air. He looked up and spied her standing in the opening. She paused for a moment and looked around. When she saw him across the room she smiled shyly and headed toward him, weaving her way through the crowd. He stood as she reached his table and waited for her to sit down.

"I'm so sorry I'm late," she said as she placed her handbag on the vacant chair beside her. "I checked on the after school arrangements for Emma and then took a phone call on my way out. I should've known better." She grimaced.

He smiled back at her, relaxed now that he knew she hadn't stood him up. "I know exactly what you mean."

They shared a look and she smiled. A blush stained the porcelain of her cheeks. Not for the first time, he marveled at how beautiful she was.

"How's Emma?" he asked in an effort to distract himself.

"She's fine. She has dance lessons straight after school and then she has piano. They're both held in classrooms on the school grounds. She doesn't finish until six. I'm afraid I'll have to leave by a quarter to." Once again, she tossed him an apologetic look.

He shrugged it off with a smile. "That's fine. I understand. Let's enjoy the time we have."

She lowered her gaze to the table and her finger traced a nervous pattern on its surface.

He cleared his throat to calm a sudden rush of nerves. "So, what would you like to drink?"

Her fingers stopped their motion and she

glanced at him. "I'll have a gin and tonic, please."

He signaled to the barman and gave him their order before returning his attention to Daisy. "How was the rest of your afternoon?"

She sighed and some of the tension appeared to leave her body. She leaned forward and rested her chin in her hand. "Oh, you know how it is. One case after another. They all blur together after a while. A lot of them were repeat offenders. We're just not doing enough to get through to these kids, to give them the help and encouragement they need."

"Yeah, I wish I knew the answer. People blame the lack of parental supervision, but there are plenty of kids this day and age who have two working parents and who come home to an empty house. They're not all in trouble with the police."

She shrugged. "You're right. Enough about that. Let's talk about something else. How was *your* day?"

"About as good as yours, I think." He chuckled.

She laughed and the sound of it was like music to his ears. He realized he hadn't heard her laugh very much, if at all, and wondered about that. All of a sudden, he wanted to know everything about her. "So," he said. "Are you a Sydney girl or did you move here from somewhere else?"

"Yes, Sydney born and bred. I was born in the Royal North Shore Hospital and I still live on the north shore, in Chatswood.

He smiled in surprise. "Really? I live in Chatswood, too."

"What a coincidence. I guess I should have known, given that you live with your uncle and he does our local bus run. I never thought about where Larry lives, but it makes sense that it would be somewhere close by." She paused and then said, "Have you ever thought about moving out? Getting a place of your own?"

The words were hardly out of her mouth when a blush crept up her neck. It was obvious she'd just realized how impertinent her words sounded. Before he could respond, she spoke again. "I'm... I'm sorry. I... It's none of my business. I shouldn't have said that."

"It's fine," he hastened to assure her. "After all, a thirty-three-year-old man still living at home? That's kind of weird." He eyed her steadily. "The truth is, I've never had any reason to leave. My uncle and I get on well and we've learned to respect each other's need for space.

"Uncle Larry has always been a bit of a private man and from the first moment I came to live with him I was made aware of that. After all these years, we've fallen into a comfortable habit, sharing meals and conversation when we both feel like it, and at other times, leaving each other alone." He grimaced. "Hell, it sounds like we're an old married couple."

"No, you're wrong! It sounds perfect," she protested.

He thought for a moment. Until Justine had brought it up in her parting arguments, he'd never really given his living arrangements any consideration. His uncle rented a comfortable home and it was convenient to Christian's work.

Actually, he knew it was high time he looked for his own place. A condo in the city held immense appeal. He could walk to work in less than ten minutes. Then again, if he was on the lookout for a wife and family, perhaps a house in the suburbs would be a better long term investment? He didn't know, but the whole idea definitely deserved serious consideration.

Their drinks arrived and they both took time out from the conversation to sample them. Christian's rum and coke burned a warm path down his throat. He set the glass down and picked up the conversation again.

"I guess it *is* probably time I looked for a place of my own. You won't believe this, but I was on the verge of getting married some months back, yet I hadn't given any thought about where the two of us would live. No wonder she walked out."

"Are you talking about Justine?"

Christian started in surprise and then recalled the conversation he'd had with Emma the night before.

He nodded. "Yes, I am. We dated for a long time. I thought she was the one. Unfortunately, she didn't feel the same way."

Daisy regarded him with a curious expression on her face. "What happened? Please tell me if it's none of my business," she added hastily.

He shrugged. "Four months ago, I would have told you exactly that, but it's funny, I don't mind talking about it now, with you. In fact, I'd prefer to talk about it. I like you, Daisy. I really like you. I'd like to spend more time with you, getting to know you. I hope you feel the same way."

He paused and studied her in silence. She reached for her drink at the same time he did and their fingers brushed. Tingles of awareness raced up his arm. He caught her quiet gasp of surprise and assumed she felt something, too. After another fortifying mouthful of alcohol, he continued.

"You heard me tell Emma last night that Justine and I worked together. We met at a conference a few years earlier and hit it off right away. Things moved quickly—we'd both seen thirty come and go. I really thought we were on the same page— wanted the same things. Ever since my parents died, I've felt there's a void in my life. I had my uncle, but it wasn't the same. I wanted a wife and family of my own. I thought Justine wanted that as much as I did."

"So, she didn't want to get married?" Daisy asked.

"Oh, yes, she wanted to get married. Just not to me."

Daisy's eyes widened in surprise. "Wow. Okay, I wasn't expecting that. Why did she spend so much time in the relationship if she knew it wasn't going anywhere? As you said, neither of you were in the first blush of youth."

Christian grimaced. "I asked myself the same question many times after she walked out." He paused and a smile tugged at his lips. "I still don't know the answer."

Daisy regarded him over the rim of her glass.

Her eyes glinted with laughter. "You don't appear too broken-hearted."

His grin widened. "You're right. It's only been four months. You'd think I'd still be wallowing in my misery, getting drunk every night and bemoaning the fact the love of my life walked out on me." He held her gaze. "And yet, I'm not. In fact, I've never felt more alive, more filled with possibilities and optimism."

Their gazes remained locked on each other and time ceased to matter. The bar and the people surrounding them faded into the background. It was as if there was no one and nothing but the two of them.

He watched her chest rise and fall in rapid succession and zeroed in on a pulse that beat frantically in her neck. Her tongue stole out and wet her lips and he followed the movement, mesmerized. His chest was so tight, he could hardly breathe and his heart thudded against his ribs. He noticed the tiny specks of tawny gold that shone in her brown eyes. He noticed everything...

"Can I get you another drink?"

Christian blinked and shook his head, feeling off balance. He looked up at the barman who hovered near their table, an expectant look on his bearded face.

"Um, no. I'm fine thanks," he managed. He looked across at Daisy. Her dazed expression filled him with a surge of satisfaction.

"N-no, I'm good," she stammered and a blush stole over her face.

"Okay," the barman replied with a friendly

smile. "Give me a holler if you need anything." He turned and walked away.

Christian drew in a surreptitious breath and slowly eased it out. He was grateful for the barman's timely interruption. It gave him a chance to take stock and re-assess. They seemed to have stepped over an unspoken line and neither knew which way was forward or even if they wanted to head in that direction. Even now, he saw the turmoil in Daisy's eyes and observed the flurry of conflicting emotions that passed over her face.

Was she thinking about her husband? About the feelings Christian's words had stirred up? Or was he kidding himself? Was he the only one who felt like the world had been turned upside down? Like his blood pounded with a barrage of emotions he had no control over and wasn't sure he wanted to stop?

He reached for his glass and the clink of the ice broke the silence that had descended upon them. Bringing the glass to his lips, he took a sip and savored the burn of the alcohol, enjoying the way it slid into his stomach, its warmth calming him.

He snuck another glance at Daisy. Her gaze remained fixed on the table. Her fingers idly traced the cardboard coaster that sat beneath her drink. He realized she was just as nervous as he was. And then, as if coming to a sudden decision, she looked up and met his gaze.

"Did you and Justine want children?"

Christian hid his surprise and nodded. "Yes, of

course. We both wanted a heap of kids. It was one of the things we had no trouble agreeing on. I grew up as an only child. I always wanted siblings. I never wanted that kind of 'only child' loneliness for my kids. Besides, siblings always have each other's backs, right?"

Daisy's eyes darkened. Her voice was husky with emotion when she spoke. "Right. I also grew up as an only child. I used to pretend I had an older brother. He was always there for me, fighting my battles, having fun, carousing with me." Her sad smile tugged at his heart.

"Did this champion of a brother have a name?"

Her answering smile chased the shadows from her eyes. "Yes, of course. His name was Drake."

Christian grinned and quirked an eyebrow. "Drake?"

Daisy's smile morphed into a chuckle. "Yes, I know. Very soap opera-ish. I think I might've even heard it on *The Bold and the Beautiful*. It sounded so strong, so reliable. So much like the name of someone who would protect me, have my back."

Christian laughed. "*The Bold and the Beautiful*," he mused. "Wow! That takes me back. I remember my mom watching that show in the afternoon while she prepared the evening meal. We used to have a TV in the kitchen. I was allowed to watch the kids' shows after I'd done my homework, but only until half-past four. That's when *Bold* came on. Mom used to be so engrossed in the storyline, she'd barely notice what I was doing. I think Ridge was her favorite character."

Daisy laughed. "Oh, yes. Ridge Forrester. How could you go past a man like that? He was everything a woman dreamed of. Tall, dark and handsome—and rich to boot. And he was just so darned nice. I was always jealous of Taylor and Brooke."

Christian chuckled, loving the blush that stole across her cheeks. She was simply adorable. He couldn't drag his gaze away. The silence between them lengthened until it became almost unbearable. He broke it by clearing his throat. "Tell me about your husband. Was he your 'Ridge'?"

Daisy's expression immediately shuttered and Christian bit his lip against a silent curse. *How could he have been so stupid—again?* They had been getting along so well, a real rapport had developed between them and he'd blown it again by asking her about her spouse.

Christian watched Daisy's face fill with sadness and he cursed silently again. Her eyes took on a faraway look.

"Pete was a good man in so many ways, but sometimes he drove me crazy. The last day I saw him alive, I told him the two of us were over."

CHAPTER 10

Daisy's gasp mirrored the shock on Christian's face. She still couldn't believe she'd told him. Until that moment, she hadn't told anyone. Not even her closest friends. Her eyes filled with tears and her heart tightened on a wave of desolation. Pete had been gone for years, but memories of their life together were as clear and fresh as if they'd happened yesterday. Their lives had been filled with love and laughter until he'd destroyed everything they'd been. And now she'd shared her heartache with a man she barely knew.

He stared at her from across the table, his expression grave. "What happened?"

"I-I'm sorry," she stammered. "I didn't mean to air my dirty laundry like that. Way too much information, right?" She tried for a smile and failed.

He continued to regard her steadily. "I'm glad you did. I want to know everything about you, the good the bad and the..."

"Ugly?" she asked, managing a brief smile.

"Never ugly," he reassured her, flashing her a grin. "What happened?" he asked again.

She sighed. She'd never intended to tell him anything about Pete and their life together, but somehow, here in the dimness of the bar, surrounded by the hum of people getting on with their lives, she wanted to. Reaching for her glass, she drained it and then looked him in the eye. "My husband was having an affair. I found out about it. He refused to discuss it. In a fit of anger, I told him I wanted a divorce. He'd been deployed and was leaving and I never saw him again. I've been living with the guilt of it ever since."

Christian blinked once and then without a word, reached out and took her hand. Engulfing it in his larger one, he squeezed it with reassuring warmth.

"That's tough," he said, his voice husky with emotion.

A sudden rush of tears almost blinded her. She lowered her gaze and gave a jerky nod. "Yes. It is."

"Why do you feel guilty? You did nothing wrong."

His quiet words, filled with compassion, brought on another wave of tears. "I sent him to war with my words ringing in his ears. We never discussed it any further. Pete left before we had a chance."

"That wasn't your fault, Daisy. And he was the one who chose to have the affair. Why are you still beating yourself up about this?"

"You don't understand!" she cried.

His expression didn't change. "I understand perfectly. You threw out some hurtful words during a very hurtful time and you didn't get a chance to take them back. Am I right?"

She nodded cautiously. "Yes, I guess so. The thing is, I didn't mean them. Well, not really. I was hurt and angry and I lashed out. Pete refused to talk about it. I wanted to rant and rave and hear him apologize. I wanted him to beg my forgiveness. I was never given the chance."

Her voice cracked with emotion and the tears that had been slowly filling her eyes spilled over and trickled down her cheeks. She swiped at them, embarrassed.

Christian's hold tightened on her hand. "Your husband was cheating on you and you never got the chance to have it out with him. You must have been furious with him and then, to not have the chance to discuss it, analyze it, find some kind of peace... No wonder you're still so upset. What I don't understand is the guilt."

"Of *course* I feel guilty! I'm sure Pete was thinking about us and the fight we'd had instead of concentrating on his job. He was killed when the vehicle he was traveling in drove over an IED. If he'd been paying better attention, it might never have happened. He might still be alive today!"

"You don't know that, Daisy," came Christian's gentle response. "Nobody can know that. It was an unfortunate accident. Pete was at war. Soldiers die. It happens. It's nobody's fault. You need to believe that."

Another wave of sad memories washed over her. As much as she wanted to believe Christian, she wasn't up to doing it right now. It had been a long day and she was tired. She also had to leave to collect Emma. With that thought in mind, she gently extricated her hand from Christian's and offered him a shaky smile.

"Thanks for the drink and for…listening. I'm sorry, but I need to go."

He nodded and pushed back his chair and stood while she collected her handbag and made to leave. She stared at him for a long time and then looked away, unsure what she felt in that moment. "You're a good man, Christian Grayson. It's been nice spending time with you."

His eyes continued to search hers. "Do you really mean that?"

She held his gaze. "Yes, I do." And realized it was true.

He held her gaze another long moment, as if searching for the truth behind her words. And then he shrugged and looked away. "Do you need a ride somewhere?"

She shook her head. "No, but thank you. I caught the train into work this morning and I can catch another one to Emma's school. There's a station only a hundred yards or so from where she is. I can walk the rest of the way."

"Are you sure? Because I don't mind giving you a ride."

She brushed off his invitation a second time, now anxious to get away. "No, it's fine." She needed time to sort out the turmoil of her feelings, including the memories of Pete. And there had been her surprising reaction to Christian when their fingers brushed against each other's... She still felt the tingling warmth of his touch and her reaction to him had been as surprising as it had been pleasant. It had been nice. No, much better than nice. She wanted to feel that way again. Wait until she confided in Sally-Ann Li about this. Her best friend would have a field day.

Still, attractive or not, she was most definitely not in the market for a man. Best, she remember that next time her heart was set aflutter by the casual brush of his warm fingers and the kindness and compassion in his bright blue eyes...

———————————

Christian opened the back door and was greeted by the faint hints of Tchaikovsky making their way up the basement stairs. His uncle loved to relax to the sound of classical music. It wasn't always Tchaikovsky. Beethoven, Strauss and Mozart all got their turn. Over the many years of Christian's childhood and even now, he'd gotten used to the music.

Closing the door behind him, he made his way into the kitchen and switched on the light. A pan almost empty of fried sausages, onion and bacon stood abandoned on the stove. There was no dirty plate or cutlery in the sink and he wagered that his uncle had either eaten downstairs or had cleaned up after himself.

A soft warm body brushed against the leg of his suit pants and he glanced down to find Sooty meowing softly at his feet. He bent down and picked up the cat, scratching it gently behind its ears.

"Hey, there little buddy. How was your day?"

The cat was a stray that had wandered into their yard nearly five months ago. It had been collarless and unloved, emaciated and scratching madly at fleas. Despite Uncle Larry's protests that he was allergic, Christian had taken the cat in. Besides, he knew Uncle Larry wasn't really allergic. He could still recall his father telling him a story about the litter of kittens Larry had found abandoned by the river. They were in a burlap bag with the top sealed. It was only a matter of time before the kittens would have suffocated or starved to death.

Christian's uncle had dragged the bag all the way back to their house. He'd hidden the kittens in the garden shed and fed them in secret. When their father finally discovered what Larry had done, he'd been livid. He used to breed rare parrots and detested any kind of cat. He hit every single kitten over the head with a ball pein hammer and had made his young son watch. Christian knew firsthand from his father's account that Uncle Larry never got over the trauma of witnessing the brutal killing of the kittens and a cat had never been brought into a Grayson household again. Until now.

Setting Sooty aside, Christian reached into the cupboard and pulled out a can of cat food. Scraping the contents into the cat's bowl, he gave Sooty another scratch while the cat began to eat.

Absently, he noticed the healthy shine to Sooty's coat and the softness of his fur. He immediately thought of Daisy and his body stirred. He hadn't been with another woman since Justine.

But it wasn't just any woman he wanted. He wanted Daisy: beautiful, funny, intelligent. She was the whole package. He only wished she weren't so filled with guilt over her dead husband. A husband who was never coming back...

Still, Christian hadn't got this far in life by giving up when the chips were down. He'd learned that persistence paid off and he was determined to win Daisy over. The fact she'd met him for a drink was a positive step.

"If she wasn't in the least bit interested, she wouldn't have shown up, right?"

He directed the question to Sooty who ignored him and continued to eat. With a sigh, he got a clean plate, went over to the stove and helped himself to the leftover food.

Lila-Jane squeezed her eyes shut to block out the music. By now, she knew exactly what it meant. Her captor would sit in the recliner facing her. With his eyes closed, he'd open the zipper of his pants and pull out his penis. Lila-Jane had never seen a real one before. It looked nothing like the ones she'd seen in the personal development books her mom had given her.

As the music reached its crescendo, the man

would gasp and groan and mutter, tugging faster and faster at his hardened length until a white fluid would gush from its end. And then he'd smile and move closer and release the bindings on one of her hands. He'd make her hold his soft flesh. He'd tighten his hand around hers and once again begin the rhythmic action. It made her feel sick and scared all at once, but there was nothing she could do. She was bound hand and foot, except for the hand that held him.

Tonight, it was different. He'd sat in his chair as usual and had taken out his dick, but before he spurted fluid all over the place, he moved and sat down in the chair that was beside her bed. This time when he put her hand around his shaft, it was hard and hot and throbbing. She tried to pull her hand away, but his fingers tightened around it.

"You've seen me do it often enough. Now it's your turn," he crooned in that strange faraway voice.

She strained to see his features behind the gaudy clown mask, but it was impossible to make out anything more than the fact he had a cloud of snowy white hair.

"Please," she whimpered. "Don't do this. Please, let me go home. I promise I won't say anything. Just let me go."

As if deaf to her pleas, he merely tightened his grip on her fingers and increased the speed of his movement. In no time at all, her hand was covered in warm, sticky fluid. She nearly gagged at the sight of it and was relieved when he released her fingers and reached for a nearby towel.

With infinite gentleness, he wiped each of her fingers clean and then offered her a drink. It looked like milk, but it tasted a little different. Thirsty, she greedily drank. Within moments, her world grew hazy and she struggled to stay awake. With a soft sigh, she succumbed to the darkness.

Larry stood staring down at the little girl asleep on his cot and felt a pang of conscience. This was the third night the child had been missing. Her mother would be going out of her mind. He wished there was some way he could help her, let her know her baby was all right. But there was nothing he could do without arousing suspicion. It was the same way every time. Besides, he took pleasure from knowing the turmoil and heartbreak he caused each time a child disappeared. Lila-Jane was no different.

He was just grateful his nephew hadn't cottoned on to what he did in the basement after so many years. Christian had wondered aloud from time to time about the children who went missing from their neighborhood, but he'd never yet connected the dots. After all, it wasn't as if kids didn't disappear in other places, places he'd never been. And no one but his nephew was aware of their connection to some of the others.

There were times when Larry wished he could get help for his affliction. He didn't want to enjoy causing parents pain. It was just that, when the urge came upon him, it was too strong for him to ignore. Sooner or later, the beast inside him took over and he was forced to act. It was just something he'd learned to live with. Including getting rid of them when he was finished.

He looked down at Lila-Jane and shook his head slowly back and forth in amusement. The little girl was so sure he believed her when she promised not to tell anyone. He saw the earnestness in her face. She was no different from all the others. And just like them, he didn't believe a word she said.

Of course she'd tell her mother, her school friends, the police. It was lucky he took precautions and kept her dosed up on Rohypnol. The drug altered her memories and interfered with her thoughts. She wouldn't be sure what she remembered and what she imagined or what had even happened at all...

Of course, he'd also been careful to blindfold her on their way into his house and had always worn a disguise, but still... She was a bright little thing. There was always a chance she'd guess who he was and then things would deteriorate faster than he could blink. It was a risk he couldn't afford to take.

The longer he kept her there, the higher the chance he'd do something or say something that would cause her to recognize him. Yes, as much as he'd enjoyed playing with little Lila-Jane, their game of love was almost up. Besides, there was always Bella Rushby. She was definitely a girl who looked like she needed a friend...

CHAPTER 11

The door to Lila-Jane's prison creaked open and her heart leaped in her chest. It had been hours since he'd visited. Her stomach was cramped with pain. She was desperate to use the bathroom and had been determined to hold it in. So far, she'd managed it, but she was pleased that the wait had come to an end.

"Please, I need to go to the bathroom. Will you please untie me?"

"Of course. I'm sorry I've been gone so long. I was busy at work and got...caught up. I had other things on my mind."

With that he moved further into the room and she noticed he held something close to his chest. As he came closer, she gasped. A young girl hung limply in his arms.

"Oh, no! What have you done?" Lila-Jane cried, horrified at the thought he'd snatched some other poor kid and brought her here to suffer like she was.

"There, there," the man crooned. "Don't upset

yourself. It's going to be fine. Little Bella was so lonely. She never had any friends. I've watched her for a long time, now. I know these things. We're going to have a lot of fun, you and I and Bella. Just you see."

As the name registered in Lila-Jane's brain, her mouth dropped open in shock. "It's Bella Rushby! You've taken Bella Rushby! How could you? Bella never hurt a fly!"

To her horror, she burst into tears and cried like she'd never stop. All the time, she kept thinking of her momma and how much she missed her. *Would she ever escape this room of horrors? Would she ever see her momma again? And what about Bella? What would become of them?*

Ignoring her distress, the man continued forward and leaned down and deposited Bella on the bed beside her. She took comfort in the fact she was no longer alone in her prison, but despaired at the thought of what lay ahead.

Please, Momma, please find me. Please come and take me home. I'm scared, Momma, so scared. And now he has Bella, too...

The words spun round and round in her head until she was dizzy with apprehension and fear. Retrieving another set of restraints, her captor quietly went about securing Bella to the bed. When at last he was finished, he leaned down and kissed the sleeping girl on the lips and smoothed back her light brown hair.

"So pretty," he mused. "Sleep my pretty girl. There will be time enough later for playing."

The words were followed by a strange cackling

laugh and the man's eyes glinted behind the mask. Lila-Jane was filled with a surge of anger. She fought against the bindings that restrained her and gritted her teeth against the frustration when they didn't budge. Her captor shifted his attention and her anger was immediately replaced with fear. His hand cupped her cheek and moved lower, across her chest and lower still.

"So, you need to use the bathroom, yes?" he crooned. His hand paused at her belly button.

She squeezed her eyes tightly shut and held her breath and then managed to whisper. "Yes."

The man's fingers continued their leisurely exploration of her belly. "Do you think you deserve to go to the bathroom?"

Once again, she managed to respond. "Yes."

"If I let you go, do you promise to be a good girl?"

Lila-Jane opened her eyes and stared at the clown mask, feeling desperate. She was about to burst. She was willing to agree to anything. "Yes, I promise."

The mask moved and she sensed his smile behind the mask. His voice was filled with satisfaction. "Good. That's what I like to hear."

His hand trailed lower, across the tops of her thighs and then slid up between the legs. She tensed and it was only by the greatest act of will that she managed not to wet herself. He stroked her through her panties and she bit back tears of shame. And then he removed his hand and chuckled. Tears of relief slid silently down her cheeks.

"All right... Let's see about loosening these restraints," he said in a matter-of-fact tone. "We can't have you soiling the bed. Not when I've just brought in our Bella. It wouldn't do to have her waking up to a mess. No, that wouldn't do at all."

Daisy woke to the sound of hammering. It took her a moment to realize it was someone knocking on her front door. She'd spent a restless night tossing and turning as images of Pete and Christian had warred in her mind.

Pete had been smiling and laughing, just like the Pete of old, and then Christian appeared and Pete's face morphed into a mask of rage. He stared at her with disappointment and accusation in his eyes. Tears rolled down his face.

"How could you?" he'd cried.

Christian merely laughed and pushed Pete away as if he were nothing. Pete's image disintegrated and was replaced with a vision of Christian. Tall and solid and resplendent in his custom-made designer suit, he brimmed with confidence. He'd shot her a sexy smile and winked at her before beckoning her with a crook of his index finger. Her heart skipped a beat when she realized she wanted to go to him...

She'd woken from the dream with a start, her heart thudding. It had taken her a long time to get back to sleep. Now the pounding was at her door and she stumbled out of bed. She glanced at the clock on her nightstand and groaned. It was a few minutes after seven. She should have been up already, getting organized for work. She wondered if Emma was awake. The knocking sounded again.

"Okay, okay, I'm coming," she shouted and reached for her robe. Pulling it over her flannelette pajamas, she pushed her feet into her slippers before making her way down the hall toward the front door.

Putting her eye to the key hole, she was taken aback to find Christian on her front porch. She hadn't seen him since their get together in the bar two nights earlier. Though he wore another designer suit, his expression was far from sexy. In fact, the drawn and somber look on his face got her heart thumping for an altogether different reason. She struggled with the lock and pulled open the door.

"Christian, is everything all right? What are you doing here? It's barely seven."

He ran a hand through his hair and from the mussed look of it, this wasn't the first time he'd done so.

"I just heard the news. Another girl's gone missing from this neighborhood. The police didn't release any names, but she fit Emma's description. I just wanted to check... I just wanted to make sure you were both okay."

A rush of warmth went through her at the realization he'd been worried about them. It was followed quickly by alarm.

"What do you mean another child has gone missing? You mean, like Lila-Jane?"

"Yes. Apparently the child was on her way home from school yesterday, just like Lila-Jane. The details are scratchy, but she didn't arrive home. Her parents called the police."

Fear coursed through Daisy at the realization that another child had disappeared. "What else do you know?"

Christian shrugged. "Not much. My uncle's already left for his bus run. I haven't been able to speak to him about it. My first thought after I heard about it was to come here."

Daisy looked at him. "How did you know where we lived?"

Christian had the grace to look embarrassed. "I asked my uncle last night. I hope you don't mind."

Daisy regarded him closely. He looked so abashed, she swallowed her instinctive protest. It was kind of sweet that he'd made inquiries about her. She opened the door wider. "Would you like to come in?"

His gaze drifted over her pajama-clad body, all the way from her neck to her fluffy pink slippers and back again. "Um, thanks, but I'd better not. You probably need to get ready for work."

She took in his charcoal-gray suit and perfectly knotted blue-and-gray striped tie. The sun had barely peeked over the horizon and yet he looked fresh and ready to go.

"You must be an early riser," she mused.

He grinned and the sight of it weakened her knees. "Yes, I guess I am. Years of listening for my uncle's alarm. I guess I got into the habit of rising when he did, even when I was a kid. It's been a hard habit to break."

"Not a bad habit though, surely," Daisy replied. "You must get a lot more done at work if you head into the office this early."

"You're right. This is the best time of day to get things done. The phones don't usually start ringing until after eight. It's amazing what you can achieve when you're not constantly interrupted by calls."

She laughed. "I'm sure. I wish I could say I had an inkling of what it's like to be in the office before eight."

"Is Emma using the bus again?"

"Yes, it's too much of a rush otherwise. I wouldn't get in for work before nine."

Silence fell between them. She peeked at him from beneath her lashes. "Are you a breakfast man?" she asked on impulse and then promptly blushed.

Ignoring her embarrassment, Christian smiled. "As a matter of fact, I am. It's the best meal of the day."

She stifled a burst of disappointment. "Oh, I guess you've already eaten, then."

His smile morphed into a grin. "As a matter of fact, I skipped breakfast this morning. I wanted to make sure you and Emma were okay." His gaze lingered on hers.

She wanted to look away, but was powerless to do so. The silence stretched between them and all the time her heart beat a frantic rhythm against her ribs. And then she remembered she was standing in her front door, in her pajamas, in full view of the neighbors—and she hastily backed away.

"I-I need to get ready for work. Emma is still in bed. The morning is always so busy. Packing lunch, finding shoes. I—"

"I understand," he interrupted, a teasing smile playing around his lips. "Is there anything I can do? Perhaps I could fry some bacon and eggs? Would that help?"

Daisy started in surprise. It had been a long time since anyone had offered to cook her breakfast. "You cook?"

Christian winked. "Yes. It's one of my favorite things to do. It helps me relax."

Daisy thought of the box of unappetizing cereal and plain toast that was her usual morning fare and then considered his offer to cook. The thought of bacon and eggs was too good to ignore.

She angled her head at him. "Do you mean it? Would you really cook us breakfast?"

"Of course. I'd be happy to throw some things together while you and Emma get dressed. It would please me greatly to know that you and your daughter have started the day with a decent plate of protein in your bellies."

Refusing to dwell on her reasons, Daisy stepped back and allowed him to enter. Closing the door behind him, she took the lead down the hallway and stopped when they came to the kitchen. He came to a halt not far behind her and she half turned toward him to speak. "I think you'll find everything you need in the refrigerator. The frying pan is in the bottom drawer under the stove. Let me know if you need anything else."

Christian threw her another grin. "This might come as a surprise, but I know my way around a kitchen. I'm sure I'll be fine."

She hesitated, still unsure how he'd come to be there at all. *Had she really invited him in to make breakfast? What was she thinking?* The only other man to occupy her kitchen had been Pete.

As if sensing her sudden indecision, Christian stepped forward and squeezed her forearm. "Hey, I don't mean to intrude. If this is too much, just say so. I'm happy to leave the way I came."

Daisy's skin tingled beneath his fingers. She immediately moved away from his touch. At the same time, she shook her head. "No, no, don't be silly. It's fine. I was just thinking, I can't remember the last time someone made me breakfast. It's... It's very nice of you."

"It's no problem," Christian said softly. "Go and get dressed. Breakfast will be ready by the time you are."

"Mr Grayson! What are you doing here?"

Daisy turned in time to see her daughter run into the room and come to a sliding halt beside the kitchen counter. Her blue eyes, so much like her father's, were wide with curiosity.

Christian leaned over the counter. "I thought I'd come over and cook you breakfast. Does that sound all right?" He wiggled his eyebrows up and down and Emma giggled.

"Yay! That sounds like fun!" She turned and

looked at her mother. "Can he stay, Momma? Can he?"

Daisy shook her head, grinning despite herself. It seemed she wasn't the only female in the Green household who was susceptible to the man's charm. She smiled at him over Emma's head.

"Okay, well, I'm going to have a shower. Emma, go get ready for school, please."

"Please, call me Christian," he said to Emma.

Emma grinned. "Okay, Momma. I promise I'll go and get dressed just as soon as I'm finished talking to Christian."

———

Christian stared at Daisy's retreating back and admired the tidy view. Even wearing flannelette pajamas and a thick winter robe, her curvy figure was still obvious. His fingers itched to bury themselves in her tousled hair and to kiss her full soft lips until she was gasping. But the shadows beneath her eyes told him she'd spent a restless night and he wondered if her inability to sleep had anything to do with him.

And then he cursed himself inwardly for being a fool. *Why would thoughts of him keep her up at night?* They barely knew each other and though their first date had gone better than he expected, they hadn't exactly parted with her promising anything more in the future.

It embarrassed him that he felt a twinge of jealousy for a dead man. *Would she ever look at him the way he wanted her to?* It irked him that he had no answer.

She was still so weighed down with guilt...

With a quiet sigh of resignation, he pulled open the door to the refrigerator and began hunting for breakfast things.

"The eggs are in that drawer," Emma offered. "And you'll find the bacon in the top part of the fridge."

"Thanks, Emma. You're really helpful. Now, where did your mom say she kept the frying pan?"

"Over there, under the stove!"

Christian nodded, recalling Daisy's words. He strode over to get it and on his way, his eye caught a life-sized picture of a man. It hung on the wall across from them.

The man looked like he was in his mid-twenties and wore full service uniform. His blond hair and blue eyes reminded Christian of Emma's. His smile for the camera was full of charm, but there was an edge in his eyes. Christian couldn't quite put his finger on the reason, but disquiet suddenly flowed through his veins.

This must be Peter Green. While he wasn't there in the flesh, it almost felt like he was. The picture dominated the room. Now that Christian had spotted it, he couldn't look anywhere without being aware of it.

"That's my dad," Emma said quietly, pride shining in her eyes. "He was a handsome and brave soldier who died protecting us and his country. Momma says he was a hero and we'll never forget him."

Christian managed a tight smile and nodded in agreement. "Your dad was very special. He was indeed a hero."

Satisfied with his answer, Emma acknowledged his comment with a grin and then said, "I have to go and get ready for school, or I'll be late. Momma hates it when we're late." And with that, she disappeared through the doorway.

Unable to help himself, Christian turned back toward the picture. The man's eyes seemed to look right into his soul, read his every thought, including the lustful ones he'd had about the soldier's wife. Inexplicable guilt washed over him and he cursed aloud.

This was ridiculous. The man was dead. Daisy was free to date whoever she wanted and so was Christian. Peter Green no longer had any say, no matter how much his presence dominated this room.

Christian shook his head at the thought. *How could Daisy bear having such a large portrait in her house? What was she trying to do? Punish herself?* The man was dead. How could having a life-sized picture of him help her accept what had happened and allow her to move on? It was as if he was still alive, watching over her, judging her...

The thought filled him with a shiver of apprehension and he wondered again at the edge in the soldier's eyes. *What had he been thinking when the picture was taken? Did Daisy see the same thing?* Or did she merely see the husband she'd disappointed and the father her daughter would never really know? Did she look at the photo and remember all the good times, or was it there to remind her of the bad times? Maybe she didn't want to forget?

With a muffled curse, Christian deliberately turned his back on the picture and busied himself at the stove. The thought of the soldier's treachery filled him with anger. He wanted to have it out with the man, perhaps even punch him in the face. *How could he have treated Daisy so shabbily? To betray his marriage vows?* It was beyond anything Christian could conceive. Still, he needed to be careful. Daisy might never be ready to move on, to put the past and her guilt behind her. He needed to protect himself before he got in too deep and lost his heart to the beautiful widow with the wide and vulnerable eyes.

CHAPTER 12

Daisy stared up at the ceiling and blew out her breath on a heavy sigh. It was way past late. The illuminated digits displayed on the clock on her nightstand told her midnight had come and gone. She'd spent another hectic day in court, arguing on behalf of her young clients, and she was exhausted. Still, sleep eluded her. Another child had gone missing off Emma's bus and though the community had been on high alert, nobody had a clue where either of them were.

A familiar wave of anxiety went through her. As soon as she'd arrived at work that morning she'd called the police to see if Marcie's little girl had been found. She received only a vague response. What she could tell from the conversation was that the police had no clues—which only made it worse. To her, it meant that the kidnapping was likely random... And that meant any child could have been snatched. Any child, including Emma.

Fear tightened her nerve endings. She'd die if

anything happened to her baby. She'd walk Em to the bus stop each morning and would make sure she was there to collect her again at the end of each day. Her little girl wouldn't be walking home on her own again—at least, not until whoever was responsible for the missing children had been caught and locked away.

She shuddered at the thought of the evil stranger who had likely taken the two little girls. It was times like this she missed having Pete around to share her concerns with. Pete would give her a cuddle and assure her he'd never let anything happen to either of his girls and she'd feel a modicum of comfort. But Pete was gone. There was no one to rely on. Except maybe Christian.

Christian.

He'd been the one to tell her about the second missing child. He'd made a special trip over to make sure she and Emma were all right. It was obvious he cared for her. She could see it in his eyes. And for the past three hours, every time she closed hers, she saw him as he'd been that morning, making himself at home.

She'd returned to the kitchen after her shower and had found him expertly flipping eggs onto a plate that already contained a pile of fried bacon. The aromatic smell filled the kitchen and made her mouth water. Emma had gotten ready in double time and the three of them had sat down and enjoyed a cooked breakfast. It surprised Daisy how comfortably the conversation had flowed between them. It felt surprisingly natural to have Christian there.

Now, after another full day of work, and in the middle of the night, in the ghostly dark and silence, she could lie to herself no longer: She liked Christian Grayson.

There, she'd admitted it.

"I like Christian Grayson," she murmured into the darkness. The words sounded strangely exciting on her lips and she was filled with a burst of anticipation. She liked Christian Grayson...and there was definitely plenty to like.

Not only was he physically attractive, he was also a decent man. He was smart and funny and kind. He had a good job. For so long, her heart and mind, her *life* had been Pete's, it was difficult to contemplate all Christian had to offer. Now, she couldn't deny that her heart beat a little faster at the thought of him.

It had been so long since she'd been with a man. So long since she'd kissed and cuddled; held and been held. Shared confidences, kept secrets, given and found pleasure of the physical kind. A surge of yearning went through her and long dormant needs stirred to life. *Was Christian the man to fill the empty space in her heart?*

Was it time to let Pete go, let her guilt go, and look toward the future? Emma had been four when her father died, but she still had memories of him and the time they'd spent together playing ball, swimming at the beach, having fun. *Would she be open to a new man in her mother's life? To a new father figure?*

Daisy sighed and rolled over. She didn't have the answers. She'd done her best to fulfill the roles of father and mother, but even she knew it wasn't the same thing as a real father. And Emma knew it, too.

Was she denying her baby something essential by refusing to let go of the past? There were plenty of single mothers who raised successful, well-adjusted children. It wasn't like a child needed a father in their life. And yet, something deep inside her wanted to give Emma the opportunity to have a good male role model.

With Daisy's parents both dead and with no brothers and sisters, her family line stopped with her. When she went, Emma would have no one. The thought was more than sobering.

A kaleidoscope of images of Christian flashed through her mind: smiling, laughing, teasing. Her heart had frozen over five years ago, but every time she and Christian were around each other, she felt a little piece of her heart begin to thaw. It was like he chipped away at the solidness surrounding it, slowly breaking through, one piece at a time.

Was she brave enough to explore their fragile relationship, to take a step forward, to leave her memories behind? What if she got her heart broken? That would be as bad as when she found out her husband was never coming home. She didn't think she could bear the pain, the agony, the desperate dark days that might come afterwards. The time when all she wanted to do was curl up and die...

Okay, so a breakup with Christian probably wouldn't affect her as badly as Pete's death. After all, they barely knew each other. But she knew herself. She knew she was someone who fell hard. She'd given herself wholeheartedly, heart and body and soul, to her husband and she'd been all of fifteen. It was just the way she was. All or nothing.

And then she remembered Emma's happy conversation over the breakfast table and the way her little girl had peppered Christian with questions. He'd answered every one of them with patience and good humor. It was comfortable, as if the three of them had done that every morning. It had been so easy. Too easy. She could see how effortlessly he could become part of their lives.

She knew he was interested in her romantically. He'd told her as much at the bar and his continued presence in their lives only supported that fact. She'd caught the surreptitious glances he'd shot in her direction when he didn't think she was looking and saw the frank interest in his eyes. No, it wasn't a matter of whether Christian wanted to pursue a relationship with her. It came down to whether she was brave enough to get involved with him.

Her shoulders slumped on another heavy sigh and she rolled over in the opposite direction, pulling her pillow with her. She rested her head on her arms and stared toward the window. The curtains had been drawn before she climbed into bed and now cocooned her from the world outside—even so, her troubled thoughts persisted.

The pros and cons of a relationship with Christian kept circling around and around in her head until she wanted to scream. *What should she* do? *Should she just let nature take its course and see where it led? Was she ready to love again? What about Emma?* Her needs were just as important as Daisy's.

Emma. Her little girl. Her baby.

The first thing to do was to talk to Emma about it. If her daughter was against the idea, that would be the end of it.

Decision made, Daisy turned onto her back with a little sigh of relief. She'd speak to Emma in the morning, before school and would ask her what she thought about it all. Daisy already had an inkling of what her daughter would say.

The thought of being romantically involved with Christian set her heart aflutter. *What would it feel like to kiss him?* The only man she'd kissed had been her husband. The thought of kissing someone else, making love with someone else, filled her with excitement and apprehension.

Though she'd maintained her fitness with regular sessions at the gym since Emma's birth, age had a way of defining one's body and at thirty-two, she wasn't in the first flush of youth. *Would Christian care that she had stretch marks across her belly? That cellulite had found its way to her thighs?* It had been different with Pete. He'd known her since she was a teenager.

Still, Christian wasn't Pete and it wasn't right to draw comparisons. She didn't want another Pete. She wanted to throw off her mantle of anger and guilt and start afresh, with someone good and kind and sexy. Someone who made her yearn for happy times, for fun and laughter. And love. She wanted to be loved. God, she wanted so much to be loved.

———

Christian glanced at his young client who sat slightly behind him and to the left of the bar table. He then widened his gaze to include the boy's mother who sat in the public gallery of the courtroom with a lace handkerchief held up to her mouth, holding back tears. In his first court appearance, Leroy Jackson had entered a plea of not guilty to several serious charges involving assault and robbery at a local convenience store. He'd denied all of the charges and had told Christian he wasn't even at the store on the night in question.

The young aboriginal boy had been identified by the police through grainy CCTV camera footage, but the footage was far from convincing. The hearing had been going for nearly two hours. The officer in charge of the investigation insisted he'd spotted Leroy wearing the same clothes a couple of hours earlier on the day of the robbery. According to the officer, the boy had been loitering around the convenience store and it had been obvious to the officer that he was up to no good.

"How do you know it was Leroy Jackson?" Christian asked.

The officer scratched at his three-day's growth and contemplated his answer. "Like I said, I drove up real close. Got a good look at the boy. It was him. I'm telling you."

"And you say that Leroy Jackson was wearing the same blue jeans and black hoodie that the offender is seen wearing in the security footage?" Christian asked.

The officer nodded. "Yes, that's right. Same as he was wearing when I saw him earlier."

Once again, Christian glanced at his client. Leroy slowly shook his head back and forth. Christian turned back to the witness.

"I put it to you, Officer Preston, that you're mistaken. It wasn't Leroy Jackson that you saw outside the convenience store a couple of hours before the robbery occurred. What do you say to that?"

The expression on the officer's face turned belligerent. "I say, you're the one who's got it wrong, Counselor. I saw that boy." The officer pointed a stubby finger at Christian's client. "I saw Leroy Jackson. The same Leroy Jackson who robbed that store, and in the process, struck the attendant over the head with an iron bar. It's just as well the lady pulled through or the boy would have been charged with murder."

The anger and disgust in the officer's voice traveled clearly across the courtroom. Christian's lips tightened in a grimace, but he kept his cool. He'd just managed to get the prosecution's main witness to incorrectly identify his client as the offender. What was more, the man was absolutely certain his identification was sound.

What the officer didn't know was that Leroy Jackson had spent the day at an amusement park, twenty miles away from the convenience store and Christian had time and date stamped photos to prove it. What was more, his client was wearing a red-and-white striped football jersey and a pair of baggy navy-blue pants. Though there were some similarities between his features and those of the offender caught on tape, the fact was, it couldn't have been Leroy Jackson.

Christian schooled his features into a blank mask and curbed his anticipation as he went in for the kill.

"So, Officer Preston. You have given sworn testimony that you are certain my client, Leroy Jackson, was the same child you saw at close range outside the convenience store a couple of hours before the robbery. The same Leroy Jackson you say has been identified in the security tape. Is that correct?"

The officer glared at him and nodded. "Yes, Counselor. That's correct."

Christian hid his satisfaction and merely nodded. "Thank you, Officer Preston. I have no further questions."

The prosecution rested their case and Christian immediately regained his feet and called Leroy Jackson. The boy confidently gave evidence as to his true whereabouts on the day in question. His testimony was followed by the tendering of several photographs taken at the amusement park by employees of the park. The pictures were the kind available for purchase as a memento of the day and clearly showed Leroy and several of his family members, enjoying a day of fun. In short order, Christian asked the judge to dismiss the case and was pleased when the judge complied.

A quiet cheer went up behind Christian. He turned to his client, who grinned. Relief showed in the whites of his eyes.

"Thanks so much," Mr Grayson," Leroy murmured, his face wreathed in smiles. "You did great."

Christian shrugged, but was pleased nonetheless. "I was just doing my job."

The boy stared at him and his eyes welled up with emotion. "You did more than that, Mr Grayson. You believed me."

Christian patted the boy on the shoulder and swallowed the lump of emotion that had formed in his throat. "You're a good kid, Leroy. Keep up the hard work at school and keep out of trouble. You're going to make a fine young man one day. I bet your momma is so proud of you."

The woman in question lumbered forward, her huge body encased in a tight floral dress. Tears glistened on her cheeks.

"I can't thank you enough, Mr Grayson," she sobbed. "You saved my baby's life." She threw herself at Christian and he held her awkwardly, his arms barely going around the tops of her shoulders.

"No need to thank me, Mrs. Jackson. I was only doing my job. You have a good boy there. Take him home and keep him safe."

The woman drew away, nodding and crying at the same time. She sniffed loudly and used the handkerchief to swipe beneath her nose. Leroy put his arm around his mother's waist and led her out of the courtroom.

Turning back to the bar table, Christian let out a

sigh. The day was over and things had turned out well. It was moments like these that kept him going, kept him believing in the career path he'd chosen. He could have made a ton more money playing corporate games with the big league, but he preferred the simple complexity of the criminal courts, dealing daily with issues that affected peoples' lives.

A lot of the time he came away feeling frustrated that not enough was being done to break the cycle of poverty and crime faced by so many of his young clients, but today he'd had a win for the little guys and it felt good. Almost as good as sharing breakfast with Daisy and her daughter.

The memory of their morning together still filled him with warmth. It had been so easy, so familiar, as if they'd been doing that kind of thing every day of their lives. He wished it were so. He was in his mid-thirties. He was tired of living the life of a bachelor, sharing a place with his uncle. It was too bad his uncle couldn't afford to meet the monthly rent without Christian's contribution.

Though Larry Grayson had held down a decent job for most of his working life, he never seemed to have any money and certainly not enough to get ahead. Larry had only rented the houses they lived in. When Christian got old enough to get a job, Uncle Larry asked him to contribute to the household expenses.

Christian was more than happy to do that. After all, if it hadn't been for his uncle's compassion and generosity when his parents died, he would have been placed in foster care, or even worse, found himself out on the street. He owed a huge debt to Uncle Larry that he was sure he could never repay and if that meant he now contributed more than his share to cover the expenses, then so be it.

When he was in his first year of law school, it occurred to him to ask his uncle about his parents' estate and Uncle Larry had admitted that Christian had inherited a sizeable amount of money. It had been kept in trust and administered by his uncle all these years. Christian had been pleased to discover the majority of his inheritance was still intact, thanks to Uncle Larry. Christian was even more willing to help his uncle out.

Still, the urge to strike out on his own was growing stronger. If things went well with Daisy, he'd definitely want his own place. He thought of his uncle's battle with the bottle and hoped if he moved out it wouldn't cause a relapse. Despite his uncle confiding in him all those years ago about his battle with alcohol, Christian had never seen him drunk. He could only hope Larry's regular solitary sessions in the basement were working their magic and keeping him strong. He wondered if his uncle's sobriety would continue in the event that Christian left home. Maybe his uncle could get a boarder, someone who also liked their privacy, but could provide companionship from time to time...

The more time he spent with Daisy Green, the more he wanted to be with her—permanently and privately.

CHAPTER 13

Larry pulled the lever on his leather recliner and relaxed back against the cushions with a sigh. He brought the crystal highball glass in his hand to his lips and sipped. The alcohol slid smoothly down his throat and he relished the slow burn. He'd convinced Christian he was a recovering alcoholic and it suited Larry to let his nephew think that way.

As far as Christian knew, Larry needed somewhere to escape the pressures of the day and the ever present lure of the bottle. It was for this reason he fitted out the basement in every house they lived in—it became his oasis from the world—at least, that's what he told Christian. The boy had believed him then and he continued to believe him—and that suited Larry just fine.

In some ways, he wished he was afflicted by an alcohol dependency. At least he'd know how to deal with that. There was plenty of support for alcoholics. Not so much for what he suffered from. He knew firsthand the truth of that. He'd sought out professional help, had attended numerous therapy sessions. All to no avail. The psychiatrist to whom he'd poured out his heart had sympathized, but had offered no real solutions.

Oh, there had been talk of meditation techniques and medication that might dull the urge, and he'd tried some of those things, but nothing really worked. The truth was, he'd always been attracted to children, even when he was a kid—a boy of twelve or thirteen on the cusp of puberty.

While his classmates were sniggering about their teacher with the short skirts and large breasts, Larry had been eyeing the fourth graders and dreaming about what it would feel like to touch them, kiss them, lick their soft skin.

He remembered his first sexual encounter as clearly as if it happened yesterday. He was fifteen. She was eight. They rode the same bus. She got off two stops before him. It had taken weeks of dreaming and then even longer to plan. One morning he hid his bike in the bushes near his stop and that afternoon, he got off and doubled back on his bike. He found her a hundred yards away from her house and convinced her to follow him into the bushes. She was small for her age. It wasn't difficult to overwhelm her.

Her tears had only excited him and even though he regretted hurting her, the experience had been everything and more than he could have imagined and left him wanting more. He was relieved when she hadn't said anything about their encounter and was even more pleased when her family moved away.

Of course, Frank had known all about it. He'd held it over Larry's head for years. Every time he wanted something, he'd remind Larry about what he knew.

'One word from me and your life will be over.' Frank would gloat and Larry would inevitably give in to his latest demand, but not without feeling angry and resentful toward his brother for using him that way. In the end, Larry had given payback and given it in spades. He chuckled at the memory. Nothing like a severed brake line to send life off course...

Still, over the years and with persistent application of the suggested therapies, Larry had managed to contain the beast for extended periods of time. It had been more than a year since the last one. But eventually the beast inside him needed attention. Its demands got increasingly aggressive until at last its hungry gaze had fallen on Lila-Jane.

He always took the time to get to know his victims and become familiar with their every move. The afternoons they were on the bus, the ones with no one home. Lila-Jane fit the bill perfectly. Her mother was distracted with the breakdown of her marriage and worked long hours besides. He'd purposefully gone back along Lila-Jane's route and had dropped her navy-blue ribbon in the bush. It was a stroke of genius and done for the sole purpose of adding weight to his claim that the missing girl had climbed off his bus.

And now he had Bella.

She didn't wear any hair ribbons in her short

dark bob, but he'd made sure her school blazer was left partially hidden beneath a bush. He wasn't sure if the police had found it yet. He hadn't listened to the news and the detectives who'd already attended upon him earlier that day hadn't offered him any information. He guessed the jacket would be found sooner or later, though, and once again his insistence the child had exited the bus at her stop would be reinforced.

Pretty little Bella. The thought of her sent a tightening through his loins and his heart skipped a beat in anticipation. Inside him, the beast flared to life. He would give the girl time to adjust to her new situation and then he'd introduce himself...from behind the safety of his mask, of course.

It was unusual for the beast to demand more than one child at a time, but that was exactly what had happened. He supposed it had something to do with his lengthy self-enforced abstinence—after all, it had been more than twelve months.

This time, when the police stopped by with their questions about the latest disappearance of a child off his bus, they'd asked to look around. Of course, he'd given his permission. After all, he had nothing to hide. The fake wall he'd purposefully installed in his basement made sure of that.

It concealed all his secrets and shielded all his lies. It allowed him to break the rules without the risk of prying eyes, even his nephew's. It was a good thing Christian was so trusting and believed everything his uncle said. It seemed impossible that he could get away with his affliction with Christian living under the same roof, but he'd been doing it for years and none of the happenings and disappearances had ever raised his nephew's suspicions.

Seizing the opportunity to take Christian in all those years ago had been a stroke of genius. When he'd planned the deaths of his brother and sister-in-law, he hadn't given any thought to their brat. He'd initially been taken aback when the estate lawyer declared there was no one else, but having listened to the reading of his brother's will, Larry couldn't help but see the advantage of having the boy. He gave Larry credibility as a decent, hardworking man getting on with his life. He'd no longer be a single bachelor living on his own who occasionally became the source of gossip. Some people wondered about a man who lived on his own...

Having the boy with him made him less suspicious. Now he was a man with a child; no longer a single man living on his own. Christian got to be raised by family and, despite the early setback of being orphaned at a young age, he'd made a success of his life. The funds he contributed, as well as the boy's generous inheritance, added to Larry's lifestyle. Things had worked out well for both of them, if Larry did say so himself.

Of course, Larry had been careful not to spend too much of Christian's inheritance. He wasn't stupid. The boy would eventually grow into a man and he'd begin to ask questions. At the time, Larry had no idea Christian would become a lawyer, and he was more than relieved that he'd kept his nephew's trust fund largely intact when the boy asked him about Frank and Amanda's estate.

He calmly showed Christian all the paperwork—the records of income and expenditure he was required to keep. There was still a sizeable portion of the inheritance remaining, as anyone would expect. Frank and Amanda's estate had been valued at over two million dollars. There was still plenty to go round. Larry should be grateful his nephew was such a generous soul who continued to pay more than his share of the bills.

Oh, yes. Larry had a lot to be grateful for. There was certainly no doubt about that. Christian had even made him sole beneficiary of his estate. In the event Larry's nephew died before he did, Larry would inherit everything... It was a tantalizing thought, but Larry had other plans for Christian and it didn't include him meeting an untimely death...

———————

Christian took a swallow of beer out of his longneck and relished the yeasty taste. It had been a long day in court and he was only now, many hours later, taking time to relax. He kept a well-stocked, small bar fridge tucked away beside his cedar locker—for that very purpose. Winning Leroy Jackson's case had been the highlight of his day and reaffirmed the reasons he did what he did for a living. There was so much wrong in the world, it was nice to have a win for the good guys occasionally.

He took another mouthful of beer and stared out the plate glass window of his office into the darkness beyond. It was late. He probably should leave for home. His uncle would be wondering where he was. Most nights they ate dinner together and caught up on each other's day. They didn't keep tabs on each other, but out of courtesy and habit, they usually let each other know if they were going to be late. It was a mutual show of respect they had for each other.

He liked to think he'd also played a part in his uncle maintaining sobriety. It was harder to hide a hangover or a relapse into drinking when there was someone sitting across from you at the breakfast table. For the best part of twenty-four years, Larry had remained sober. Every time he thought about it, Christian was filled with pride, and though his uncle rarely mentioned it, he was sure Uncle Larry was grateful to him for being there.

As they seemed to do of late, his thoughts drifted to Daisy and Emma and then he remembered the other missing girl. The story had made the morning papers. The second missing child had been identified as Bella Rushby, an eleven-year-old schoolgirl who caught Uncle Larry's bus.

The connection to his uncle troubled him. Though not all of the missing kids over the years had ridden on Uncle's Larry's bus, some of them had. The police hadn't drawn attention to it at the time and Christian hoped they wouldn't do so now. It wasn't his uncle's fault those kids disappeared on their way home.

Uncle Larry loved the kids who traveled to school on his bus. He knew every one of them by name. He knew their likes and dislikes. He knew the ones who had plenty of friends and those who sat alone. He'd always have a special word and a kind smile to the lonely ones.

Christian remembered the few times his uncle raised his voice to the bigger boys down the back. It was only when they needed it and they quickly fell back in line. Everyone knew when Mr Grayson was serious and they loved and respected him for it. He loved and respected them back. He loved his job and it showed. There were many times over the years during the school holidays that Uncle Larry moped and grouched around the house. To Christian's relief, school would eventually go back in session. Uncle Larry was happiest when he was behind the wheel of his bus.

With a quiet sigh, Christian finished the rest of his beer and then dropped the bottle in into the recycling bin. Not bothering to tidy up the papers on his desk, he switched off the banker's lamp near his elbow then stood to retrieve his jacket. With a last glance around his office, he opened the door and left.

Daisy blew her breath out on a sigh and stared across at her best friend. Sally-Ann Li had caught her in the corridor between their offices and had asked if she had time for coffee. Even after discussing Christian with Emma and having her little girl give the idea a thumbs up, she was still torn about making a decision and she could really do with her friend's advice.

"Sure," she agreed.

They'd found an empty table at a café not far from their building and both of them had ordered skim lattés. The drinks arrived and they both took a few sips before Sally-Ann hit Daisy with a question.

"So, what's going on? Are you in trouble?"

Daisy shook her head. "No, it's nothing like that."

"I read the paper this morning. Another young girl's gone missing. Are you worried about Emma?"

"Of course I am. The child catches Emma's bus. So far, the police don't have a clue where she could be. They're not ruling out the possibility the disappearances could be related."

"That's right. There was another little girl last week. Have they found her yet?"

Daisy grimaced. "No, only what they think might be one of her hair ribbons. It was found in a bush along her route home."

"Her poor parents must be going insane," Sally-Ann said quietly.

"Yes. I'm friends with the child's mother. Her marriage broke down over a year ago. She's on her own. She's really having a tough time of it."

"I can't imagine." Sally-Ann touched her belly that was slightly protruding. She'd recently married James Shepherd, a detective who worked in the city. She'd confided in Daisy only a week earlier that they were expecting. Daisy couldn't be happier for her friend.

"How's Emma taking the disappearances?" Sally-Ann's question broke into Daisy's thoughts. "She's okay, I guess. A little scared and confused and, like the rest of us, she's wondering where poor Lila-Jane and Bella are. We just want them to come home, safe and sound. Everyone does."

The two women fell silent and both of them took another sip from their mugs. With a quiet sigh, Sally-Ann sat back in her chair and eyed Daisy.

"So, if you're not in trouble and Emma's fine, why do you look so tired and out of sorts?"

Daisy shot her friend a rueful grin. They'd been friends long enough that Sally-Ann recognized when she was feeling down or unsettled, or both. She'd known Sally-Ann when Pete was still alive and her friend knew most of the ups and downs they'd faced. Sally-Ann had been the shoulder Daisy had cried on when she'd been given the news of Pete's death and she wouldn't have found the strength to return to work and carry on if it hadn't been for Sally-Ann's support and encouragement.

"You're right. The problem isn't with Emma. It's with Christian Grayson."

Sally-Ann frowned. "The new guy?"

"Well, he's been here about four months."

"Yes, I think he started while I was away on my

honeymoon. From all accounts, he must be good looking. And around the water cooler, I hear he has most of the female staff in a lather."

Daisy laughed. "Yes, I guess you could say he's good looking."

Sally-Ann shot her a shrewd look. "Don't tell me you're one of the females whose heart is all aflutter?"

Heat crept across Daisy's cheeks. She busied herself with her coffee.

"Daisy?" Sally-Ann's tone was insinuating, demanding an answer.

Daisy sighed and decided to come clean. After all, that was why she'd agreed to coffee in the first place, wasn't it? She needed her friend's advice.

"Okay, so I find him attractive. What's the big deal?"

Sally-Ann sat forward, her eyes wide with astonishment. "Did I just hear correctly? Did you just say you found Christian Grayson attractive?"

Daisy shrugged self-consciously, almost regretting she had confided in her friend. "Yes, so what of it?"

Sally-Ann shook her head slowly back and forth, her expression incredulous. "So *what?* Is this my friend, Daisy Veronica Green, admitting to having feelings for a man? A man who is not her husband who passed away five years ago?"

A reluctant grin tugged at Daisy's lips and she poked her tongue out at her friend. Sally-Ann promptly burst into laughter and clapped her hands gleefully.

"Oh, my goodness! This is *wonderful* news! I

never thought I'd see the day when you finally *noticed* a member of the opposite sex, let alone admitted to feelings of attraction! Wait until I tell James! He's going to be as thrilled as I am!"

She reached for her phone and pushed back her chair. "Here, let's get a selfie. I want to preserve this moment for all time."

With that, she came around to Daisy's side and bent low until they both fit on the screen. Daisy's grin widened at her friend's antics. Sally-Ann snapped the shot.

"Right," Sally-Ann said as she settled herself back across the table. "Now, tell me everything."

Daisy reached for her coffee mug and took a healthy sip, buying time. Now that the moment was upon her, she wasn't quite sure what to say.

"We met by chance the evening Lila-Jane Morrissey disappeared. She's the first little girl to go missing," she added, seeing Sally-Ann's frown.

"Okay. How did it happen?"

"It's a little complicated. Christian's uncle was driving the bus that Lila-Jane caught home from school. Apart from whoever took her, he was the last person to see her. Larry—that's Christian's uncle—and Christian came by Marcie Morrissey's place to see if there was anything they could do. Emma and I were already there. We got talking and... I guess things went from there."

Sally-Ann's eyes gleamed with keen interest. Daisy could tell her friend wanted more. She swallowed a sigh and continued. *After all, how was Sally-Ann meant to offer advice if she didn't know everything?*

"The thing is, Sal, we really like each other. A couple of days ago, he came over and made Em and I breakfast. It was so sweet. I can't remember the last time a man made me breakfast. In fact, I don't think I've ever had a man make me breakfast, not even Pete."

"That paragon of virtue," Sally-Ann commented dryly.

Daisy ignored her friend and continued. "Anyway, I haven't felt this way about a man since Pete, and it's tearing me up inside. Every time I close my eyes, I see Christian grinning at me in my kitchen, looking way sexier than any man has a right to. Then I see Pete looming over me. He's only a shadow, but I know that it's him.

"He's reminding me of all we had together and how he wished he was still here, by my side. And then I get overwhelmed with guilt and I don't know where to turn especially when I get to work and Christian emails me something cute. I get confused all over again."

Sally-Ann nodded slowly, her expression filled with compassion and understanding. "Why are you feeling guilty? Your husband's been dead five years. I don't mean to be insensitive, but there it is. You didn't die with him and neither did Emma. You owe it to her to start living again and what better person to do it with than a good man like Christian Grayson?"

Daisy was already shaking her head *no*, even before her friend finished. "You don't understand!" she cried.

"What don't I understand? That you're a

beautiful woman in the prime of her life who has wants and needs like everyone else?"

Daisy blushed, but maintained her stubborn stance. "It isn't that easy, Sal! There are things—" She stared across at her friend. "There are things you don't know."

"What things?" Sally-Ann asked gently.

In stilted sentences, Daisy told her about Pete's affair.

CHAPTER 14

Shock flooded Sally-Ann's face. "Oh, Daisy! I don't believe it! You poor thing! I had no idea! I mean, I knew Pete was sometimes aloof and spent hours holed up in his den, but I thought that's all it was. I didn't realize he was seeing someone else. Why didn't you tell me?"

Tears filled Daisy's eyes and she shrugged helplessly. "I don't know. I guess I was ashamed. I mean, my husband had sought out the company of another woman. What kind of wife did that make me?"

Sally-Ann glared at her from across the table. "Don't you *dare* talk like that, Daisy Green! None of that was your fault. Pete made the decision to cheat on you. He alone bore the responsibility for what happened after that. You did what any other sensible woman would do if their husband betrayed them like that."

Daisy sniffed and reached for a tissue in her handbag. Wiping her eyes, she drew in another fortifying breath.

"I know. In my head, I know you're right, but my heart keeps telling me different."

"What did you do when you found out?" Sally-Ann asked softly.

"We had an almighty row. Pete refused to discuss it with me. I found out she was one of his colleagues. They both happened to be on leave at the same time. When I tried to find out why and how long and whether it was over, he clammed up; simply refused to speak to me. He threw a few things in a bag and left. He stormed out of the house and told me he wasn't sure if he'd be back."

She paused as the awful memories washed over her. "By then I was so worked up and mad as hell, I spoke without thinking. I told him to keep on walking. That I wanted a divorce."

Sally-Ann gasped. "Oh, my goodness! Daisy, I had no idea!"

Daisy nodded sadly. "I don't think I actually meant it. In fact, I'm *sure* I didn't mean it. I said the words in anger. I wanted to lash out at him and hurt him, like he'd hurt me.

"He stayed away for two whole days and I had no idea where he was. I rang his cell and left messages. I sent texts. He didn't reply. And then he came home the night before he was due to leave for his next deployment and he packed his bag and slept in the spare room. I tried to talk to him, but once again he refused to discuss it. He left early the next morning. It was the last time I saw him alive."

Her voice cracked with emotion on the last few words and tears slid down her cheeks. Sally-Ann stood and moved closer and gave her an awkward hug. "Oh, Daisy! You poor baby! I can't believe you've been living with this on your conscience for the past five years! Why didn't you tell me? Why didn't you let me help you by sharing the burden? You should not have had to bear this all alone!"

By now, the tears coursed freely down Daisy's cheeks. She could barely find the energy to wipe them away. Memories of those awful final days with her husband came rushing to the fore. The anger, the pain, the hurt, the disappointment. They washed over her in waves. She hiccupped on a sob, embarrassed to have lost control. She was in public, for goodness sake! She needed to get a grip!

"It's all right, Daisy. It's all right."

Sally-Ann's quiet reassurances and gentle stroking of her hair made the tears fall faster. It had been so long since she'd felt anyone truly cared. Her parents had died from natural causes—both of them had been in their seventies and had long suffered from diabetes. She'd been thirty when her mother died and her dad followed shortly thereafter. Emma could barely remember her grandparents.

As for Pete's family—they'd never approved of their marriage. She hadn't seen them since the evening when Pete announced their engagement. To this day, she didn't know what she'd done to incur their wrath, but there it was. To have someone care for her now, really care, shattered her armor and control.

Sally-Ann remained standing, shielding her from the public's view and for that, Daisy was grateful. Gradually the sobs subsided and her friend slowly withdrew.

"Are you all right?" Sally-Ann asked quietly, concern still shadowing her eyes.

Daisy sniffed and nodded. "Yes, I'm fine. I'm sorry for blubbering all over you. I haven't cried like that in a long while."

"I think you needed to have a good cry."

Daisy nodded. "I think you're right." She smiled a tremulous smile and it was reflected on Sally-Ann's face. She drew in a deep breath and sighed.

"Thank you for listening and for...everything."

Sally-Ann's smile filled with warmth. "Any time."

A moment of silence fell between them and then Sally-Ann cleared her throat. "So, I gather this is the reason you're so confused about your feelings for Christian Grayson?"

Daisy nodded and lifted her gaze to her friend's. "Of course! I think about Christian and how much I like him and how much I'd like us to spend time together and then I remember Pete, how much I loved him and believed in him. And how he betrayed my love and my trust. And the awful way we parted—the guilt from that just about tears me apart. And then I think about how he cheated on me and I wonder if I can ever trust a man again. It isn't fair to Christian—he's done nothing to deceive me, but the uncertainty is there, just the same. I don't know what to do." Once again, Daisy was close to tears.

"Enough!" Sally-Ann almost shouted, her voice stern.

Daisy blinked in surprise. "Excuse me?"

"I said, enough," Sally-Ann repeated in a slightly milder tone. "That kind of talk is ridiculous and won't get you anywhere. It won't make you feel any better and it sure as hell won't bring your husband back."

Daisy gasped as if she'd been slapped. Sally-Ann looked unrepentant.

"Don't look at me like I've run over your favorite puppy," Sally-Ann grumbled. "I'm sorry, okay? But your circular thinking called for some radical intervention." She sighed heavily.

"You're my best friend, Daisy Green, and I love you. It kills me to see you beating yourself up like this! Pete died in a terrible accident. He was a soldier at war. Tragic things happen. You can't ever believe you had anything to do with his death. Thinking like that is destructive and will only cause you grief.

"Okay, so it's unfortunate you guys had a big fight right before he was deployed, but shit happens, right? You can't blame yourself. You have to let it go, put it behind you, accept it. There's no other way for you to move forward, with Christian or with anyone, until you do."

Daisy drew in a ragged breath, feeling as fragile as fine blown glass. In her head, she knew what Sally-Ann said was right. Logically. It was her heart that was harder to convince. Still, she felt a faint kind of peace softly invade her heart and for the first time, she didn't feel so agitated at the thought of Pete and his untimely death.

Could she finally accept that she wasn't responsible for what had happened and let her guilt subside? Could she finally give herself permission to move on with her life, to learn to trust and seek out love again?

An image of Christian smiling at her flooded her mind and she closed her eyes against the wonder of it. She wanted to get to know this man better, to be the recipient of more of his smiles—and maybe more of his breakfasts, too.

––––––––––––––

Daisy drew in a deep breath and squared her shoulders, searching for the courage to knock on Christian's office door. She'd already cleared it with his secretary, who had confirmed that he was in. Daisy worked on the opposite side of the building, so she could hardly use the excuse she was just passing by.

What she was about to do sent waves of nervousness rushing through her, but sometime during the early hours of the morning, after tossing over all that Sally-Ann had said, she'd made a decision: It was time to put Pete and their life together behind her and look toward the future. She owed it to Emma and...she owed it to herself.

Holding on to her courage, she rapped sharply on the closed panel and immediately gained a response.

"Come in."

With a fresh rush of nerves surging through her,

she opened the door and walked straight into Christian's office. He looked up from where he sat behind his desk and his eyes widened in surprise.

"Daisy! How are you? To what do I owe this pleasure?"

Now that the moment was upon her, she could barely get out the words. Heat crept up her neck and spread across her cheeks. She hastily averted her gaze.

"I-I wanted to thank you for breakfast the other morning. I've been so busy, I haven't had a chance to stop by."

"You thanked me already that morning," Christian replied. "There's no need to thank me again. It was just breakfast."

She drew a little closer and came to a halt a few feet from his desk. "No, that's where you're wrong," she said. "It was more than just breakfast. It was an act of kindness and caring and... I need you to know, I really appreciate it. It's been a long time since I've received attention like that from anyone."

Christian nodded slowly and from the expression on his face, it was obvious he understood.

"I'm honored to have been invited into your home and to have been allowed to make you breakfast," he replied. He paused and then his voice gentled to such a degree it almost brought tears to her eyes.

"I understand how difficult it must be to accept your husband is never coming back, Daisy. It was like that when my parents died and though everyone says how resilient children are, I can tell you, I did it tough for a long time."

A surge of tenderness went through her as she thought of the little boy Christian had once been, abandoned forever by those he'd loved the most.

"You're so lucky your uncle was willing to take you in," she whispered. "He obviously did well by you. You're a successful lawyer with a good job and you seem to be reasonably well-adjusted, despite your rocky past. Your uncle should be congratulated on that."

"You're right. In fact, I was thinking the same thing recently. How lucky I've been. Uncle Larry was thrust into parenthood overnight and came without any training. I don't think he did a half-bad job." Christian followed his words with a grin and Daisy found herself smiling back.

"I agree. He didn't do a half-bad job," she said.

The gazes held and lingered and Daisy's heartbeat took off in a rush. Once again, nerves clogged her throat. Her gaze fell to his full lips and not for the first time she wondered what it would feel like to kiss him. She blushed at the direction her thoughts had taken, and looked away.

As if sensing her inner turmoil, Christian pushed his chair back and came around his desk toward her. She held her ground and when he reached her and stopped, there was barely a breath of space between them. With his thumb and index finger, he gently tilted her chin until she was forced to look at him.

"I want to kiss you, Daisy," he said plainly.

She could barely breathe. Her heart hammered in her chest. But she realized her reaction to his words was more from nerves than from fear. She wanted Christian to kiss her. And she wanted to kiss him back. The discovery left her feeling scared and exhilarated, all at once.

Christian stared at her, waiting for her response. It was a testament to the kind of man he was that he wouldn't make a move without her consent. She gazed at him with all the confusion and need she felt inside and offered him a hesitant nod.

"I want to kiss you, too, Christian."

His blue eyes immediately darkened with emotion, and his hands found their way to her hips. He drew her close. Their clothing brushed and she gasped from the sensation of his warm hard body against hers.

With infinite slowness, his head descended and when his lips brushed hers, it was as soft as a whisper. Even so, that slightest touch was enough to ignite her. Her heart beat so hard she thought it might thump right out of her chest. Her lips tingled where they met his. She was scared and enthralled and awestruck. She never wanted it to stop.

And then, just as quickly as it had started, the kiss was over. Christian pulled back and released her chin. With eyes dark and unfathomable, he stared down at her, as if gauging her reaction. Her breath came fast and so did his. She saw the tiny fluttering of a pulse in his strong neck. It pleased her to know that he was as affected by the kiss as she was. Somehow, it made her feel good that this thing between them was as important to him as it was to her.

She drew in a deep breath and eased it out as her arms crept up around his neck. Pulling his head down to hers, she caught the flare of surprise and need in his eyes an eternity before she touched her lips to his. This time, though it was still very much a kiss of exploration, she kissed him properly. She traced the outline of his lips with her tongue and then nibbled on the fullness of his lower lip. She kissed the corners of his mouth and then moved once again to savor the fullness of his lips.

Once again, his arms tightened about her and a groan escaped his lips. He kissed her back with equal fervor and before they knew it, they were tightly wrapped in each other's arms. It was as if a firecracker had exploded inside them and their blood had burst into flames. The kiss deepened, exploded with passion. Neither could get enough.

Daisy's nipples tightened with need and she felt the hard evidence of Christian's desire pressing against the softness of her belly. Some part of her brain whispered that they were in his office and that maybe this wasn't such a good idea, but she ignored the warning.

And then Christian lifted his head and broke the kiss and both of them were gasping for air. He released his hold and her arms slid from around his neck. She took a step back and tried desperately to regain some control.

"Wow," Christian murmured. "That was... That was... Wow."

Daisy laughed shakily and swiped a hand across her lips. They felt full and swollen and tingly. Now that the moment of passion was over, she couldn't help but feel embarrassed by her forwardness. "I... I'm sorry," she stammered. "I didn't mean for it to get out of control like that."

Christian closed the distance between them and placed his hands on her shoulders. His gaze was intent. "Please don't apologize for anything that happens between us, Daisy. I was as involved and affected as you were." He laughed then admitted, "The ferocity of it took me by surprise, too. But that's a good thing. It's nothing to apologize for. We're two people coming together and I find you incredibly attractive. I'm over the moon that you feel the same and want to spend time with me. There's nothing wrong with that."

She saw the sincerity in his eyes and managed to nod. "You're right. I guess I'm not really sorry. I wanted this as much as you did. I guess I just wasn't expecting it to be so..."

"So great? Is that what you meant to say?"

She looked at him and nodded again. "Yes. I guess I wasn't expecting it to be so great." She looked down, a bit embarrassed.

"I understand," he replied. "I guess I'm selfish enough to want you to say that it was never quite like that with Pete."

Daisy thought of her life with her husband and the love that they'd shared. Initially their passion for each other had been every bit as strong as what she'd just experienced with Christian, but it had been so long since Pete had held her, kissed her, spoke gentle words of love and toward the end, things hadn't been so great...

She guessed it was the guilt that had kept her so loyal to his memory and so adamant that she not move on. But as Sally-Ann had said, it was time to put the guilt behind her, to forgive herself for the part that she had played, to take a chance and learn to live and love again.

———————

Lila-Jane felt the girl stir beside her and swallowed a burst of excitement. Bella had been asleep for most of the time she'd been there. The only time she'd woken, she'd been dazed and confused. Lila-Jane supposed the man with the clown mask must have given her something, just like he'd given something to her. But now, it seemed the girl was finally waking. Lila-Jane wanted to ask her a million questions, to find out if the girl had any idea where they were.

"Bella! Bella! Open your eyes! Bella, can you hear me?"

Lila-Jane had recognized her straight away. Though Bella was in the year ahead of her in school, they caught the same bus. The girl was pretty quiet and usually kept to herself, but Lila-Jane had always admired her glossy dark hair.

Bella's eyes slowly opened and Lila-Jane grinned in excitement. After the hours and days she'd spent there alone, it was great to be sharing her fear and apprehension with someone else. She didn't relish the idea of telling Bella exactly what went on there, but she was pleased for the companionship, nonetheless.

As Bella's gaze focused, her eyes grew large

with surprise. "Lila-Jane? What are *you* doing here? People are looking for you everywhere! We even held a prayer vigil and everybody came. There were candles and singing and praying. It was beautiful. Except for your mom. She couldn't stop crying."

Lila-Jane blinked back a rush of tears at the thought of her mother. She was filled with a yearning so great it snatched her breath.

Momma, where are you? Please hurry! I'm here, Momma! I'm here!

The words reverberated through her head, but she bit her lip and steadfastly remained silent. She didn't want to scare Bella before it was absolutely necessary.

"How did you get here?" she asked the newcomer.

Bella frowned. "I don't know. The last thing I remember is Mr Grayson telling me he'd received a call from my mother to say she was running late from work. I was to stay on the bus and come home with him. My mother would collect me from there."

"Does your mom know where Mr Grayson lives?" Lila-Jane asked.

"I'm not sure."

Lila-Jane frowned. Fragments of memory teased at the surface, vague and elusive. "I think Mr Grayson told me my mom was running late, too," she said slowly. "I remember thinking I could just get off and walk home like I always do, but Mr Grayson insisted my mom wanted me to wait at his house."

Bella stared at her with wide eyes. "Do you think we're at Mr Grayson's?"

Lila-Jane considered the idea in silence. Now that she came to think about it, the man with the clown face was the same height and build as their bus driver. He also had a cloud of white hair. Lila-Jane had seen it poking out behind the clown mask and when the man had turned his back on her.

"Maybe," she conceded.

"Have you seen anyone since you've been here?" Bella asked.

"Yes. A man comes every now and then to bring food and let me use the bathroom. He wears a mask so I can't see his face."

Bella looked curious. "What kind of mask?"

"A clown mask."

"Does he say anything to you?"

"Sometimes."

"Has he told you why you're here?"

Lila-Jane shook her head. She'd worked out why she was there. Her captor was one of those evil men her mother had warned her about. The kind who did naughty things to little children. She shuddered at her recent memories. No sense alarming Bella before she had to.

"I want to go home," Bella said in a small voice.

Lila-Jane reached out as far as the restraints around her wrists allowed and managed to squeeze the other girl's hand. "Me, too," she whispered.

CHAPTER 15

Christian barely noticed the warm sunshine and bright blue sky that evidenced another mild winter day. He was on his lunch break and he'd come outside with a vague notion of buying Daisy flowers. The kiss they'd shared in his office had just about blown him away. His mind was full of her.

He wanted to stride over to her office and repeat the experience, but it was a wiser move to put some space between them before he ended up embarrassing them both. He wasn't sure what had changed her mind after their conversation about her husband, but it was clear she'd come to the decision to put her old life behind her and look toward the future.

Why else would she have come to his office and kissed him? Why else would she have agreed to meet him for lunch? Except she'd just texted to say her case had run overtime and now she couldn't make it...

Or was that just an excuse? Was she even now

regretting the decision to get to know him better? Was this her way of backing away, putting space between them? If she didn't want to see him, why didn't she just come right out and say so, dammit! Why go through the pretense of telling him she was running late? It's not like he was forcing her to go to lunch. He only wanted to spend time with her, as much time as possible, but if she didn't feel the same way...

He groaned in frustration. Several people standing nearby gave him strange looks and he quickly schooled his features into a blank mask. He and Daisy weren't even officially together and already she was doing his head in. He liked her. He *really* liked her. *But how could he take that next step forward if he didn't know how she felt?*

A direct approach was called for. There was nothing else to do. He'd never been interested in playing games and he suspected she wasn't, either. Decision made, he tugged out his phone and quickly dialed her number. Even if the case had run overtime, she should be on her lunch break by now. To his relief, she answered on the second ring.

"Christian! It's good to hear from you."

His heart thumped hard against his ribs. He drew in a deep breath and blurted out, "Daisy, I can't bear not knowing how you feel about me. That kiss we shared... It was amazing... I want us to go out together, date, get to know each other. I want to know everything about you. I can't stop thinking about you. But I need to know if you feel as crazy and confused as I do.

"An insecure part of me wants to run and hide from this madness, but most of me just wants to spend time with you. My heart beats so hard when I'm near you. It's like a shot of adrenaline is pumped straight into my blood. I'm excited and nervous and confused all at once. This all might be a little too much for you. I'm probably coming on too strong. It's too soon, isn't it? I—"

"It's all right, Christian. I understand. And I... I feel exactly the same way. Scared, confused, excited... Our past colors how we see things, and that's generally a good thing. But this time it feels like something I've never experienced or believed in before. It's been so long since I felt even close to this way. It scares me half to death. But... I want to get to know you better, too."

His breath escaped in a rush. Until that moment, he hadn't even realized he'd been holding it. "I-I'm so glad," he managed.

"It would be nice if we could go out to dinner sometime," she quietly suggested.

"Of course! Name the time and place."

"It's a little difficult with Emma. I'd have to find a sitter. Unless..."

Her voice drifted off. Christian waited for her to continue. When she didn't, he couldn't help but prompt her. "Unless...?"

"Unless you'd like to come over to our place? I could cook. Fair's fair. You cooked us breakfast and I'd like to return the favor."

His heart filled with warmth and he smiled so hard his lips hurt. He wanted to shout his happiness from the rooftops—and probably would have if he hadn't been standing in the middle of Martin Place surrounded by busy shoppers and people having lunch.

With an act of will, he kept his voice even. "That would be nice."

———————

Daisy moved the curtain slightly to one side and peeked out the front window. The street below was bare of traffic. Christian was nowhere in sight. She stifled her disappointment. It wasn't like he was late. Well, not really. Five minutes wasn't really late. Perhaps he was one of those people who didn't care so much about being punctual? She wasn't one of them, but she knew plenty of people who were. It could be a little irritating at times, but nobody was perfect.

Turning away from the window, her gaze snagged on the life-sized portrait that hung from her living room wall. Her hand came up to her mouth on a silent gasp. She'd forgotten it was there. She'd never wanted the picture. Pete had commissioned it months before his death. He wanted everyone who came to their house to know how proud he was to be serving his country.

She could still remember the phone call from the photographer who had done the work. He'd called her three weeks after Pete had died to tell her the picture was ready to be collected. Emma had fallen in love with the portrait and insisted on hanging it in the living room where everyone could see her daddy, the war hero. Daisy didn't have the heart to tell her no.

A light rap on the door sent her thoughts about Pete scurrying and she nervously patted down her hair. She'd washed and dried and brushed it an hour ago until it fell in soft, shiny waves.

"You look beautiful, Momma," Emma announced, watching her get ready.

"Thank you, baby. You look very pretty in your dress, too. I've always loved that color on you."

Emma grinned with pleasure. "Pink's my favorite."

Daisy bent over and kissed her daughter on the nose. "I know."

Emma giggled and Daisy's heart rejoiced at the sound. She hoped her little girl would feel just as happy as she did about Christian coming around.

The knock sounded again and Daisy hurried to open it. Christian stood on the other side of the doorway with a bouquet of brightly colored gerberas in his hand.

"Good evening, I'm sorry I'm late. My car's being serviced and Uncle Larry was out. I should have known better than to rely on public transport running on time."

Daisy's heart skipped a beat at the sight of him. Dressed in a light-blue polo shirt and Levis, he looked every bit as good as he did in a suit.

"Don't worry about it," she replied, brushing his apology away. "It's fine."

"Just so you know, I'm usually very punctual," he added. His eyes gleamed with good humor. "I promise."

She laughed at his teasing. "Well, that's good to know, because I am, too."

"No, you're not, Momma! You're *always* running late!"

Daisy blushed as Emma appeared at her side, but Christian merely laughed. Shaking her head, Daisy stood back and invited him inside.

"These are for you," he said and handed her the flowers.

Once again, heat crept across her cheeks, but this time the response was more from pleasure than embarrassment. "Thank you. They're beautiful. You shouldn't have."

Christian merely shrugged. "I wanted to."

She led him down the hallway and into the open-concept kitchen and living room and then headed toward a dresser to collect a vase.

"Something smells good," Christian commented, looking around.

"Mom's been cooking all afternoon," Emma announced. "She wasn't sure what kind of food you like to eat, so she's made a little bit of everything."

The heat in Daisy's cheeks intensified and she averted her gaze from Christian's amused one. Keeping her back to him, she pretended to be busy adding water to the vase and arranging the flowers.

"I hope you like East Indian food," Emma continued.

"As a matter of fact, I *love* Indian food," Christian replied. "The spicier the better."

"Good," Emma replied with satisfaction.

"Because Momma's made all my favorites. Butter chicken, beef vindaloo, and best of all, garlic naan bread."

"Sounds delicious! I love naan bread, too."

Daisy set the vase of flowers in the middle of the table and stood back to admire the results. "You really shouldn't have, Christian. These are way too much."

He moved closer. "I wanted to. Beautiful flowers for a beautiful woman. It sounds corny, but it's true."

His gaze tangled with hers, the blue of his irises turning to cobalt. Her heart tightened with emotion and she blinked back a rush of tears. Christian stared at her, as if trying to read her thoughts.

"No one's ever brought me flowers," she whispered, her voice husky with emotion.

As if sensing her fragility, Christian merely murmured, "You deserve these."

"We're having satay chicken kebabs for starters," Emma announced with a wide grin, breaking the mood. "I hope you like them, Mr Grayson."

Christian laughed and looked back at Emma. "I do like kebabs, Emma and I thought I told you to call me Christian."

The little girl looked embarrassed and then grinned. "Sorry, Christian."

"So, Emma. Satay chicken kebabs for starters, Indian food for main. What about dessert?"

His eyes glinted with mischief as he looked at Daisy over Emma's head. Emma stared at him seriously. "For dessert, we're having a four-stack chocolate cake with fresh whipped cream and strawberries. I helped Momma ice it! I can't wait to take a bite!"

Once again, Christian shot her a teasing grin. "It sounds like your momma's been busy. I can't wait to try it all."

Emma smiled and ran over to the table and pulled out the chair at its head. "Sit here, Christian."

He shot Daisy a searching look, but she carefully schooled her expression so that it didn't reveal any of the inner turmoil. It hadn't occurred to her that Emma would invite him to sit in Pete's seat. She gave him a nod.

Christian continued to search her face for answers. "Are you sure?"

"Yes, of course I'm sure," she said firmly.

Emma promptly seated herself to his left and with her elbows on the table, rested her chin in her hands. She stared up at Christian adoringly. "You've got nice eyes, Christian."

His gaze remained on Daisy. She felt the heat of it all the way down to her toes. After a long moment, he told Emma, "Thank you, Emma. You have nice eye, too!"

The little girl dissolved into a fit of giggles. A smile tugged at Daisy's lips. It was so good to see her baby laughing. For a long time, there hadn't been enough laughter in their house. Somehow this all felt so right. She was filled with a surge of determination to spend time with this good and decent man and perhaps even allow herself to fall in love with him...

The thought sent a shaft of emotion straight to her heart, but instead of fear, she was filled with anticipation. The tiny burst of hope that miraculously ignited inside her felt wonderful.

Could she trust these burgeoning feelings? What if he failed to live up to his promise and ended up breaking her heart? Where would she be then? And what about Emma? Her daughter was already half in love with Christian. Was it right for Daisy to bring her defenseless child into this? To risk Emma's heart, too?

As if aware of her morose thoughts, Christian shot her another look of concern. His eyes darkened and questions were obvious in his gaze. Unwilling to spoil their evening, she shook her head a little and offered him a smile of reassurance.

"Who's ready to eat?" she asked and with forced gaiety, headed toward the kitchen.

CHAPTER 16

Christian stared after Daisy and wondered what had upset her. He wished he could ask, but knew now wasn't the time or the place. His best guess was that she was thinking about her husband. Again.

It was a shame Emma had suggested Christian sit at the head of the table. Given a choice, he would have sat anywhere else. He didn't want to replace Emma's father and hadn't enjoyed the uncomfortable moments before Daisy turned away to serve the food.

"Do you need a hand with anything?" he asked, keeping his tone mild.

"No, thanks," she replied in a dismissive tone, keeping her back to him. "I have everything under control."

A moment later, she returned with a plate of delicious-looking chicken skewers. In her other hand, she held a small dish of satay sauce. The smell was mouth-watering.

"This looks delicious," he said and offered her a

grin. To his relief, she smiled in acknowledgement. Whatever had been troubling her earlier seemed to have passed.

"Can we start now, Momma?" Emma asked, reaching for a kebab.

"Sure, honey. Just as soon as we say grace."

Christian shot her a look of surprise, but duly bowed his head. He'd been raised by his parents in a Catholic household, but religion had gone by the wayside when he moved in with Uncle Larry. He occasionally wondered why his father had practiced his faith, when it was obvious Uncle Larry did not, but that was just the way it was.

"Would you like to say grace?" Daisy asked, glancing at him shyly.

Christian blinked in surprise, but then smiled. "Of course." Closing his eyes, he prayed: "Dear Lord, thank you for the food that we're about to enjoy. Please bless the people in this house and most importantly, the cook."

When he opened his eyes, tears glinted in Daisy's eyes. "That was lovely, thank you," she said.

"Can we eat now, Momma?"

Daisy laughed. "Of course, Emma. Now you can eat."

Needing no further encouragement, Emma reached over and began to fill her plate. "One at a time, Em. You might not eat that much."

"But I'm starving! I could eat a horse!" the little girl groaned in an exaggerated way.

Daisy smiled. "All right, then, but take it easy, okay?"

They ate together in a comfortable silence until Emma asked, "So, you told us you didn't have any kids with Justine, but do you want some someday?"

Daisy choked on a bite of chicken and turned red. Christian smiled, amused. "Yes, Emma. I'd love to have some kids. Why?"

"Because I always wanted a brother or sister," the little girl stated calmly.

Once again, Daisy choked. Christian hid his grin. "Are you all right, Daisy?" he asked, widening his eyes innocently.

She tried hard to glare at him, but he caught the glint of amusement in her gaze. She reached for a glass of water and took a couple of swallows before replying. "I'm fine, thank you."

"Good. This chicken is delicious, by the way," he added, tossing her a wink.

A becoming blush stole across her cheeks, making her look utterly adorable. He wanted to push away from the table and take her in his arms and kiss her senseless, right there at the dinner table.

Of course, he did no such thing, but it was an effort to continue calmly eating while his jeans had become uncomfortably tight.

"How was work today?" he asked. "Your case ran overtime?"

"Yes," she replied. "Judge Sperry came down with a migraine. He adjourned for a couple of hours. It put the whole caseload behind."

Christian grimaced. "Too bad. I hope your client didn't run off."

Daisy chuckled. "It sounds like you've been there before."

Christian grinned. "You bet. Judge Sperry's renowned for cutting short the day's events when it suits him. Several times I've had to talk my young clients into hanging around. I don't think Judge Sperry realizes the effort it takes sometimes to get them there."

"Either that, or he doesn't care," Daisy responded dryly and then followed it with a smile.

Dinner followed, with pleasant conversation. This was their first real meal together, not counting breakfast, but like the first time they'd eaten together, it felt like they'd been doing this forever. Christian was filled with a quiet satisfaction and could only hope Daisy felt the same way.

"Is it time for cake, now?" Emma asked hopefully as she carried her plate to the sink.

Daisy laughed gently. "Yes, honey. If you still have room, we'll have cake."

"And ice cream?" she asked.

"But we have whipped cream, remember?"

The girl looked at her slyly. "Can I...have both?"

Daisy laughed again and this time Christian joined her. Daisy's daughter was too cute for words. Daisy shook her head slowly back and forth, still smiling. "You're incorrigible, Emma Green."

Emma frowned. "What's in...cor...?"

"Incorrigible," Daisy finished. "It means you're hopelessly persistent, you don't give up until you get what you want."

"Is that a bad thing?" the child asked.

Daisy's expression filled with tenderness. "No, honey. It's not a bad thing at all."

Satisfied, Emma nodded and returned her attention to dessert. "Can I help you cut the cake, Momma?"

The dishes were rinsed and stacked in the dishwasher and the leftovers had been put away. Emma had gone to brush her teeth and ready herself for bed. She came back in to say goodnight and Daisy quietly excused herself to tuck her daughter into bed.

Christian suggested he make coffee and Daisy gave him a grateful nod. "That would be nice," she said and then followed Emma down the hall. A few moments later, she returned.

"That didn't take long," Christian murmured as he opened cupboards, looking for coffee mugs.

"Third door on the left," Daisy replied. "And no, it didn't take long at all. I think she wore herself out with all that chatter." She threw him a rueful glance. "I'm sorry about all those questions. She..." Daisy shrugged helplessly.

"Hey, she's a child. Don't beat yourself up about it. Besides, I didn't mind. It's refreshing to talk to kids like her. They have no filter."

Daisy laughed, relieved he hadn't been offended. The coffee percolated and Christian filled two cups. After asking her how she liked it, he added cream and sugar. At Daisy's suggestion, they moved into the living room and both took a seat on the couch and set their mugs on the coffee table. Their fingers brushed as they did so and Daisy inhaled sharply, surprised by the power of his touch.

Most of the light came from a small lamp she'd turned down low. With Christian's thigh less than a foot from hers and her heart already in overdrive, she was suddenly filled with an inexplicable rush of nerves.

Daisy had left the draperies open and the streetlights shone through the window and gently illuminated the room, casting shadows across the floor. It added to the intimate atmosphere and heightened her awareness of the man who sat too close. The mood between them over dinner had been so comfortable, but they'd also had Emma watching their every move. Now she was tucked up in bed with her door closed and they were suddenly alone.

"Thank you for dinner," he said quietly, breaking the silence that had fallen between them.

She smiled nervously. "Yes, it was nice."

"Emma's such a great kid."

Daisy's head bobbed up and down. "Yes, yes she is."

Christian moved an inch or two closer and Daisy's heart skipped a beat and then took off at a gallop. He reached out and as if in slow motion, she watched his hand move toward her face. Slowly, gently, he cupped her cheek and turned her face toward his.

"Beautiful," was all he said.

She dragged her gaze up to meet his and her breath hitched at what she saw. Even in the dimness, his eyes burned with need. An answering flame of desire ignited inside her and surged through her veins until every nerve ending felt like it was on fire. When his thumb stroked her skin, softly, slowly...the tantalizing touch almost drove her wild.

His hand slid around her head to caress the nape of her neck. Slowly, inexorably he drew her nearer until their lips were inches apart. He paused and she saw the question in his eyes. Once again, he was waiting for permission and his consideration for her filled her with a rush of warmth. She only had to say the word and he would stop. He had no idea that stopping was the furthest thing from her mind.

Turning to face him fully, she reached for him. With her hands on his shoulders, she came naturally into his embrace. It was like she was meant to be there, fitted tightly against his chest. And then his lips found hers and all thoughts but the heat of his kiss and their closeness fled from her mind.

The kiss started slow and gentle as he nibbled his way across her tender flesh, but almost immediately, she opened her mouth, deliberately deepening it. He groaned and buried his hand in her hair and at the same time, his tongue tasted hers. Kissing and tasting and touching, they explored each other with increasing fervor as heat traveled through their veins.

Daisy's hands eased from his shoulders and

splayed across his chest. The firm muscles of his pectorals tightened beneath her touch. With a groan of impatience, he shifted until she was sitting in his lap. She gasped at the evidence of his desire jutting against her butt.

Suddenly mindful of the child who lay asleep not far away and of how fast things were moving, Daisy pulled back and placed a finger against his lips.

"I'm sorry," she whispered, her breath coming fast. "I want this as much as you, but I have to think about Emma."

Christian dragged in a deep breath in an effort to control his own harsh breathing and nodded. "I understand."

Daisy held his gaze. "I'm not sure that you do. It isn't just because she's sleeping down the hall. I have to think about what's good for her, long term. I don't want to jump into this and then have my heart broken—or hers. I'm responsible for her welfare and I take that responsibility seriously."

Christian nodded. "I wouldn't expect you to feel any other way. It's one of the things I like and admire most about you."

Daisy's shoulders slumped in relief. She'd expected such a reaction from him and her faith in him hadn't been misplaced.

"Thank you. It means a lot to me that you understand where I'm coming from," she murmured.

Christian leaned over and kissed her soundly on the mouth. "I've already told you how much I like you, Daisy Green. I meant it then and I mean it now. I'm here for the long haul. We'll take things slowly until you're sure. However long it takes."

Emotion flooded her heart and she had to blink back tears. *How had she gotten so lucky to have this wonderful man come into her life?* After years of darkness and desolation, he was filling her life with light. Even better, he treated Emma just as well as he treated her. She couldn't ask for anything more.

———

Lila-Jane listened to Bella's quiet whimpering and wanted so much to offer her comfort. Until now, she hadn't remembered the details of what the man had done to her, but after seeing him with Bella, her nightmares had come true. She felt dirty and scared and angry and she wanted her Momma so bad. She'd lost count of the number of days she'd been there and not knowing how much longer the nightmare would go on was even worse.

"*Shh*, Bella. Don't cry. He's gone now."

She was met with silence and then a tiny voice said, "How long before he comes back again?"

"I don't know," Lila-Jane answered honestly. "Sometimes it's hours. Sometimes it feels like days. It's hard to tell in here. The only window is so high up, you can barely tell if it's day or night. Do you know how long I've been in here?"

"It's been about a week, I think," came Bella's soft reply.

Lila-Jane shook her head in disbelief. "A *week*? Is that all? It feels like I've been here forever."

"I wonder how long he's going to keep us here," Bella murmured.

"Who knows? I tried to ask him once why he'd brought me here, but he merely smiled. At least, I think he smiled. It's hard to tell what's going on behind that mask."

Bella shuddered on the bed beside her. "It's so creepy. I never want to see another clown again." She paused and then continued thoughtfully. "But I think you're right. I looked at him really hard this time and I think it *is* Mr Grayson."

Her voice had dropped to a frightened whisper. Lila-Jane's hands tightened into fists. She understood exactly how Bella felt.

Why would their trusted, friendly bus driver kidnap them and hide them in his home? No one would believe the things he'd done to them or that he was involved in their disappearance. He was the last person they'd be looking for. Mr Grayson had a kind word and a cheery smile for everyone. He knew all the kids by name. He once joked that he knew everything about them just by listening to their chatter day by day.

At the time, she'd thought nothing of it, but as her head cleared of the ever present fuzziness, his words took on a sinister edge. *Had he been planning this all the time? Was that the reason behind all his questions?*

The thought sent her spiraling into a depression so dark, she despaired she might ever return to normal. How would she ever look at life the same way? Mr Grayson had changed her forever.

"We have to believe the police will find us," Bella said, her voice getting stronger. "They formed a huge search party when you went missing. According to the news, they're still looking for you. Your mom gave interviews on all the TV stations and there were pictures of you in the newspapers. I'm sure my mom will be just as frantic and won't give up until I've been found."

Lila-Jane heard the growing confidence in Bella's voice and prayed to God that her friend was right.

Please, Momma! Please don't give up looking for me! Please! Please, I want to come home.

The sound of a cat meowing startled both of them.

"Did you hear that?" Bella asked.

Lila-Jane nodded. "Yes. It's a kitten. I've heard it before."

"Have you seen it? What color is it?"

"No, I haven't seen it. I only heard it through the door."

"Here, kitty, kitty," Bella called softly.

The meowing got louder and even Lila-Jane's heart skipped a beat.

"He's coming closer!" Bella whispered.

"Yes." And then Lila-Jane felt something soft brush against her fingers where they hung over the side of the bed. She jumped, startled.

"I think it just touched me!" she cried.

"Really? I want to see!"

Lila-Jane felt Bella straining against her bindings. A moment later, the girl gave up with a defeated sigh. "It's no use. These ties are too tight. I can barely move."

"Mine, too," Lila-Jane agreed.

"Call to him, Lila-Jane," Bella pleaded. "He might come back again."

Lila-Jane drew in a deep breath and eased it out slowly. She yearned to feel the softness of the kitten again. In this room of evil and despair, the kitten seemed so safe and normal—and free.

"Here, kitty, kitty, kitty," she said. "Here, kitty, kitty, kitty." She waited a moment, but felt and heard nothing.

"Is he still there?" Bella's voice was filled with hope.

Lila-Jane shook her head and sighed in disappointment. "I don't think so."

"Where did he go?"

"I don't know," Lila-Jane replied.

"How did he get in here?"

"I don't know."

"It couldn't have been through the window. We would've seen!"

Lila-Jane thought for a moment. "You're right. The man must have left the door a little way open." A wave of excitement went through her. "We need to try and get free of these bindings," she said.

Bella nodded. "Yes, but mine are pulling so tight. I don't know how I'm ever going to get free of them. And my head hurts so much. Everything looks so fuzzy."

With renewed determination, Lila-Jane pulled on her restraints, but they refused to give. With tears in her eyes, she slumped against the mattress and silently admitted defeat.

"Don't worry, Lila-Jane," Bella whispered. "He'll slip up again and then we'll be ready. We're going to get out of here! I promise.

Lila-Jane mulled over Bella's words. She wanted so much to believe them, but she'd been in here so long. She'd just about given up hope.

CHAPTER 17

Larry sat back in his leather recliner in the basement room that was visible from the bottom of the stairs. With a sigh of contentment, he took a sip of his drink. The girls had fallen silent—at least, he thought they had. It was difficult to tell behind the soundproof wall he'd installed for that very purpose. Little Bella had been everything he'd hoped and he looked forward to many more hours of fun. And he still had Lila-Jane...

Having two girls at the same time filled him with burgeoning excitement. He'd have to remember to add to his supply of Rohypnol. With the two girls there, he'd need double the dosage. Already, he'd been forced to use half of what he normally would for each girl and wondered how effective a half dose would be in putting them out and interfering with their memories.

He had a contact who supplied him with the tablets. He'd met the man online in one of the secret chat rooms he hung out in and they'd struck up a conversation. The man promised to supply him with everything he needed to elicit the greatest pleasure during his pursuits. They both knew what he referred to.

Rohypnol had been part of the deal. Not only did it cause dizziness and confusion while the victim was under the influence, it also caused memory loss. Such a thing was important to Larry's plan because he didn't intend to keep them forever...

He usually only kept them a week or two. He made sure they were doped up with pills before he loaded them into his car. He'd drive for hours and drop them off in a park or on the edge of a clearing, sometimes many hundreds of miles away. By the time they regained consciousness, they were usually so dazed and confused they could barely remember anything about their time with him. And that's the way he liked it.

It had been his preferred modus operandi for years now, and it had worked every single time. There had only been one unfortunate incident when a child had reacted badly to the drug. Nikki Carlin had ended up going into cardiac arrest and had died right there in his basement. It was lucky he managed to keep calm and dispose of her body without being discovered. And all the while, his nephew slept, oblivious, upstairs...

Of course, that was the reason he'd snatched Nikki in the first place. Christian had been way too close to the girl, spending every waking moment with her. Larry wasn't too proud to admit he'd been jealous of the attention the boy paid her, just like the way he'd been jealous of the attention Frank had paid Amanda.

Christian was meant to hang out with his uncle, going fishing, playing ball. That was the way it was supposed to be. He was meant to be the brother Frank had never been. Instead, the boy had begun to spend all his time with Nikki. Well, Larry soon put an end to that.

The soft meow of Sooty snagged his attention and he leaned down and gave the cat an idle scratch between the ears. He'd never been fond of cats. Not since he was a kid. Sooty had been Christian's idea. In fact, Larry had done his best to dissuade his nephew from bringing home a cat by saying he was allergic, but Christian would have none of it. In the end, Larry had given in, but only because Christian knew he didn't have an allergic reaction and Larry couldn't come up with another reason to say no.

Now he was glad he had. The cat would come in handy, especially when he knew it spent so much time with Christian. The boy could hardly step through the front door without the cat brushing up against his legs. Larry hardly saw the animal through the day, but the moment Christian arrived, the cat appeared. He intended to use that to his advantage. Oh, yes. He did indeed.

Just then, he heard the latch of the front door open and close above him and then he listened to the steady sound of Christian's boots as he walked across the wooden floor. Larry glanced at his watch. It was late. It was Christian's third late night in a row. He'd barely seen him over the weekend just gone. He wondered if the boy was simply busy at work or if there was something else that had stolen his attention.

Perhaps he'd found a new woman? Larry had been pleased when Christian told him his relationship with Justine had broken down. For a long while, things had appeared serious between the two of them and Larry worried that he might have to do something to prevent Christian from moving out.

Though Larry was now a much older man and people didn't seem to talk so much about older men living on their own like they would have when he was younger, he still preferred to have his nephew living with him, to give him a blanket of credibility, trustworthiness and an alibi, if ever needed. After all, one could never be too careful. It was the reason he'd created the scrapbook and left it in the bottom drawer of Christian's desk.

Leaning over, Larry picked up the remote control for the stereo system and tuned the music to one of his favorite classical songs. Christian would hear it playing and, no doubt leave him alone. It was a routine Larry had established long ago to keep the boy's curiosity at bay. *After all, how much time could one spend in a basement without arousing suspicion?*

A few moments later, he heard another door open and close and then he heard the sound of water in the pipes as it made its way to the shower. It was all good. Christian was preparing for bed. Larry breathed out quietly and took another sip from his drink, relishing his solitude.

———————

Christian scrubbed shampoo through his hair until it was a soapy lather. Enjoying the invigorating thrum of the hot water on his bare skin, he tilted his head back and rinsed the suds from his hair. He'd spent another pleasant evening with Daisy and Emma. That night they'd enjoyed fried chicken, mushy peas and creamy mashed potatoes for dinner. Afterwards, they'd played some board games. He couldn't remember the last time he'd experienced so much excitement over Monopoly. It had been fun, and when Emma was tucked into bed, Daisy had returned to the living room and they'd ended up on the couch. Like teenagers, they'd kissed and petted and generally did things to drive each other wild, all the time, knowing it wouldn't go too far that night.

At the thought of Daisy and her lush body pressed against his, blood surged through his veins and centered in his groin. His cock came to life. It felt like he'd been carrying an erection around for three days—ever since their first dinner. Whenever they spent time together, they inevitably ended the night cuddled up on the couch and luckily he'd managed to hold onto his self-control. He'd promised to take things slowly and he'd keep that promise, if it killed him.

But here, in the privacy of his bathroom, he

allowed himself to seek the relief he so desperately needed. Soaping his hand, he stroked his cock until it hardened. He cupped his heavy balls, overflowing with unfulfilled need. He thought of Daisy and her luscious breasts, straining against her shirt. The way her nipples pebbled when he stroked them. Tonight, she'd let him undo the top three buttons of her blouse and slide down the straps of her bra. He'd taken one nipple and then the other into his mouth and slowly suckled.

She'd gasped at the torment and her eyes had darkened with desire. It had been all he could do not to drive himself into her right then and there. Instead, he'd taken her hand and had pressed it against his raging erection and had sighed in relief when she fondled him through his Levis. At one stage, she popped his button and slid the zipper down. Her hand had slipped inside.

Soft and warm, her fingers had encircled him, working their way up and down his shaft. He'd been in heaven. And then she bent her head and took him inside her mouth. He leaned back against the couch in ecstasy and agony all at once. She licked and sucked and squeezed and pulled, until finally it got to be too much.

"I'm gonna come if you keep that up," he growled and she'd hastily pulled away.

"I'm-I'm sorry, Christian. I didn't mean to drive you to the point of no return. You made a promise that we'd take things slowly and I'm the one making things difficult for you. It isn't fair of me."

After pulling his underwear up over his cock, he tugged up his zipper. "Don't apologize. It's fine, I promise," he assured her. "I'm a big boy. I'll live. I promised we'd take things slowly and we will. Nothing happens before you're ready."

She averted her gaze and her cheeks flushed red, but he could tell she was pleased he'd called a halt to their heavy petting. They'd been seeing each other regularly and he was pleased with the progress they'd made. He noticed some of the pictures of Pete had disappeared from around the house, although the life-sized portrait was still in the living room. It felt strange making out with her while her husband stared at them from a few feet away, but he didn't have the heart to suggest they move to another room and the picture didn't seem to bother Daisy.

As his hand move faster along his shaft, the need inside him built. He pictured Daisy in his shower, naked with soapsuds running between her breasts. She stared at him with eyes that were heavy with desire. Her mouth parted and she beckoned him closer. A moment later, he reached his climax and collapsed against the shower wall with a groan.

Toweling dry, he put on a clean pair of boxers and made his way down the hallway to the bedroom. His uncle's door was open, but the room was empty. Christian could hear the familiar music drifting up the stairs from the basement. With a sigh, he closed the door to his room and threw himself across his bed. He was tired, but his mind wouldn't let him rest.

Images of Daisy flooded him. Even though he'd showered, her scent seemed to cling to him, filling the air. He'd keep the promise he'd made to her, but he didn't know how much longer he could stand being so close to her without having her. Then again, anything worth having was worth waiting for and Daisy Green was definitely worth waiting for. If it meant he came home with blue balls, yet again, it was a sacrifice he was prepared to make. And that was all there was to it.

Daisy stared unseeingly at the pages spread across her desk. With yellow highlighter in hand, she'd been reading over the record of interview given by her most recent client and underlining anything significant. Fourteen-year-old Clinton Toomey had been charged with break and enter and was due to appear in court for the first time later that afternoon. Daisy had been doing her best to come up to speed on his case, but so far, she kept getting distracted.

Every time she read a sentence the words all ran together as memories of the night before came back to her. She and Christian and Emma... Spending another lovely evening at home... Sharing a meal and then a game... But it was what happened after Emma was tucked up in bed that kept flaring to life in Daisy's mind and stirring up much more salient emotions.

True to his word, Christian had called a halt to things before they got out of hand and she admired his restraint. She was certain he wanted her as much as she wanted him and the fact that he respected her enough to stick by his promise spoke volumes about his character.

As she remembered the feel of his hard body pressed against hers and his lips kissing her all over, a warm flush rose from her feet and swept upwards and across her body. A need far too long denied centered between her legs and she squirmed in her chair.

For heaven's sake, she was at work! This wasn't the place for idle fantasies—or any fantasies, for that matter! And certainly not when the object of her fantasies sat in his office on the opposite side of her building. So close and yet, so unattainable... *Or was he?*

Could she come up with a plausible excuse to stop by his office and say hello? Maybe she could even risk it all and kiss him? In broad daylight. In his office. Again. The thought sent a thrill of excitement arcing through her and all of a sudden, she was eager to see it through.

Pushing away from her desk, she went to her locker and refreshed her makeup and ran a brush through her hair. She giggled at the effort she was making just to go and say hi, but couldn't deny the fluttering of nerves and anticipation that filled her belly at the thought of marching into his office, taking him by the tie and tugging him toward her. She'd plant her lips on his and kiss him like there was no tomorrow and then promptly turn and leave—all without saying a word.

She smiled, hardly daring to believe she was actually going to do it. Such naughty spontaneity was so unlike her and it left her heady with excitement. It was time to throw the old Daisy Green over and begin again—starting now.

Decision made, she strode across her office in her three-inch heels and opened the door. With a quick word to her secretary, advising the woman she was stepping out for a few moments, Daisy headed for Christian's office.

Christian doodled on the legal pad in front of him and wished he could stay focused enough to do something worthwhile with his time. He had a pile of letters to write and emails to respond to and yet he was sitting here wasting time, thinking about Daisy. It had been the same for the past four days. Ever since they'd begun dating.

His fixation on her was causing havoc to his productivity levels. He was way behind meeting his monthly budget target. Just as well the previous three months he'd exceeded the budget set by the partners or he might be forced to answer some uncomfortable questions.

The door to his office opened and he looked up, only half interested in who it might be. At the sight of the woman before him, his heart stuttered in shock.

"J-Justine! What are you doing here?"

Christian's ex-girlfriend strode confidently across his office and came around to his side of the desk. Her short, tight skirt and clingy sleeveless blouse emphasized her tidy figure. Her makeup had been impeccably applied, as usual, and she'd added lighter touches to the ends of her dark blond hair. The months since they'd parted had treated her well. She looked better than ever.

He pushed his chair away from his desk and her smile widened. Taking his approach as an invitation, she planted herself in his lap and draped her arms around his neck. Before he knew what was happening, she kissed him on the mouth.

"Justine!" He gasped, almost surprised beyond words. Not that he should have been. His ex-girlfriend had never been lacking in confidence. She had a good body and she knew it and she didn't shy away from using it to her advantage. Right now, it was plastered against him and her tongue was doing its best to make its way past his lips.

He turned his head and wrenched his mouth away. At the same time, he reached for her arms and loosened them from around his neck. She promptly started nibbling on his ear lobe.

"Justine! Stop!"

She pulled back, managing to look both surprised and upset at the same time. "What's the matter, babe? You used to love it when I did that."

With gritted teeth, he pushed her off his lap. She stood somewhat reluctantly and frowned at him. "Okay, I understand that it's been a few months since we split and the last time we spoke I told you I'd met someone else, but the truth is, things didn't work out. He wasn't the man I thought he was and it got me to thinking about us—you." Her expression turned petulant.

"You see, Chris, I never knew what we had together until I broke us apart. We were so good together. You're a good and decent man. Can't we just forget about the last few months and go back to the way things were?" She reached for his hand. "Christian Grayson, will you marry me?"

Christian stared up at her in surprise. He almost laughed, but swallowed the impulse just in time. Her expression was somber and earnest. She was dead serious about taking up where they'd left off...and beyond. It was as if the past four months had never been. Still, there was no point being nasty about it by laughing in her face. He might have gotten over her far quicker than he could have imagined, but there was no need to be mean.

Gently extricating his hand from hers, he slowly shook his head. "I'm sorry, Justine. I truly am. While I'm flattered by your proposal, I'm afraid it's just too late. Over the time since we separated, I came to realize my feelings for you weren't as strong as they should have been for you, the woman I'd expected to spend the rest of my life with."

Her mouth gaped and her expression turned stricken. "But, Christian! I said I was sorry. That other man didn't mean anything to me! I realized almost right away that I'd made a mistake throwing our love away. I've wanted to call you for weeks, now. I was trying to find the courage..." Her voice drifted away.

He stared at her, gentling his tone. "I'm really sorry, Justine. You and I... We're over. It was never meant to be. I think we should be grateful we discovered this before we made the mistake of getting married. We would have been miserable. What kind of life is that?"

The anguish in her face increased. He could almost feel her panic. "No! You can't mean that, Chris! Please, don't say we're over! Haven't you heard of new beginnings? We could start over again. Forget about the past four months. Forget about what I said at the time. We can—"

"No, Justine. We can't."

Her eyes reflected her desperation. "Yes! We can! We—"

"I've met someone else," he blurted out. He hadn't meant to hurt her like that, but she'd given him no choice.

She reeled back in shock. "You've met someone else? It's only been a handful of months since I left. How could you have moved on so quickly?"

Christian shrugged, uncomfortable about discussing his relationship with Daisy. "I don't know. It just happened. Who are we to determine the way love works?"

Her eyes widened. "Love? How could you be talking *love*? You couldn't possibly have fallen in love with someone in such short a time. You and I were together for the better part of three years and in the end, you still weren't sure you loved me. I won't believe you've fallen in love with someone else so quickly!"

Her expression became thoughtful and her tone became matter of fact. "No, it must be a rebound thing. It happens all the time. I understand, Chris, and I forgive you. Move in with me and we'll forget this ever happened. You must be ready to leave that old place of your uncle's, anyway. I never did understand why you've stayed living with him all these years. My condo in Bondi is so much more appealing. I'm even prepared to make room for your clothes in my closet. In fact, we can go there straight after work. What do you say?"

He stared at her in disbelief, but maintained his good humor. "Haven't you been listening to me, Justine? Whether it makes sense to you or not, the truth is, I've met a wonderful woman and I've fallen in love with her. We've been dating for the past week and... It's been the best week of my life."

Her expression began to crumble and tears glinted in her eyes. He took pity on her and softened his tone. "We had a great time together, Justine, but you need to accept it's over. We weren't meant to be. It's no one's fault, it's just the way it is."

"No!" she wailed and once again threw herself at him. She wrapped her arms around his neck and planted her lips on his.

He squirmed against her and did his best to turn his head away, but she remained insistent. Such was his concentration to escape the attention of the woman in his arms, he barely registered the brief knock on his door and it was only when a loud gasp sounded from across the room that he blinked and managed to drag his head away. He stared into Daisy's startled face, her eyes wide with shock and disbelief.

Struggling harder against Justine's hold, he finally managed to disentangle himself. Pushing away, he stood and adjusted his clothes. At the same time, he sent Daisy a beseeching look.

"Please, Daisy. This isn't what you think."

CHAPTER 18

Christian swiped his hand across his mouth, feeling the need to rid himself of the taste and touch of Justine. Catching sight of the smear of red lipstick on the back of his hand, he flushed with guilt. Meanwhile, Justine, with admirable composure, stepped forward and held out her hand toward Daisy.

"Hi, I'm Justine. Christian's girlfriend."

"Ex-girlfriend," Christian corrected through gritted teeth.

Daisy look like she'd been blindsided. As if in a daze, she shook Justine's outstretched hand. "Daisy Green," she murmured. "I work on the same floor."

"It's nice to meet you, Daisy. I suppose you've come here to talk about work. Well, I better be going. She reached up and pecked Christian on the cheek. "I'll see you later, babe."

"Just hang on a minute," Christian replied, his anger surfacing at last. "You're not going to get away with that."

He circled his desk and came to a stop beside

Daisy. Reaching out, he drew her close against his side. She tensed and tried to pull away, but he merely tightened his hold. There was no way he was going to let her walk away without hearing his explanation.

"Justine and I are *over*," he stated, staring hard at his ex-girlfriend. "She arrived here unexpectedly and did her best to convince me to give things another go. When I told her we were done, she tried to convince me another way." His lip curled up in disgust. "I don't know what else you want me to say, Justine, but I'm with Daisy now, and like I told you, I've fallen in love with her. You and I are over. Finished. Forever. I'm sorry things didn't work out for you and the other guy, but we're never going to be a couple again. I'd appreciate it if you think about that next time you get the urge to barge into my office. In fact, it would be better for both of us if you stay away altogether."

Justine's eyes widened in surprise and hurt. A moment later, she let out a sob and then spun on her heel and left without another word. The office fell silent. Christian hazarded a glance in Daisy's direction and was relieved to see the shock and disbelief had faded from her eyes.

"Did you mean it?" she asked quietly.

"That Justine and I are over forever? Yes, of course I did. I haven't seen her since we broke up and that was months ago. I don't know why she dropped in here unannounced and why she thought we could pick up where we'd left off. It's strange to say the least, but that's exactly what happened."

Daisy nodded. "I believe you."

"You do?"

"Yes. You've given me no reason to believe you'd lie."

Christian smiled in relief. "I'm glad to hear it."

"But that's not what I was referencing when I asked if you meant it," she added quietly.

"Okay," he replied, trying to think back to what else he'd said.

Taking pity on him, Daisy offered him a tight smile that disappeared almost before it had formed. "No. I meant... Did you mean it when you said you'd fallen in love with me?"

Christian stared down at her and his heart tripped over at the uncertainty in her eyes. He turned her around to face him fully and held her gaze. "Absolutely." He took a deep breath. "Almost from the first moment I saw you."

Her smile was slow in coming, but when it did, it lit up every aspect of her face. "Good. Because I've fallen in love with you, too."

His heart skipped a beat. He stared at her in surprise, hardly daring to believe it. "You have?"

She laughed and nodded. "Yes, I have."

She lifted her arms and draped them around his neck. His hands tightened on her hips and she came naturally into his arms, as if she was meant to be there. He held her close and kissed her once, twice, three times before passion overtook them. She opened her mouth and he opened his and their tongues danced in the heat of her mouth. She pressed herself against him and he reveled in the feel of her soft breasts crushed against his chest. His cock filled with blood and began throbbing, and his need became even more desperate than before. With an effort that was almost beyond him, he slowly ended the kiss and pulled back.

"You drive me crazy, Daisy Green. Any more of that and I'm going to completely lose control, office or no office."

She grinned unrepentantly, looking just as dazed as he felt. "I love that I can stir you up so much that you lose control, and in the middle of the work day, no less," she teased. "Why don't you come over tonight? We could have a celebratory dinner."

His heart leaped at the promise in her eyes, but he cautioned himself to continue going slow. After all, that's what he'd promised. "I'd like that," he murmured. He pressed another lingering kiss on her lips.

They were both breathless when they drew apart. Daisy shot him a grin. "Maybe you should pack your toothbrush and a change of clothes."

Larry smiled down at the two children who snored quietly on the bed. He'd given them both a healthy dose of Rohypnol twenty minutes earlier and all signs indicated they were fast asleep. With a little luck, the effects of the drug would take ten or twelve hours to wear off. Plenty of time for what he had planned.

He'd already finished with the scrapbook, adding the stories about the latest missing girl. Pictures of Bella were splashed all over the media. The police had few clues to go on. They knew from the school blazer they'd found where Larry had left it that she'd climbed off the bus. As to her current whereabouts, they didn't seem to know. In the meantime, she slept as peacefully as a newborn in his basement a few blocks away from her house. He chuckled at the irony.

Reaching over, he undid the restraints around Lila-Jane's wrists and then turned his attention to those around her feet. He checked the bindings that held Bella tight and was satisfied with what he found. She wouldn't be going anywhere.

Next, he picked up a blanket that he'd brought down with him to the basement and wrapped her in it, taking care not to cover her face. He didn't want her suffocating before he could dispose of her. That wasn't in his plan.

Tenderly, he picked up the little girl and carried her up the stairs. He almost stepped on Sooty in the dimness. The cat let out a meow and scurried out of his way. He made his way across the living room on silent feet. He wasn't sure why he was being so quiet. After all, apart from the sleeping Bella, the house was empty.

Years of habit. That's what he guessed, at least. He'd learned a long time ago how to live a stealthy life. His cautiousness had protected him well in the past. He slid open the back door and walked across the deck. A few more steps and he was in the garage. Flipping open the tailgate, he gently laid the child on the tray of his pickup. No sense putting her on the back seat, because he could be pulled over by a highway patrolman, inquisitive as to why he was on the road at such a late hour. Best to keep the girl concealed until the very end.

Backing slowly out of the driveway, he turned the pickup into the street and headed north. His goal was to leave her on a popular walking track inside the bowels of Ku-ring-gai Chase National Park. It was an area he'd frequented before and it had proved a successful hiding place in years gone by. The trails were popular with bush walkers. It would only be a matter of time before Lila-Jane was found. At this time of year, the forest could be chilly, but the blanket was sure to suffice to keep her warm.

He reached down and switched on the radio and then turned the dial until he found a classical music station he liked. Humming along with the haunting notes of the orchestra, he was filled with a peace he often struggled to find.

It was weird. He felt the best he ever did at the moment when he was finished with one of his kids. An indescribable calmness came over him when he had them in the back of his truck and was taking them toward freedom. It was like he finally had some control over the beast. He didn't know what that said about him, but he hoped it showed he had some redeeming qualities. After all, he'd never meant for Nikki Carlin to die.

His use of Rohypnol was another indication of his compassion. He used it to confuse their memories and help them forget about the time they spent in his basement. After all, he didn't mean to traumatize them for the rest of their life. Of course, the mind-altering drug also served to confuse their memories of the events. He only hoped the half-strength dose he'd been forced to administer until he could increase his supply would suffice. It wouldn't do for him to be found out after all these years.

His thoughts slid to Christian and the fact his nephew was out late yet again. The boy had mentioned at the breakfast table that morning that he was seeing another woman and this time it felt so right. He'd even mentioned he'd started looking for another place.

The words sent a tremor of fear through Larry's heart, but he steadfastly forced the feeling aside. Christian had dated women before. He'd never gotten serious enough to move out. Larry just had to remember that and hope this current relationship would be no different.

And then, Christian had confided that Larry knew the new woman in his nephew's life. "Her name is Daisy Green," Christian continued. "You remember, you met her and her daughter at Marcie Morrissey's house the night Marcie's little girl disappeared. Daisy works with me at Sydney Legal. Her daughter's name is Emma. She catches your bus."

"Oh, yes, of course. I remember now," he managed to say. Recalling the way Christian had looked at the Green woman, a fresh wave of panic touched his heart.

Christian had spent time, a lot of time, talking to the woman the evening of the prayer vigil. Larry had stood by and watched his nephew smile and laugh and carry on conversation with both Daisy and Emma. The little girl with the bright smile and bouncy blond curls was as cute as could be. And her mother—well, what could Larry say? He could well understand Christian's interest in the woman and the fact they were now dating, meant things had moved faster than he could have expected.

What if this woman managed to lure his nephew away from him at last? He'd be left alone in his house, with no one for company except his children who lived in his secret room downstairs. What if he once again became the strange old man who lived alone at the end of the street, the subject of rumor and ridicule? That was a risk he couldn't take.

He'd spent decades maintaining his cover, sliding under the radar, getting away with appeasing the beast. He'd be damned if he'd be discovered now. He wasn't sure how he'd accomplish it, but he'd make certain Christian's relationship with the Green woman would come to an end, one way or the other.

His headlights swept over a road sign that indicated the turnoff to the Kur-ring-gai Chase National Park. Slowing his vehicle, he took the turn and eased himself along the gravel path. A mile into the forest, a parking bay emerged. He pulled over and climbed out.

Leaning over the tailgate, he pulled out Lila-Jane Morrissey. He was relieved to see she was still asleep. Moving slowly, with the child still wrapped in the blanket, he headed toward the walking path. He walked for half a mile before depositing her on the grass in a clearing. She wasn't directly visible along the path, but once the sun came up, anyone coming along would spot her soon enough.

Now that the final moment of farewell was upon him, he was filled with a surge of emotion. He leaned over the inert body and pressed a soft kiss against her cheek. Tears burned behind his eyes. Tenderly, he wrapped the blanket around her more tightly to ward off the winter chill. He brushed the hair out of her eyes.

It's been nice knowing you, Lila-Jane," he whispered. "I can't wait to see you back on the bus."

———

Daisy bustled into the kitchen with shopping sacks in her hands. She deposited them on the counter and then headed back to her car for more. She passed Emma in the hallway, on her way in. The child carried a sack in each arm, as well as her school bag.

"Why all the special preparations tonight, Momma?" the child grumbled. "It's not like Christian hasn't been here before."

Daisy paused with her foot on the top step of the front porch and turned to look at her daughter. "You're right, honey."

She'd hoped to wait awhile for this conversation, but she supposed now was probably as good a time as any. After all, if the night went well, like she hoped it would, she might very well invite him to move in with them. Such a decision couldn't be made without consulting Emma.

With a quiet sigh, she let the door close and came back to her daughter. "You like Christian, don't you?" she asked, linking her arm through Emma's and leading her to the couch in the living room.

"Yes. I told you that when you asked last time," Emma replied, taking a seat beside her mother.

"Well, I like Christian, too. I like him a lot."

"He's nice, Momma."

Daisy drew in a deep breath and eased it out. She reached up and stroked her hand through Emma's hair. The little girl frowned.

"Momma, what are you doing? Why are you acting so strange?"

Daisy laughed, but it sounded a little rusty. "I'm sorry, honey. I don't mean to act strange. See, the thing is, Christian and I really like each other. In fact, the two of us have fallen in love."

Emma's eyes widened. "Does this mean he's going to be my father? Can he come to school when they celebrate Father's Day? That would be so cool! I'd be like lots of the other kids."

Daisy's heart clenched with sadness at Emma's words, but the excitement on her face at the thought of taking Christian along on Father's Day warmed her through. She hadn't realized how such a little thing could mean so much to her daughter. Emma had never said anything... Then again, Daisy hadn't ever thought to ask.

"Is Christian going to move in with us? Are we going to be a real family at last?"

Once again, Daisy's heart tightened with emotion. "Would you like that?" she managed.

Emma nodded with enthusiasm. "Yes! Do you think he'd want to take me to the park and play ball? In summer, we could go to the beach. Or to the movies. Or the arcade. Or anywhere. Do you think he'd want to do those things, Momma?"

Daisy looked down at her daughter, at the earnestness on her face and her eyes filled with tears. For so long, she'd been blind to Emma's need to have a father. Her daughter was such a good little girl, never complaining, mostly happy. But it was obvious the thought of having a father in her life was everything she'd dreamed of.

Daisy put her arm around Emma's shoulders and pulled her close. She pressed a kiss on her hair. "You'll have to ask him, honey, but I think he'd be only too happy to do those things. We could do them together, like a real family."

A lump of emotion lodged in her throat and she had to swallow in order to speak. She couldn't remember the last time she and Emma had been part of a real family. Pete was away so often, they were never like other families, even back then.

"What about the picture of Daddy?" Emma asked softly.

Daisy frowned. "What do you mean? We have lots of pictures of Daddy."

"Yes, but I mean the one on that wall." Emma

turned and pointed to the life-sized portrait. "It's pretty big, Momma, and if Christian's going to move in, it might be best if you took it down."

Another lump clogged up Daisy's throat and tears now burned in her eyes. "Do you want me to take it down, honey?"

Emma stared at her solemnly. "Yes, Momma. I think you should. It wouldn't feel right and I'm sure Christian would be happy to see it gone."

Daisy thought about it a moment and nodded. "You're right. I think it's time to take it down."

"Don't throw it away!" Emma cried, looking suddenly panicked.

"I won't throw it away, honey. I promise. I'll find somewhere to put it in the garage."

Relief spread across Emma's face and then she smiled. "I'm glad."

Daisy hugged her daughter tight. "Me, too," she whispered.

Christian knocked on Daisy's front door and tried to quell his nerves. He didn't know why he was so nervous. It wasn't like he hadn't had dinner there before. But on those other occasions, Daisy hadn't told him to pack a toothbrush, nor had she looked at him with such promise in her eyes. He was sure he hadn't misread her meaning. Tonight, he'd know the true delights of heaven sharing a bed with the woman he loved.

He'd taken special care choosing his wardrobe

and was dressed in a soft blue chambray shirt and Levis. His boxers were black Calvin Klein, silky to the touch. He'd brushed his teeth twice and had flossed and had even gargled with mouthwash, leaving nothing to chance. It was a bit ridiculous seeing as how he hadn't even eaten yet, but there it was.

The door opened and Daisy stood there, resplendent in a long-sleeved, red woolen dress. The stretchy fabric clung to her in all the right places. Almost immediately, the blood rushed to his groin.

"Good evening," she murmured and then quickly averted her gaze.

He smiled. It eased his nerves to know that she was feeling just as edgy as he was. It told him that this evening was special to her, just as it was special to him. It was more than just another dinner date.

"Would you like to come in?"

He blushed, unaware until that moment that he was staring at her. "Of course." He stepped over the threshold and handed her a bouquet of flowers and a bottle of her favorite wine.

She smiled in delight. "Flowers and wine! How lucky am I!"

She kissed him lightly on the cheek and his skin tingled from her touch. That only served to send the blood pumping faster through his veins. All of a sudden, he didn't give a damn about dinner. In fact, the meal couldn't end fast enough.

"Christian! There you are! I've been waiting for you for hours!"

Christian laughed as Emma appeared in the hallway. He ruffled her curly hair and shot her an affectionate grin. "It's good to see you, too, Em. How was school?"

She groaned exaggeratedly and rolled her eyes. "School is boring. I can't wait until I'm a grown up and I don't have to go anymore."

Christian laughed again. "Well, you have a fair way to go yet, squirt. Hang in there, all right?"

"*All right,*" Emma replied, dragging out the sounds.

"Good girl. Now, what have you cooked me for dinner?"

The dark clouds immediately dissolved from Emma's face and she smiled in excitement. "You're not going to believe it! We took forever in the shops! Mom's cooked all your favorites!"

"Wow, she must've been busy!" He glanced in Daisy's direction. The woman dressed fit to kill, merely smiled.

"So, there's roast chicken, and gravy and creamy mashed potatoes. There are peas and roast pumpkin and fresh garden beans." Emma looked at him pointedly. "*I* cut the beans."

"Well, thank you, Miss Emma. I'll be sure to try some."

"And then, afterwards, we're having pecan pie and homemade vanilla ice cream. I've already tried some. It tastes great!" Emma grinned.

"It all sounds delicious," Christian commented and this time he winked at Daisy. With his gaze still on hers, he added, "I can't wait to sample every little bit."

His comment elicited a blush from Daisy. It stole across her neck and flooded her cheeks. She turned, as if flustered, and busied herself in the kitchen.

As he walked into the living room, his gaze was immediately drawn to the empty wall directly across from the table. A faint outline, like a shadow on the paint, was the only indication that there had once been a picture hanging there. His gaze zeroed in on Daisy's. She saw the question in his eyes and nodded. He smiled back at her and his heart filled with warmth.

Removing the portrait of her husband was such a huge step forward in their relationship, probably even more significant than her invitation to stay the night. He'd gotten used to having Pete watching their every move and he'd been determined not to let it affect him. But now, Daisy had removed it. To where, he didn't know. And it didn't matter. The fact was, she'd taken it down on the eve of their first full night together. It was an encouraging sign.

"Well, something smells good," he commented and once again, Emma regaled him on their cooking feats. He listened with only half an ear, his attention focused on Daisy. She moved with quiet elegance from the sink to the stove and back again. Lifting lids on pots, sampling food, murmuring to herself. She had a dusting of flour on one cheek and he itched to wipe it off. And then he acted on that impulse and moved toward her.

She looked up at him in momentary surprise and then relaxed as he reached out and tenderly turned her to face him and wiped the flour from her skin. Her eyes widened at his nearness. When her gaze fell to his lips, desired ignited inside him. Unable to resist, he bent his head and kissed her.

"Momma and Christian are kissing," Emma sang in a singsong voice.

They broke away, smiling. It warmed Christian through that Daisy didn't seem to care. Up until that moment, she'd been careful not to show him any sign of affection for him while Emma was around, but something had changed in recent hours and his heart sang.

CHAPTER 19

Daisy's hand shook slightly as she poured two glasses of wine. Handing one to Christian, she joined him on the couch. Dinner and dessert had been eaten and the dishes cleared away. Emma had enjoyed a quick bedtime story before Daisy tucked her in and switched off the light.

"Is Christian staying here tonight, Momma?" Emma had asked as Daisy pulled up the covers to her chin.

"I think so, honey. Is that all right?"

"That's fine. I like knowing Christian's here. He makes me feel safe."

Daisy's heart swelled with tenderness and she leaned down and kissed her daughter goodnight.

"I love you to the moon and back, baby," she whispered.

Emma grinned. "I love you more."

Now, seated beside Christian on the couch, Daisy stole a glance at him and was surprised to find him staring at her. "W-what is it?" she stammered.

He continued to gaze at her. "Have I told you how beautiful you look tonight?"

His voice was low and husky and sent a shiver of desire running through her, centering in her core. He hadn't even touched her, and yet she tingled with need. It had been so long since she'd been loved by a man.

Right from the beginning, she'd been drawn to him, with an inexplicable need that defied definition. At the time, she'd been determined to ignore it, feeling guilty for having feelings like that. After all, if she hadn't sent her husband back into a war zone with her harsh words ringing in his ears, he might still be alive.

The guilt she'd carried with her for so many years was hard to ignore. So was the wariness that came from being betrayed. She would never have guessed Pete would cheat on her and yet, he had. She'd believed, if she couldn't trust him, a man she'd loved most of her life, there was no one she could trust.

But slowly and surely, Christian had knocked down her defenses until she had nothing left. He'd forced her to examine her existence and to question what had gone before. Like Sally-Ann had told her—harsh words or not—she wasn't responsible for Pete being killed. She finally accepted that as the truth. Her husband had been dead five years. He'd be dead forevermore. She was still very much alive and so was her little girl.

Christian had gently forced her to see the reality of their lives and she realized she'd been merely going through the motions for the past five years. It hadn't been that she didn't accept that Pete was never coming home. It was more that she didn't accept she deserved to find happiness with anyone else.

Her guilt over the way they'd parted followed him to the grave. Who knows? If Pete had survived and returned from his deployment, they might not even be together now. Their marriage might have become a statistic, like one in every three Australian marriages did and they would have gone their separate ways and done the best for their daughter.

But he *had* died and she was left with the all-consuming guilt. Until Christian came along, she didn't realize it had been eating her up inside. But now he was there and she'd never felt more alive and from the spark of desire that ignited in his eyes as his gaze traveled over her, he felt the same way.

He reached out and slowly trailed his finger up her arm. He started at her wrist and though she wore long sleeves, she still felt the heat his finger left behind. He arrived at her shoulder and then eased across and began tracing the neckline of her dress. The soft wool sank into a deep V that shadowed the softness of her breasts. Slowly, Christian's finger stole across her skin. He dipped into the valley between her breasts and then his finger climbed upwards again.

Over her collarbone and up to her shoulder and down the other side, he didn't pause until he got all the way down her other arm and finished at the wrist, just above her other hand. The whole time, he kept his gaze on hers, willing her not to look away.

Her heart beat fast; her lips went dry. She couldn't have dragged her gaze away if she tried. And all the time, he remained silent. It was the most erotic thing anyone had done to her.

Leaning forward, he gently nuzzled her neck. "Is Emma asleep yet?" he murmured.

The moment his lips touched her skin, Daisy was beyond coherent thought. All she could think of was how good his mouth felt on her flesh. Then his words connected in her brain and she somehow managed to respond.

"I went and checked on her while you were loading the dishwasher. She was definitely asleep."

"Good," came his muffled response as he focused more attention on her neck. Licking and sucking, he covered every inch of her bare skin and then started moving lower, across her chest. His hands joined in the exploration and cupped each one of her breasts. The pads of his thumbs found her nipples and as he began to stroke back and forth, she gasped.

She arched into his hands, unable to help herself. A needy heat centered between her legs. Her heart thumped so loudly, she was sure he could hear it—and she couldn't care less. All that mattered was how he made her feel and the need that burned inside her. She squirmed on the couch and reached for him, needing to feel all of him, up close.

With a groan, he followed her willingly down as she dragged him into her arms. With her back against the couch, she laced her hands behind his head and kissed him for all she was worth. It was a kiss of awakening, sweet and soft and tender, but the moment his lips moved on hers, the passion between them ignited in every way.

Mouths opened and tongues entwined. They kissed like they couldn't get enough. With her fingers clutching at his hair, she stroked and tasted and touched. She loved him and he loved her. *How had life gotten so sweet?* She still couldn't believe he'd stumbled into her life and that she'd fallen headlong into his heart.

It was so wonderful it brought tears to her eyes—or it would have, if she hadn't been so distracted with other things—like Christian nibbling at her earlobes while his fingers caressed her breast. And the feel of his erection, hot and hard against her belly, reminding her how long it had been since she'd made love.

His hand slid down her thigh and then pushed up the hem of her dress. She tugged his shirt out of the waistband of his jeans and slid her hand underneath. The warmth of his skin sent desire spiking straight to her core. Gliding upwards, over taut pecs and a scattering of chest hair, she found his nipples. First one and then the other, she scraped back and forth with her nails.

"That feels so good," he murmured.

Slowly, his fingers moved to the center of her heat and then his fingers flicked over her panties, tracing over the most intimate part of her through the silk. Up and down, round and round, the action so erotic it drove her wild. She wanted to feel his skin on hers, without the barrier of underwear.

Squirming against his hand, she tried to communicate her needs. He chuckled in her ear. "Do you like that?"

"Yes," she breathed. "I like that very much."

"What about this?"

His fingers pulled aside her panties until his bare skin was pressed against her heated flesh. He delved into her moist softness, stroking slowly. She shivered with pent-up need and clung to him, her exploration of his chest forgotten. With her breath coming faster, she pressed herself into his palm.

"You're so wet," he murmured, his voice thick with desire.

"It's all because of you," she breathed.

With a low growl of possession, he gathered her up in his arms. Once again, his mouth found hers and he kissed her thoroughly. With hearts pounding, they pulled apart and stared at each other in the dimness.

"I want to make love to you, Daisy."

She held his gaze. "I want to make love to you, too, Christian."

His eyes darkened to a beautiful cobalt and gleamed with white-hot desire. He kissed her again and then easily swung her up in his arms.

"Which way to the bedroom?" he muttered, his voice husky with need.

"Second door on the right," she replied. With her arms around his neck, she clung to him, breathing in his scent.

He turned the doorknob and nudged the door open with his shoulder. The room smelled heavenly—courtesy of the frangipani-and-cinnamon scented candles she'd lit in there earlier. She'd changed the sheets and had fluffed up the pillows and even had hoovered the carpet. The room with its pretty white damask bedspread and matching curtains looked like a picture out of a glossy home magazine.

But it could have been a barn for all the notice Christian took. She would have been disappointed if it weren't for the look of fierce concentration on his face. All of his attention was fixed on her. It was like he stared into her soul. His eyes burned with the need to have her. The muscles in his arms were tense beneath her thighs. And then he was lowering her to the bed. She lay back against the pillows and sighed with contentment, reaching for him.

He followed her down and immediately zeroed in on her lips. With her arms clasped behind his neck, she met him kiss for kiss. The heat that had barely banked between them ignited once again and her heart pounded from the excitement of it.

Pulling slightly away, Christian stared at her, his breath coming fast. "I think it's time we got you out of that dress. As amazing as it looks on you, I'm sure the view is even better underneath."

He reached down and took the hem in his hands and slid it up her legs. The soft woolen fabric complied without a sound of protest. Over her thighs, exposing her black lace panties and higher, until her matching bra was visible. She watched the desire flare in Christian's eyes and saw the tension in his face. Finally, he pushed the dress over her head and tossed it onto the floor without breaking her gaze.

Coming up on his haunches, he stared at her, his eyes wide with wonder. He reached down and traced the curve of her breasts with his fingers. Over her flat belly and lower still until he cradled her mound and then, like they had before, his fingers slipped inside the silk of her panties and stroked.

This time, her legs fell open, inviting him to touch his fill. His finger slid lower until he found her opening and with his gaze still on hers, his finger glided inside.

She gasped from the unfamiliar feel of his attentions. Not content merely to be inside her, his finger began to stroke. And then he inserted another and she clenched her hands into fists. Mindless pleasure consumed her, making her forget everything and everyone but him.

Her entire world narrowed to Christian and the magic he created. Over and over, he stroked her, until she cried out in torment.

"Please, I can't take anymore! Please, I want you inside me." She reached up and popped the button on his jeans and struggled to pull down the zip. At last it complied and she reached through his underwear and encircled his thick cock in her hand. She sighed with relief and was filled with anticipation at the feel of his impressive hard length.

And then she tried to stroke him, but the jeans

and boxers got in her way. Making a sound of frustration deep in her throat, she sat up and helped him undress. Without bothering to undo buttons, he pulled the shirt off over his head and tossed it aside. Standing up, he shucked his jeans and underwear over his hips and then stepped out of them, leaving them on the floor. She had a brief moment to admire the sheer hard length of him, her gaze scanning him from head to toe, before he rejoined her on the bed.

Lying beside her, he gathered her close and then kissed her softly on the mouth. Unlike their previous fiery kisses, this one was slow and tender. His tongue came out and traced her lips before slipping inside to explore the warm recesses of her mouth. She reveled in the touch and taste of him, but right now, it wasn't enough.

Moving against him restlessly, she reached down and took hold of his cock. Now free of the restrictions of his clothing, she was able to stroke and squeeze as she liked. She ran her hand along the length of him, from the moist tip to the base of his balls and then she did it again, only this time, she tightened her hold.

"*Mm*," he groaned against her hair. "That feels so good."

She smiled in satisfaction. "You like that, huh?"

He grinned back at her. "I like that a lot."

She chuckled and renewed her efforts and it wasn't long before they were both breathing hard. His excitement fueled hers and the need inside her grew until she didn't think she could stand it. As if able to read her thoughts—or perhaps he was at the brink, too—Christian reached down between them and loosened her fingers.

Pushing her gently onto her back, he positioned himself between her legs. With the fire at its peak, she opened them eagerly and waited for him to take her. To her disappointment, he remained motionless, merely staring down at her with hooded eyes. She moved impatiently beneath him.

"What's wrong?" she uttered.

"Nothing's wrong. I'm merely remembering this moment. It feels like I've waited my whole life for you. I want to savor every minute. This is the first night of the rest of my life. We're going to be together forever. I feel it in here." He pressed a fist against his heart and she melted.

Could he be any more perfect?

With that, he leaned down over the side of the bed and retrieved a condom from the pocket of his jeans. She watched while he sheathed himself and then settled himself back between her thighs.

Slowly, his cock probed her entrance and she braced herself for the feel of him. Inch by inch, he eased inside her. He felt so strange and unfamiliar and yet, wonderful all the same. With excruciating care, like she was a virgin and this was her first time, he moved inside her.

Finally, he was all the way in and he paused there, relishing the moment. Daisy looked down at the place where the two of them were joined and then at the utter bliss on Christian's face and knew that he was right. They belonged together and they'd be that way until the end of time.

With his desire-filled gaze still on hers, he began to move his hips. In and out, smooth and strong. He was making love to her with every stroke. She stared at him, transfixed, unable to drag her gaze away. The universe had disappeared and all that was left was them. They were each other's sun and moon, they were each other's everything. As Christian picked up his pace, she clung to his broad shoulders, trusting him to take her with him over the other side.

The heat inside her continued to build until she was a furnace from the inside out. Christian continued to thrust in and out and his gaze never wavered from hers. He reached for her hands and entwined their fingers and still, his gaze held hers. The tension on his face and the increasing speed of his movements told her he was getting close.

The need in her core became more urgent and she squeezed his fingers tight. And then, as he cried out and tensed over her, she reached the peak of her release. Tumbling over the other side, her cries of relief mingled with his. Collapsing on top of her for a moment, he fought to regain his breath. And then he rolled onto his side, taking her with him.

Gradually, their breathing returned to normal and he smiled in contentment and gathered her in his arms. "That was everything I dreamed of, and more," he whispered.

She returned his smile and nodded. "You're right."

Daisy stared at the witness statements in front of her and tried to concentrate. Apart from being sleep deprived, her head just wasn't in the right space. She kept thinking of the hours she'd spent in Christian's arms. It had been the most wonderful night of her life.

They'd made love two more times during the night and it had been in the early hours of the morning before they'd both fallen asleep, satisfied smiles on their lips. He'd been so wonderful, so patient and loving and generous. And fun. He was everything she could have dreamed of and she couldn't believe she'd waited so long to find out just how generous he was. And so good in bed, she almost wet her pants thinking about his sexual prowess. She was head over heels in love with him and even better, her daughter liked him, too. The world couldn't get more perfect.

Thoughts of their intimacies the night before sent need rushing through her. Squirming in her chair, she crossed her legs in an attempt to stem it. She was at work. Such amorous thoughts were totally inappropriate. Besides, she could hardly march across the floor into his office and demand that he assuage her need. She'd already stolen so many glances in that direction since she'd arrived, she was developing a crick in her neck.

With a sound of impatience in the back of her throat, she pushed away from her desk. She tried to distract herself by grabbing her coffee cup, telling herself she just needed a strong hit of caffeine. Without a second thought she headed past her secretary and continued down the hallway toward the tearoom. Rounding the corner, she spied Christian coming toward her from the other direction. He also held a coffee cup. Her eyes widened in surprise, even as her heart increased its speed.

"Good morning," she said, doing her best to keep her voice even. They'd agreed over breakfast that they would keep their relationship secret around the office, at least for a while.

"Indeed, it is an *excellent* morning," he replied, shooting her a brilliant smile.

She blushed and averted her gaze, but was filled with a rush of pleasure. She could still feel the memory of his touch the night before...

He was dressed in another custom made suit that fitted him to perfection, but in her mind's eye, all she could see was his naked chest covered in a scattering of dark-blond hair and the strong, firm length of his legs that had wrapped themselves around her. And of course, his equally firm and impressive manhood that had given her so many hours of pleasure.

As if sensing the direction of her thoughts, his gaze lingered meaningfully on her breasts, outlined beneath her cashmere sweater. The pale pink color complemented her olive skin tones and went well with the steel-gray color of her skirt.

"I see you're in need of coffee," he said, indicating the cup her hand.

"And you, too," she replied.

"Yes, I had a late one last night. I'm not sure what time I fell asleep." He winked.

Her heart skipped a beat, but she kept her

expression neutral. "Me, too. I think I've been working too hard. I just couldn't switch off last night. There was so much going on in my head and my body... She grinned. "Still, I can't say it was all bad."

"Not all bad?" he replied. "That sounds a little...disappointing."

She was quick to shake her head. "Oh, no. Don't be mistaken. There was nothing disappointing about why I couldn't sleep."

"That's good to hear," he replied. The teasing grin was once again in evidence.

"Yes, you have no reason to worry," she added. "In fact, I was very much taken care of." She stretched and covered a yawn. "Despite my lack of sleep, I don't think I've ever felt better."

They turned and walked together toward the tearoom. "So, what's on your calendar this morning?" he asked.

"I'm not in court, thank goodness," she replied. "But I have a mountain of statements to read through. I have a trial starting in less than two weeks and I'm barely halfway through those statements."

He grimaced. "I feel for you. All I have on is a sentencing hearing in the local court. Oh, and of course, I have client appointments. We never seem to run out of those."

She laughed and he laughed with her. The mood between them was so easy and relaxed. She was glad. Though it wouldn't have changed her mind about sleeping with him, she had worried a little that things might become difficult between them in the office afterwards. She needn't have worried.

Christian was daydreaming. It wasn't the first time he'd done it that day. In fact, Judge McDonald had called him to account during the sentencing hearing and he'd been embarrassed to realize he'd let his mind drift off. Fortunately, it hadn't affected his client's outcome and the young offender got off with a three-month good behavior bond. It was a good result for someone who had already been before the courts on similar offenses and no doubt would come before them again.

The rest of the day had dragged slowly forward and it felt like five o'clock would never come. He still had a couple of appointments to keep before he could call it a day. His thoughts kept turning to Daisy.

She'd surprised him that morning by asking him to move in with her and Emma. Of course, he'd said yes. Earlier in his life, he might've been concerned they were moving too fast, but with Daisy, everything felt so right. He wanted to wake up beside her every morning and go to bed with her every night. The hours of their lovemaking had been nothing short of wonderful and he couldn't wait to explore their relationship more. Even this morning, when he'd woken in her bed, there hadn't been any awkwardness between them.

And then later, at the office. It was as if they'd been together forever.

He'd only recently broached the subject with his uncle. Larry had barely responded to his news that he and Daisy were dating. His uncle seemed even less interested in his comment that he might move out, although perhaps he'd gotten good at hiding his true thoughts. Christian knew for a fact his uncle liked having him around. The man often commented on what a good team they made.

Now with Daisy offering to open her house to him, the need to find a place of his own had disappeared. At least, for now. He didn't intend to spend the rest of his life living in the house she'd shared with another man, but he would put the proposition of moving to some place new to her and him when things had settled down. Right now, their relationship was so new and fragile. Best not do anything to upset it.

The phone at his elbow peeled and he distractedly reached over and picked up the receiver.

"Christian Grayson."

"Christian, it's Daisy." At the sound of her voice, his heart skipped a beat. He wanted so much to see her. Though she was only on the opposite side of his floor, he could hardly go running over there without a reason. She'd asked that they keep their relationship secret from their work colleagues, at least for the time being, and he respected her request.

"It's nice to hear from you, Daisy. What can I do for you?"

"I'm wondering if you can do me a favor," she said. "I just had a call from the jail. One of my young clients has been arrested and is asking for me. He needs me to attend a bail hearing."

"How can I help?"

"The thing is, it's almost time for Emma to get off school. I'm not going to make the bus in time. I'm wondering if you could meet her at her bus stop? She gets there a little after four."

Christian glanced at his electronic diary and slowly shook his head. "I'd really like to help you out, but I'm afraid I have back-to-back clients this afternoon. One is already waiting for me outside."

"Oh, I see." He heard the disappointment in her voice. Another thought occurred to him.

"Listen, how about I call my uncle? I could get him to take her home. You could pick her up from his place. Would that be all right?"

"Yes, that would be great. Do you think Larry would be willing to do that?"

"I'll call him now. I'm sure he won't mind. It's not like it's out of his way. Emma can just stay on the bus and go home with him at the end of the run."

"Thank you, Christian. I appreciate the suggestion. That sounds like a good plan. Ever since those young girls went missing, I just haven't wanted her walking home on her own. You can't be too careful."

"You're right. It would be unimaginable if something were to happen to her. I'm sure Uncle Larry would feel that way, too. I'm certain he'll have no trouble watching her until you arrive."

Daisy sighed in relief. "Thank you again, and

please, thank your uncle. He'll be going above and beyond what's expected and I'll be really grateful if he can."

"Hey," Christian replied, his voice softening with unexpected emotion. "That's what family is for and I hope before too long you and I are family."

Chapter 20

Larry checked his side mirror before putting on his indicator and changing lanes. The bus was almost full and the kids were as noisy and rambunctious as they usually were this time in the afternoon. The day had been warm and sunny, defying the usual winter temperatures and his passengers were in high spirits.

His phone vibrated in his pocket, momentarily distracting him. With the next stop right up ahead, he ignored his cell until he brought the bus to a halt. Flicking the lever, he opened the door.

"See you tomorrow, Thomas. Have a good afternoon."

"You, too, Mr Grayson. See you tomorrow." The fifth grader waved and smiled.

Larry retrieved his phone from his pocket and glanced at the screen. The call had already diverted to voicemail, but he could see it was from Christian. Without bothering to dial into his message bank, he merely returned the call.

"Christian, sorry I missed your call. What's up?"

"I just left you a message," his nephew replied. "I need a favor."

Larry shrugged. "Sure."

"It's Emma Green. Her mother's been caught up at work and won't get home in time to meet her daughter off the bus. With the disappearances of those other two kids, she's a little spooked and I don't blame her. I told her you might be willing to let Emma stay on the bus until the end of your run. Daisy could collect her from home. Would that be all right?"

Larry glanced through the rearview mirror at the little girl in question. She was seated in her usual spot, four seats from the front. She normally sat next to Henrietta Ridley who talked incessantly, but as luck would have it, today Henrietta was at home sick with the flu. Emma sat quietly all alone.

She was such a cute little thing with her mop of golden curls and she was always so polite. She never failed to say good morning, or to thank him for the ride. So sweet. So pretty... He felt a stirring in his loins.

Christian had asked him for a favor. The child's mother had been delayed. It would be a shame to put her out at her bus stop and risk her coming to harm. Not when there was another alternative. After all, he was free all afternoon. He couldn't think of a better way to while away a few hours than in the company of sweet little Emma Green.

"Of course," he replied. "She's more than welcome to stay on the bus and I have no problem taking her back home. Does her mother know where we live?"

"I'll give her the address," Christian replied. "And thanks, Uncle. I really appreciate it. I can't imagine Daisy will run later than five or six, but it won't matter to you if Emma's there a bit longer, will it?"

"No, of course not. I have nothing more planned for this afternoon but to go home and put my feet up."

Christian laughed. "I'm sure you deserve the rest. I don't know how you put up with that noise day in and day out. I can hear them from here."

"You're right," Larry chuckled. "I guess I've gotten used to it over the years."

"Well, thanks again, Uncle Larry. I'll let Daisy know not to worry. You have everything under control."

With anticipation running through his veins, Larry ended the call. Climbing out of his seat, he made his way down to where Emma sat. Her eyes grew wide at his approach and most of the kids fell silent. It wasn't often he came down the back. Pitching his voice low so that he wouldn't be overheard, he addressed the little girl.

"Emma, I've just had a call from your mother. She's running late at work."

The child's face fell. "Oh, not again."

"Yes. But she's asked if you wouldn't mind staying on the bus until the end of the run. You can come home with me and she'll pick you up from there."

Emma eyed him uncertainly. "I guess so. Are you sure that's what she asked me to do?"

"Yes, honey. I'm sure. And do you know what? I

have a new litter of puppies. You could see them when you come home. I'm sure they'll be awake. They normally feed about this time."

Emma's eyes widened with interest and a smile played around her lips. "Puppies? Really? I *love* puppies."

Larry grinned and ruffled her hair affectionately. "Well then, you're going to have fun at my place this afternoon."

With a final fond smile, he turned away and regained the driver's seat. Thoughts of the delights that lay ahead of him filled his mind. It was fortuitous that he'd so recently disposed of Lila-Jane. Though Bella still inhabited the bed, there was plenty of room for one more. The fun they were going to have! He couldn't wait! The fact that this time his plaything was Daisy's Green's daughter made it all the more sweet.

Somehow, he'd make sure the police looked squarely at his nephew. Of course, they wouldn't find any evidence of his involvement in the child's disappearance, but he *had* known her mother was running late... And then there was the scrapbook... A decent search by the police of his house would uncover it. Of course, there was no proof it was Christian's, but if it *were* found in the bottom drawer of his desk...

Larry chuckled. He hoped the questions raised by the police and Emma's mother would be enough to drive a wedge between her and Christian. Their fledgling romance would come to an end quicker than he anticipated. Not only would he have another plaything, but he'd also put an end to any thoughts his nephew had of moving out. It was a win-win situation. His smile morphed into a grin.

———————

"There it is! My place! We'll see the puppies soon."

Emma stared out the window at the neat brick-and-tile home pointed out by Mr Grayson. The front yard was newly mown, but there was not a flowerbed in sight. The house sat a fair distance back from the curb. The bus driver continued to drive the bus forward until they turned at the next corner and turned again into a back lane. He pulled the bus up outside behind the same house.

He turned to face her. "Sit tight. I won't be long. I just have to open the gate." With that, he climbed off the bus and walked toward a high steel fence.

Emma looked around her. It was strange being on the bus all by herself. The silence was weird. Until Lila-Jane and Bella had disappeared, she'd never been the last to get off. And now she'd gone all the way to the end of the bus run, to where Mr Grayson kept his bus. It was strange, but also a little exciting. She looked forward to seeing the puppies. For once, she didn't mind that her momma would be late.

With a creak of protest, the gate swung inward and a moment later, Mr Grayson climbed back on the bus. Lumbering forward, he drove the bus into the backyard. Switching off the ignition, he turned to face her once more.

"We're home. You can climb off now. Just give me a moment to close the gate and I'll take you inside, show you the puppies."

Emma's heart skittered with excitement. There was nothing in the world she loved more than puppies. It had been so long since she'd been allowed to walk home. The puppies belonging to the Owens family were probably nearly grown. She missed them.

A few moments later, Mr Grayson shut and locked the back gate and quickly returned to her side. Ushering her through the garage, they climbed the steps that led into the house.

"Would you like a glass of milk and some cookies?"

She nodded and took a seat at the kitchen counter. The bus driver went into the kitchen and took a glass out of the cupboard. Next he went to the fridge. Emma swiveled in her chair and looked around her. They were in an open-concept kitchen and living room. The hardwood floors were polished to a high sheen. She thought of the puppies and giggled.

"I bet they have a fun time on those floorboards," she commented, turning back to Mr Grayson.

He came toward her with a glass of milk and a plate of cookies in his hands. "Who's that?"

"The puppies, of course," she replied.

"Oh, yes, of course! The puppies. You wouldn't believe how much fun they have on these floors." He chuckled.

Emma grinned. Reaching over, she picked up the glass and took a long drink. The day had been unseasonably warm and she was thirsty.

"Have a cookie," Mr Grayson urged, pushing the plate toward her.

Chocolate chip. Her favorite. She reached for one. She'd only managed a couple of bites before she started to feel awfully strange. Her head felt foggy, like she couldn't think. She opened her mouth to say something, but the words wouldn't come.

What was happening to her? She'd never felt like this before. *Was she coming down with something?* Her friend Henrietta had the flu. *Perhaps she'd caught something from her friend before she had sense enough to stay home from school?*

"Are you all right, Emma?"

Emma stared at Mr Grayson and tried to make him out. His face had gone all blurry and his voice sounded kind of echoey, as if it came through a long tunnel.

"I... I... I feel strange. My head feels all funny. I think I'm going to be sick."

Mr Grayson hurried around the counter, reaching her side just as she toppled backwards on the chair.

Larry stared down at the small child he held in his arms and felt an overwhelming wave of tenderness. She was so beautiful, so innocent and she'd fallen straight for his story. It was the non-existent puppies that had tipped her over the edge and of course, the fact that her mother had given her permission to be there.

Mothers could be so trusting sometimes, couldn't they?

Daisy was the only person in the elevator as it ascended to her floor. After attending a last-minute bail hearing for Ferrell James and managing to get him released, she'd returned tired, but triumphant to the office. The time was well past five. On her way up, she dialed Christian's number. He picked up on the second ring.

"Hi, I'm on my way home now. How did you do?" he asked.

"Good. Ferrell made bail and I've just arrived back in the office. I'm going up to drop off my files and collect my coat and bag. It's turned chilly out there."

"Yes, after the beautiful day we had, it's a shock to the system now that the wind's picked up."

"How did you do with your uncle? I take it he was okay about taking Emma home with him?"

"Yes. It was no trouble at all. I'm not far away from the house now. I'll go and check in on them."

Daisy breathed a soft sigh of relief, grateful things had worked out all right and that her baby hadn't been forced to walk home alone. "Great. And thanks again for approaching your uncle about this. I really appreciate it."

"No trouble at all. Did you get the address details I texted earlier?"

"Yes."

"Good. I'll see you soon."

Daisy ended the call. A moment later, the elevator *dinged* indicating it had arrived at her floor. Stepping out, she dropped her files on her desk and just as quickly retrieved her coat and bag from her locker. A few minutes later, she exited the room, eager to see Emma and Christian.

CHAPTER 21

Christian opened the front door and made his way through the quiet house. He found his uncle out on the deck. Larry turned toward him at his approach.

"Hey there, nephew. How are you doing?"

"I'm fine, thanks uncle. Where's Emma?"

Larry frowned. "Emma got off the bus at her bus stop."

It was Christian's turn to frown. "What you mean? I thought you were going to bring her here? Daisy's on her way over to collect her."

"I know that's what we talked about but when I got to her bus stop, there was a woman waiting there. She said she was a friend of Daisy's. I spoke to Emma and she seemed willing to go with the woman. I asked the child specifically if she wanted to stay on the bus, but she told me the woman was a friend of her mothers and she'd be safe to walk home with her."

Christian shook his head, perplexed. Daisy had said nothing about a friend being available to meet Emma off the bus. *What was going on?*

Unsettled, he pulled out his phone. "I need to call Daisy," he said. His uncle merely waved in acknowledgement and headed back inside. She answered on the third ring.

"Christian, I've only just left and I'm stuck in traffic. I'll be there as soon as I can. What would you like to do for dinner?"

Christian swallowed. There was no easy way to do this. "Daisy, Emma's not here."

There was a moment of shocked silence and then Daisy spoke again. "What do you mean, she's not there? Of course she's there! You spoke to your uncle. He agreed. She was going home with him."

Christian was nodding along as she spoke. "Yes, I understand what we agreed and that's what I thought had happened. But, you see, Emma didn't come here. Uncle Larry told me there was a friend of yours waiting for her at the bus stop and Emma insisted it would be safe to walk home with her. He let her off the bus. He's upset at the fact he might have done the wrong thing."

"A friend? Who was it?"

"I don't know. Uncle Larry didn't recognize her, but Emma appeared willing to go with the woman. He didn't think anything of it."

"The only person I spoke to about making arrangements for Emma was you. There's no way someone should have been there to meet her off the bus. Oh, my goodness! Something's happened to her! I just know it! She's been taken, just like those other girls. I'm calling the police!"

"Daisy, I understand your concern. I'm concerned, too, but I think I should go around to your place first and make sure she isn't there. After all, perhaps she was met by a friend at the bus stop? You could be worrying about nothing.

"Listen, Uncle Larry and I will go and retrace her route, see if we can find anything. You've only just left the office. We'll get there faster than you. I'll call you as soon as we find her. She must be there. After all, where else can she be?"

His words echoed in the silence that met him on the other end of the phone. "Are you still there, Daisy?"

"Yes, I'm still here." Her voice was dull, as if she was already imagining the worst.

"Call the police if it makes you feel any better, honey. Given what's happened around your neighborhood lately, I'm sure they won't mind if it turns out to be a false alarm. I'll tell Uncle Larry what's happened and we'll leave right away. We'll find her, okay?"

"Okay." Once again, her reply was a dull monotone. He couldn't imagine what she was going through. He only hoped her concerns would be for nothing. Unfortunately, there was no way of knowing until he got to her house.

And then Daisy spoke again and her voice cracked with emotion. "Please, get around there right away. I'll try the house number. Maybe she'll answer it. I'll be there as soon as I can."

Larry stared down at the two little girls who lay side by side on the bed. Leaning down, he brushed the blond curls off Emma Green's forehead. She was gently snoring. He smiled tenderly. The Rohypnol had done the trick.

As if sensing his presence, Bella blinked and opened her eyes. Almost immediately, she gasped and fear chased shadows across her face. She turned her head and spied Emma.

"Oh, my goodness! What have you done! Why is Emma here?"

Larry's tender smile widened behind the clown mask. "She's come to join us in our games. The three of us are going to have so much fun. She's going to be sleeping a little while longer, but soon..." He let out a gleeful cackle that sent a fresh wave of fear rushing across Bella's face. The little girl paled and he laughed even harder.

"Where's Lila-Jane?" she asked, fear pinching her lips.

"She's gone."

The child turned even paler. "Gone where?"

"She's gone home. Well, she might not be home, yet, but I guess she'll get there eventually." He laughed until the tears ran down his cheeks.

With a sense of urgency, Christian strode in from the deck. At the same time, he called out for Uncle Larry. He was met with silence. Checking the kitchen and living room, he then walked down the hall. The bathroom and toilet were also empty. The only place he hadn't checked was the basement.

In all the years he'd lived with his uncle, he'd never once broken his uncle's rule about disturbing him down there. Still, this was an emergency. They needed to find Emma and Uncle Larry knew better than he did the route she would have taken to walk home. It would save them both a lot of time if his uncle came with him.

He was halfway down the stairs when he spied Sooty. The cat was carrying a scrap of fabric in his mouth. Curious, he squatted on his haunches and picked the cat up in his arms.

"What have you got there, boy?" he asked, giving Sooty a scratch.

Pulling the fabric out of the cat's mouth, he frowned. It was a navy-blue satin ribbon, the kind of ribbon that a little girl might wear in her hair. Something tugged at his memory, but whatever it was remained elusive and he gave up. A child he cared about was missing. He didn't have time to work out what it was. Instead, he put the ribbon in his pocket and continued on his way down.

Larry appeared a moment later, pulling the basement door closed behind him. At the sight of Christian, he pulled back in surprise.

"Christian! What are you doing down here? I was just on my way up. Is there something wrong?"

"Yes. Well, maybe. I just spoke to Daisy Green. She's confused about the change in plans—about someone meeting Emma off the bus. She can't think who it might have been. We need to retrace the route Emma would have taken after she got off the bus and make sure she arrived home. Did you recognize the woman who met her at the bus stop?"

"No, but like I told you before, Emma was happy enough to go with her. I would never have let her off if I'd felt there was a need for concern."

Christian nodded and felt a modicum of comfort. His uncle would never knowingly place one of his kids in danger. Besides, Emma was a bright girl. She wouldn't have gotten off the bus and gone with a stranger. She must be at home. There was no other explanation.

With a surge of impatience, he turned and headed back up the stairs. He glanced back at his uncle. "Hurry up. Let's go."

Daisy accelerated through the rush-hour traffic and cursed the slightest delay. She'd already tried to phone home and no one had answered. She didn't want to jump to the conclusion Emma wasn't home, because sometimes the little girl was in her room with her headphones on listening to music or watching a movie on her iPad, but listening to the phone ring out and then having the answering machine kick in sure hadn't done anything to reassure her that everything was all right.

Yet another stoplight turned red ahead of her and in frustration, she hit the steering wheel with her fist. It had been nearly twenty minutes since she'd spoken to Christian. He should have reached her house by now and would know if Emma were home. *Why hadn't he called?*

She squeezed her eyes shut and shook her head, trying her best to get her tumultuous thoughts under control. She was letting her imagination run away with her. It was just that, ever since she'd been told Emma had gone home with a stranger, the blood in her veins had run cold. After all that had happened recently in their neighborhood... First Lila-Jane, then Bella. Now her little girl might also have gone missing. Fear constricted her chest. Unable to stand it a moment longer, she picked up her phone and dialed the police.

The officer she spoke to told her they'd send someone over to talk with her and assured her that most missing children turned up safe. By the time Daisy ended the call, she felt a little calmer. Hopefully Emma had merely gone home instead of staying on the bus and would turn up safe and sound like the officer said and Daisy could put this nightmare behind her.

The lights changed and her Honda surged forward. With half a mind on the road, she wracked her brain as to who the unknown friend who'd met Emma could have been. Daisy was an only child. She had close friends, mostly work colleagues, but like she'd told Christian, she hadn't told anyone else about her predicament. No one but him knew she was running late and wouldn't be there in time to meet the bus.

Try as she might, she couldn't think of anyone Emma would have been happy to go with, especially when the bus driver had given her the message that she was to stay on the bus and her mother would collect her from his home. It was confusing and frightening and too many questions kept circling in her brain. All she wanted was to find her baby and hold her close. Weaving her way through the traffic, a silent prayer ran through her head.

Please, baby. Please be at home...

Daisy rounded the corner at double speed and accelerated to the end of her street. With a screech of the brakes, she came to a halt outside her house. Christian and his uncle were on foot and had just lifted the latch on her front gate. Breathless with fear, she climbed out of her car and ran toward them, fumbling in her handbag for her house key as she went.

With shaking hands, she inserted the key into the lock and immediately pushed the door open. Christian and his uncle followed.

"Emma? Where are you, honey? I'm home."

Daisy half-ran down the hallway, almost skidding in her high heels. She poked her head into the kitchen and living room, but Emma was nowhere to be seen. Next she ran down the hallway to Emma's room. Nothing.

"Emma! Where are you? Answer me!"

Increasingly panicked, Daisy checked in every room. The last place to check was the small backyard and as she surveyed the modest courtyard, her hopes of finding her daughter safe and sound at home disintegrated.

Christian approached her silently, his face grave with concern. "Did you call the police?" he asked quietly.

"Yes, they told me they'd send someone around." Christian's uncle came up behind him. Daisy turned to him. "Tell me about the woman who was waiting for her at the bus stop?" she demanded. "What did she look like? Have you seen her before?"

Larry regarded her somberly. "No, but like I told Christian, Emma seemed to know the woman. She got off the bus quite willingly and I saw them walking away together."

"Which direction?"

"In the direction of your home."

Daisy's shoulders slumped on a desperate sigh. Her thoughts were a confusion of fear and terror and she tried desperately to sift through them and think. *Who could the woman have been and why would Emma go with her?* It didn't make sense.

A brisk knock on the front door snagged her attention. Her heart skipped a beat and she hurried back to the door. Two plainclothes detectives crowded the doorway. It took her a moment to realize they were the same officers who'd attended Marcie's premises.

She ushered them inside, unable to believe she was now the distraught mother in this situation. *She* was the one with a missing daughter. *She* was the one panic stricken and doing her best to remain calm enough to answer their questions.

Her head spun. The older detective—Detective McLennan, she seemed to recall—shot her a look of concern and urged her to sit down. She stumbled to the couch, the same couch she'd made out on with Christian only the previous night. In such a short amount of time she'd gone from being deliriously happy to having her world disintegrate into pieces. The emotional shift down had been at a breakneck speed.

Had it only been a couple of weeks since she'd attended Marcie's home? It felt like a lifetime. *Poor Marcie.* Her baby was still missing and now Daisy's daughter was, too. Stricken with overwhelming pain and anxiety, she buried her face in her hands and cried through her pain. Christian stepped forward and put his hand on her back, rubbing it gently, rhythmically, offering silent comfort.

"What's that in your pocket?" Detective McLennan asked.

Daisy stopped mid-sob and sat back, confused. The detective was pointing to Christian. He looked just as confused as she, but pulled out a piece of blue ribbon. Daisy gasped. It looked just like the one the police found in the bush after Lila-Jane disappeared. She stared at him and icy dread settled like a stone in her chest. *What was he doing with Lila-Jane's ribbon?*

Unable to help herself, she wrenched away from him and opened her mouth and screamed.

"Oh, my goodness! It's *you*! I can't believe it! All this time, it was *you*!" She turned to face the police officers. "It's him! He has to be the one behind the kidnappings."

She thought back to all that had happened since she'd met him. His arrival at Marcie's house, offering his help. He'd also turned up at the prayer vigil and at the time, she'd been touched by his show of support.

But what if there was more to it? What if he'd been there not as someone offering to help, but as the perpetrator, wanting to keep an eye on proceedings? She remembered watching a TV program once where the narrator of the program pointed out how the perpetrator of a crime often hung around, close to the scene, in order to garner information. They did it under the auspices of wanting to help, or being curious, but really, they were there to keep abreast of the facts. To stay ahead of the law.

She knew from other true crime documentaries she'd watched that the police took special note of the bystanders at a crime scene and especially those who appeared overly interested or concerned about an investigation. More often than not, that person had more than a passing interest in what was happening.

And then there was his uncle's comment that same evening about how much Christian loved little girls. According to Uncle Larry, Christian was always playing with them when he was a kid. And now he had Lila-Jane's hair ribbon...

Did he still have a fascination for little girls? Was

that what this was all about? She gripped the arm of the couch in fear, unable to look at him. All of a sudden, the recent disappearances of Lila-Jane Morrissey and Bella Rushby and the facts surrounding them raced through her brain.

Christian's uncle had the bus run. It meant Christian had access to those children. He would know their bus routes and their timetables. Perhaps sometimes he even caught his uncle's bus home? The presence of the bus driver's nephew wouldn't have been too much cause for concern. In fact, most of the kids probably wouldn't have noticed if he'd been on the bus. Emma had never mentioned him riding with them, but that didn't mean it hadn't happened.

Christian's work as a defense lawyer regularly placed him outside the building throughout the day, with court appearances and the like, it wouldn't have been too difficult for him to have made the bus ride after school and pass his absence off as a delay in the courtroom.

But what of Larry Grayson? Wouldn't he have found it strange that his nephew wanted to accompany him on his run? And what explanation had Christian given his uncle when he'd gotten off the bus with one of the children? No, that didn't make sense. It couldn't have happened that way. Not unless...

Maybe they were both involved?

Daisy's thoughts spun in a whirlwind of confusion and fear. Her heart beat fast and she didn't know which way to turn. *Were Christian and his uncle involved in the disappearance of those girls, or was Daisy way off the mark? Had she been totally wrong about both of them?* She'd thought of Larry as a sweet old man who seemed to really care about the children who caught his bus. And Christian—he'd come across as so good and kind. *How could she have been so wrong?*

Daisy glared at both of the Grayson men. "Where is she? What have you done with her?" Her accusations filled the house.

Christian looked shocked to his core and turned stricken eyes in Daisy's direction. "Daisy, I swear! You've made a mistake! It isn't what you think! It isn't me!"

She glared at him, tears still sliding down her cheeks. "Then how do you explain why you have Lila-Jane's ribbon?"

His expression became desperate. "I didn't know it was hers! I found it on the stairs that lead into our basement. My cat was playing with it. Please, you have to believe me."

Both officers came alert and looked at each other. "Get over there now," the detective ordered. "I'll take him back to the station and call for backup. I want a thorough search of that property."

In short order, Christian was handcuffed and taken away, all the while pleading his innocence. Larry looked shell shocked. He stood nearby, wringing his hands, his expression reflecting his devastation. "Daisy, you have to believe me. I had no idea about any of this. I'm just as shocked as you..."

Daisy was overwhelmed with disbelief. Any

moment, she expected to shatter into a million pieces. Her life had been destroyed. It would never be the same again. She couldn't believe she'd trusted Christian, fell in love with him, invited him into their lives. Now he had her daughter, her little baby girl. All she could do was hope and pray he hadn't done anything to her and that the police would find her in time.

A fresh wave of sobs tightened her chest. Air was in short supply. She gasped and wheezed and finally screamed and then sobbed like her heart was broken. She was barely aware of the room emptying. All she knew was when she finally raised her head, she was alone.

CHAPTER 22

L arry cast a furtive glance over his shoulder and quickly climbed into his pickup. They'd left it at Emma's bus stop and had walked all the way to her home. It had been Christian's idea. He wanted to retrace her route. All the time, he'd peppered his uncle with questions about the woman Emma had met. It had driven Larry crazy, but with an effort he played along. He couldn't afford to let his guard down.

Spying Christian halfway down the stairs to the basement had given him the fright of his life. A few more seconds and he'd have caught him in the room. Larry would have been in the process of locking the concealed door and would have been caught red-handed. Still, Sooty's role in it had gone down just fine. Larry had given the cat Lila-Jane's ribbon in the hope he'd take it to Christian. And he had. When Larry had spied the scrap of satin hanging from his nephew's pocket, he'd fought hard to hide his smile of satisfaction.

In the end, the ribbon was his savior. It had

placed the suspicion directly on his nephew, giving Larry time to escape. Then of course, there was the scrapbook. No doubt the police would find it during the course of their search. Christian would be stuck in an airless interview room answering questions for hours, yet.

Of course, the evidence against his nephew was purely circumstantial and a good lawyer would have the case thrown out. It had never been his idea to see his nephew go to jail. After all, it suited him better to have him live with him. But Christian was planning to move out anyway. He'd given no thought for how it might destroy Larry's life. That's when he saw that his nephew didn't really care for him at all and certainly didn't have his back. It was like Frank all over again. Christian was willing to walk away from everything his uncle had given him, and for what? A woman.

Because of his nephew's thoughtlessness, Larry was going to have to go it alone and once again risk the suspicious glances and the chatter behind his back. Still, he was now a man in his fifties. Men his age weren't quite so conspicuous, living on their own. He'd make up some story about nursing his wife through terminal cancer. Unfortunately, she'd recently died. It was the reason he'd moved into a new neighborhood. He wanted a fresh start, away from their life together and the sad, sad memories...

It was a good story and he was sure his new neighbors would fall for it. After all, most people only saw what they wanted to see. It's just the way it was.

It was a shame there was no time to return to the house and pack a bag. The police would be swarming the place by now. He needed to leave immediately, to disappear for a while. It was a good job he'd done it so many times before. He'd gotten good at it over the years...

Lila-Jane woke to a splitting headache. She blinked, but the world around her remained hazy. Slowly, she became aware of the dampness of the ground soaking into her school dress and the smell of wet earth close to her nostrils. She tried to move and realized she was no longer restrained. It was also obvious she was no longer in Mr Grayson's basement.

Abruptly, she sat up and then cried out in pain. Cradling her head between her hands, she breathed through the agony that tormented her. It felt like her head had been split open. As the pain resided, she became more and more aware of her surroundings. The darkness was slowly penetrated by a million twinkling stars. Deeper shadows morphed into trees. She was somewhere out in a forest and from the utter silence that surrounded her, she was a long way from anyone else.

He let me go! I'm alive and he let me go!

The sudden realization she was free, hit her hard. Tears flooded her eyes and poured down her dirty cheeks. She struggled to her feet and just as quickly fell flat on her face. Her legs were so weak from lying down for so long, they couldn't take her weight.

Breathing hard and with a concerted effort, she forced herself to stand. This time, her legs held firm and after a few moments, she took a step. And then another and another until she was half-running down the dirt path. She could barely see in front of her, but it didn't matter. She was free and she was going to find her mother.

The street was filled with emergency vehicles—police cars, ambulances, even a fire truck. All of them were flashing red and blue and white strobe lights, flooding the night with light. Daisy pulled up in her car on the opposite side of the street and stared at the pandemonium.

Uniformed officers swarmed the front lawn of Christian and Larry's house. Curious spectators lined the street. She'd checked that the address was the same as the one given in the text Christian sent her a lifetime ago. It matched. Pushing open the door, on unsteady limbs, she made her way up to the front door. Her progress was blocked by a well-built uniformed officer.

"I'm sorry, ma'am. You can't go in there."

She found the strength to glare at him. "My name is Daisy Green. I think my daughter's being held captive inside. Please let me pass. I need to see her. I need to know she's all right."

Despite her best intentions, her voice had risen in pitch with each sentence until it cracked with emotion on the last few words. Tears welled up in her eyes. The officer remained unmoved, but she saw a flash of sympathy in his gaze.

"I'm sorry, Ms Green. I truly am. I wish I could let you in there, but I can't. The police are conducting a thorough search of the premises. No one's allowed inside."

His words sounded like they were reaching her through a barrel of molasses, but his meaning registered just the same. She couldn't go inside and find her baby. She had to wait and see what the police might find. And just like that, her distress boiled over and she crumpled at his feet. Huge sobs wracked her body and she was powerless to make them stop.

And then a shout of triumph went up through the crowd and slowly registered in her brain.

"They've found them!"

"It's them!"

"They've found the missing girls!"

Daisy stopped mid-sob and lifted her head, staring back at the house. And then she noticed the officers who stood on the front porch each holding a little girl in their arms. Emma was sound asleep, but there was no mistaking her blond curls. With a cry of relief, Daisy jumped to her feet and ran toward them.

"Emma! Oh, Emma! Baby! My baby!" She shook the officer's arm none too gently in her eagerness for a response. "Please tell me she's all right?"

The officer smiled back at her and her knees

went weak with relief. "Yes, ma'am, she's gonna be fine. She's sleeping off some kind of sleeping pill, but I'm sure she'll be right as rain, just like her friend. We got lucky. We got here in time."

"W-where was she?" Daisy managed, staying close.

"We found a fake wall in the basement. The girls were behind it, tied to a bed."

Daisy's mouth opened in horror, but her words dried in her throat when Emma blinked and opened her eyes.

"Oh, Emma! *Sweet child!* It's Momma! I'm here, honey! I'm here! You're safe now. I'm here. Thank goodness you're all right! Did he hurt you, baby? Please tell me Christian didn't hurt you!"

Emma looked at her strangely. "Christian? What has he got to do with anything and why would he hurt me?"

Daisy frowned in confusion. "Didn't Christian bring you here?"

"No. The last thing I remember is Mr Grayson offering me milk and cookies. I think I fell asleep in his kitchen. I might have even fallen off the chair. The next thing I knew, the police were breaking down the wall."

"Mr Grayson, the bus driver?" Daisy asked.

Emma nodded. Daisy frowned. *If it wasn't Christian, who was it?* The only other person Emma had mentioned was Larry...

Before she could fully form the thought another uniformed officer came over. He addressed the officer who held Emma, but Daisy heard every word.

"We've just received a call. Lila-Jane Morrissey's turned up at the Hornsby Police Station. Some people found her wandering alone along the road. It seems as though she was dumped out there in the national park."

The officer who held Emma nodded. "We've spoken to the other little girl who was inside—Bella Rushby. She confirmed Lila-Jane had been held captive with her and that Larry Grayson's the man responsible for keeping them there. We also found some blister packets of what could be Rohypnol. The lab will tell us for sure. We can only assume the dosage wore off at some time, enough for the girls to recognize Grayson and remember him. Bella assures us he was the only one she had contact with. We've taken Christian Grayson in for questioning, but it's quite possible Larry Grayson was acting alone. We've have patrol cars out looking for him now."

Daisy stared blankly in shock, trying to take it all in.

Larry Grayson.

Uncle Larry. It had been the bus driver all along. Not Christian... Christian likely didn't have anything to do with it... *Oh, God. What had she done?*

Christian eyed the hard-nosed detective who glared at him from across the table. The officer's companion had a far more affable look. Christian understood what they were doing. He'd watched enough shows to recognize they were doing their best to play good cop, bad cop. Only, he wasn't falling for it. He hadn't done anything wrong and there was no way in hell they were going to get him to say otherwise.

The bad cop drew in a breath. He leaned back in his chair and, stretching out his legs, casually crossed his ankles. "So, Mr Grayson, tell us again about Bella Rushby and Emma Green. It's true that you're dating Emma Green's mother, isn't it?"

Christian gritted his teeth and held on to his patience with difficulty. "I've already told you, I had nothing to do with the disappearance of those girls. I don't even know Bella Rushby."

"But you know Emma Green, don't you?"

"Yes."

"And you know Lila-Jane Morrissey." This came from the good cop.

Christian held his temper and kept his tone calm. "No. I don't know Lila-Jane Morrissey."

"Then how do you explain the ribbon?" Bad Cop asked.

"I don't know. I found it on the steps leading into the basement of my home."

"So you said."

"It's the truth."

"And what about the scrapbook full of newspaper clippings? Why would you keep that?" Bad Cop asked.

Christian frowned in confusion. "I don't know what the hell you're talking about."

"Yeah, that's what they all say," Bad Cop added with a smirk.

"It was found in the bottom drawer of your desk. At least, we assume the desk belongs to you. There were volumes of legislation and old case law scattered all over it, including over the top of the scrapbook, concealing it."

Christian continued to regard the officers steadily. "I still don't have any clue what you're talking about."

A knock on the door sounded loud in the small confines of the interview room. The door opened and another officer poked his head in. "Sarge, can I have a word?"

Bad Cop looked like he wanted to deny the request, but Good Cop got to his feet and left. He came back a few moments later. "You're free to go."

Christian started in surprise. "What happened? What made you believe me?"

"It seems the missing girls have been found—all three of them. They've been interviewed independently and they're all saying they believe it was Larry Grayson who kidnapped them and held them captive in the basement. We also found a clown mask in a cupboard outside the room, the one they say he wore. DNA testing will confirm if it was his or not."

Christian heard the words and felt like he'd been sucker punched in the chest. Shocked, he gasped for breath. *Uncle Larry...? It couldn't be and yet... It made an awful kind of sense. All the missing children. All the times they'd moved. The basement where he was forbidden to go. The renovations... It seemed so obvious now.*

He was filled with a sudden sense of urgency. He needed to call Daisy. He didn't blame her for what she'd said. He probably would have jumped to the same conclusion. She was upset and angry and she panicked when she had to deal with the facts she had. And then he paused. Uncle Larry had kidnapped her baby. *What if she blamed Christian, too? What if she blamed him for his uncle's evilness? What if she never wanted to see him again?*

In the circumstances, he couldn't blame her if she felt that way. That thought filled his mind even as his heart rebelled. He needed to go and apologize and then disappear from her life. There was nothing else to do.

––––––––––––

Daisy's stared down at her sleeping daughter and brushed the hair from her eyes. It was way past late and yet she couldn't bring herself to go to bed. She'd gone with Emma in the ambulance and had been by her daughter's side during the lengthy medical examination and even lengthier questioning by the police. But now it was all over, and Emma had been released into her mother's care.

To Daisy's relief, the doctor had advised that in her opinion, Emma hadn't been assaulted. They'd reached her in time. The news was music to Daisy's ears. She'd sagged with relief and had thanked the doctor before taking her baby home.

Even still, it would take a long time for Emma to recover, but Daisy was determined to do everything she could to help her.

Sliding down the wall near Emma's bed, Daisy rested her head against the mattress. She was so tired, but her head still spun, filled with images of Emma and also of Christian. Detective McLennan had called her a few hours earlier. Christian had been cleared of all suspicion.

Lila-Jane had confirmed it had been his uncle who had kidnapped her and hurt them in the basement. It upset and angered Daisy to listen to the details, but she made herself do it for her daughter's sake. If she was to play a part in Emma's healing, she had to know everything.

She thought back to the way she'd treated Christian when she believed he was involved, the hurtful accusations she'd tossed. She'd been consumed by fear and anger. She didn't know what to think. Though she hadn't wanted to believe he *was* involved, the evidence at that point in time said something different. Now that she'd been given the truth, she really should call him and apologize. She'd said some awful things to him—none of which he deserved.

A sound broke into her thoughts and it took her a moment to realize someone was at the front door. She frowned. It was after midnight. *Who would be knocking on her door at this hour?*

The knock came again, this time a little louder and with a sigh, she got to her feet. Padding down the hallway in her slippers, she peered through the peephole.

Christian.

Her first impulse was to spin on her heel and ignore him. It was way too soon! She couldn't bear to face him! He was innocent of any wrongdoing, but still... It had been his *uncle!* And right under Christian's nose! *How could he have been so blind?*

The knock came a third time and something inside her broke. With trembling hands, she undid the security lock and slowly swung open the door. He stood on her porch looking so forlorn and dejected, the anger inside her died. This was no more his fault that it was hers. They'd both been innocent victims in Larry's evil game.

"I'm sorry," he whispered and tears glinted in his eyes.

"I'm sorry, too." Her voice was equally soft.

"You have nothing to be sorry for," he replied. "This is all on me. All this time, it was my uncle. My *uncle!* I can't believe it. I don't *want* to believe it! And yet, I have no choice."

He paused and shook his head. "He told me he was a recovering alcoholic. I was only nine at the time. I believed him. That was why he forbid me to go down to the basement. He said it was his peaceful place and helped him stay off the bottle. It turns out, he was lying. He was hurting little girls and one of might have been the girl who was my best friend. I can't believe I fell for it. I feel like such a fool."

She regarded him steadily and tears slowly filled her eyes. "I can't believe it, either. He got away with it for so many years! So many stolen children!

So many broken dreams! It just doesn't seem right."

Her voice cracked with emotion and before she knew what was happening, he'd taken her in his arms. Somehow, the two of them stumbled inside and fell down on the couch. They held each other, joined by tragedy, and cried quietly through the night.

The sun had just poked its head over the horizon when she and Christian stirred. The house was still and quiet. Daisy guessed that Emma was still asleep but that wasn't good enough. She stood and walked to her little girl's room and checked on her. When she returned to the living room, the sun was coming up and she saw that Christian had dark shadows beneath his eyes— eyes filled with love and tenderness and sadness as he watched her approach him.

"I'm not sure how you feel about me anymore, Daisy, but I love you so much it hurts. I understand if it takes you some time to rediscover the special place I held in your heart. I had nothing to do with my uncle's deeds and yet, I'll feel responsible for them for the rest of my life. All I ask is that you give me some hope that one day, you'll forgive me and see past what he did and love me like I love you."

Tears burned in her eyes. Despite everything, she did still love him and she'd already forgiven him—after all, he'd done nothing wrong. There was nothing to forgive.

"I love you, Christian. I won't deny it will take some time to come to terms with what has happened, but it wasn't your fault. I don't blame you for the actions and pain inflicted by your uncle. You're not responsible for him. If you're willing to give me time, I'd like for us to remain friends and in the future...who knows?"

His answering smile was tremulous and his eyes lit up with hope. "You don't know how happy that makes me," he whispered. "I want nothing more than to love you and Emma and keep the pair of you safe for the rest of your lives."

He leaned forward hesitantly and she willingly met him halfway. Their lips touched in the gentlest of kisses and with it, a promise for their future.

EPILOGUE

Christian emptied his pockets and reached down and took off his shoes. Tossing his things into the plastic bin provided, he pushed it onto the conveyer belt that would take it through the security screening. He'd entered the jail on so many occasions to see clients that he had the routine down pat and even nodded greetings to a couple of the corrections officers he recognized, but it still jolted him to realize he was there to visit his uncle.

It had been a month since Larry had been arrested and this was the first time Christian had brought himself to the point where he could visit. For weeks, he'd gone over and over in his mind all that had happened and tried to work out why he hadn't put it all together earlier. He'd lived with the man for most of his life. He should have known what his uncle was up to. If he'd been more observant and less obedient, he might even have saved some of those poor little girls.

Daisy had tried to comfort him, telling him his uncle's evil actions weren't Christian's fault. Just like it wasn't her fault her husband had been killed on active duty. She'd finally learned to accept the fact Pete's death was an unfortunate accident and Christian needed to come to the same realization where his uncle was concerned.

"You're right to go through, Christian," one of the corrections officers said.

Christian nodded his thanks and walked through the metal detector and out the other side. Collecting his things, he headed toward the visitors' room.

Uncle Larry was already seated when Christian arrived. He looked up at his nephew and smiled.

"Christian! I thought you were going to leave me in here to die! It's been a month already! What's taken you so long?"

Christian stared at his uncle in disbelief. *Could the man honestly think he'd forgive and forget what he'd done, just like that? Was he delusional?*

"I need you to represent me," his uncle continued with barely a pause. "The lawyer the court appointed me is useless. He couldn't even get me bail." Uncle Larry spat toward the floor in disgust. Christian held onto his temper.

"I'm not going to represent you, Uncle. In fact, I had to force myself to come here today. It's only because Daisy urged me to do so. I have so many questions and until I get the answers, I'll never have any closure."

Larry smirked. "Closure? Who needs closure? What kind of bullshit is that?"

Once again, Christian held onto his temper. His hands curled into fists and he slowly counted to ten.

"Why, Uncle? Why did you do it?"

Larry held his gaze and slowly shook his head. "Why not? It made me feel good."

Christian swallowed the bile that rose up in his throat. "Were you always attracted to little girls?"

"Yes. Right from the very start."

"And Nikki? Were you responsible for her disappearance?"

"Little Nikki," Larry murmured, his voice soft and dreamy. "She was so sweet."

Anger ignited inside Christian. His face went hot. "She was a beautiful, innocent child! She was my friend!"

Larry eyeballed him. "Exactly."

Christian reeled back in shock, hardly able to believe what he'd heard. "You mean, you targeted her for that reason?"

"You were much too close to her, Christian. You spent every waking moment by her side. We used to do so much together until Nikki came along." He shrugged. "She had to go."

His voice vibrated with anger. "You killed her, didn't you?"

Larry held his gaze. "Not on purpose."

Christian leaped up from his chair, intent on jumping on his uncle. With a sheer act of will, he managed to refrain. His chest heaved with the effort.

"Why? Why were you jealous of a little girl? She was my friend!"

"Like I said, she took your attention away from me, just like your mother."

Christian frowned. He stared at his uncle and his heart skipped a beat. "What do you mean, my mother?"

"Frank and I should have been the best of friends. He didn't like me much as a kid and he liked me even less when your mother came along. The two of them loved to roar off together in Frank's car, leaving me behind. It was a game to them. I'd hear them laughing all the way to the end of the street."

He took a breath and glared at Christian. "So, I fixed them. I made sure I had the last laugh."

As his uncle's words exploded into his brain, Christian gasped in shock. "W-what are you saying?" he stammered, not really wanting to know.

Larry chuckled. "You're a smart boy, Christian. You graduated top of your class. I'm sure you know exactly what I mean."

"You're talking nonsense. My parents died in a car accident."

"Yes. It's funny what can happen when you don't have any brakes."

Christian's eyes widened as a fresh wave of shock ricocheted through him. "You... You tampered with their vehicle? Is that what happened?"

"Nothing less than they deserved. They should have learned to be nicer to me. Perhaps they'd still be alive."

Christian's head was reeling. His uncle had just admitted to killing his parents. The man was more evil than he could ever have imagined. He couldn't believe they shared common blood, that for so many years, they'd lived under the same roof. He felt sick to his stomach. Unable to stay there another moment, he spun on his heel to leave.

"Christian! Where are you going? You have to get me out of here!"

Ignoring his uncle's desperate plea, he continued across the room.

"Christian! Come back here! After all I did for you! You ungrateful wretch! Don't leave me here! I'm sick! I need help! This is a sickness, something I can't control! Please, I need to be in a hospital, not in a jail. You know what they do to people like me in jail! Christian! Come back!"

His uncle's cries of desperation followed him all the way out. Eventually they were silenced when the heavy steel door closed behind him. He leaned against it, breathing hard, his mind in a whirlwind of confusion. He'd come there for answers and he supposed he'd gotten them, but it would take him a long time to accept that he had no blame in what had happened. He guessed he'd have to take his cue from Daisy and let her help him heal. Just like she'd let him help her. She was the only good thing to come out of all of this.

At the thought of his woman, he was filled with tenderness and slowly, the tension and rage inside him eased. Daisy would see him through this. She and Emma would be the family he never had. He already loved them like they were his own and would continue to do so until he drew his last breath and hoped they'd do the same.

Note To Readers

I do hope you have enjoyed reading Christian and Daisy's story. If you've enjoyed this book, please feel free to leave a review for Ordinary Evil at Goodreads and your favorite digital retailer. Every review is very much appreciated.

Receive a free book when you sign up for my newsletter if you would like to receive news on upcoming stories, release dates, book launches and other snippets. I love to receive feedback from my readers. Please feel free to contact me at chris@christaylorauthor.com.au

The Ties That Bind is the next book in The Sydney Legal Series.

Here's a sneak peek:

Trey Walker is living high on life. A successful lawyer at the prestigious Sydney Legal law firm, he's dangerously good looking, drives a vintage red Mustang and has his pick of women. Life couldn't get much better. Then Trey receives an urgent call from his identical twin brother.

Wade Walker's life has never been easy. He might have been born with looks to die for, but so far things haven't worked out. In and out of dead end jobs and keeping company with even more unsavoury friends, he can only look at his twin brother in awe and wonder how Trey got there.

One thing though, he's always been able to rely on Trey and the night of Saturday, September fifth is no different. In a tight situation, Wade calls on Trey and once again, Trey comes to the rescue. Only this time, things don't quite go as planned.

A woman has been raped and all of a sudden, the police are there, asking a whole bunch of questions. Trey steps up to the plate and is taken away in handcuffs for his efforts. Wade is left to wonder if his brother will be able to talk his way out of this scrape...

Kyiesha Munro has a reputation at Sydney Legal for being the best damned defense attorney in the firm, but her rise to the top has been far from easy. As the first aboriginal woman to be offered a place on the District Court bench, she knows too well what it takes to get there. When Trey seeks her out to represent him against rape charges, she's initially taken aback.

There isn't a woman under forty employed at Sydney Legal who hasn't heard of Trey Walker. With killer looks and a body that would get any woman's heart racing, he has a reputation around the office for being a ladies' man. Though Kyiesha isn't immune to his charm, she refuses to be taken in by a pair of sexy eyes...

But then she hears Trey's story and she's convinced he's been wrongly accused. She's determined to do all she can to prove his innocence and at the same time, protect her heart. Trey Walker is dangerous, but not in the way the police think. Of that there is no doubt.

CHAPTER 1

Wade Walker surveyed the dimly lit bar. It was crowded with people as it was most Saturday nights. The young and rich and beautiful, the people with more money than sense. Most of them didn't lift a finger through the week, except to attend their hairdresser or masseuse, but still, they liked to let their hair down on the weekends. Tonight was no different.

He moved on silent feet, working the crowd like a pro. A wave here, a smile there and for that pretty girl, a wink. She'd been eyeing him all night, although she'd made a fair attempt at hiding it. Seated at the bar beside an equally attractive woman he guessed was probably her friend, she'd stolen moment after moment to watch him and his progress around the room. He could tell she was intrigued by him. From his mannerisms and his popularity with the crowd, he was *someone*. She just didn't know who. And it was killing her.

Moving inexorably closer to her on the pretext for refreshing his drink, Wade narrowed the distance between them until he was only a few feet from where she was perched. His gaze swept over her long, tanned legs. They were crossed at the knees and one Christian Louboutin-shod foot moved up and down to the heavy beat of the music. The short black leather mini skirt was almost indecent as it rode high up on her thighs. It was coupled with a sheer black lace corset that was threaded with leather ties all the way up her back.

She looked sexy as hell and was the reason he'd chosen her out of a crowd full of strangers to while away a few pleasant hours. It was obvious she was out for a good time, and so was he. *What better way to spend a Saturday night?* He sidled up to the bar and pretended not to notice them. It was a trick he'd perfected long ago. A beautiful woman expected to be noticed, *needed* to be noticed. She was put out when things didn't happen that way and it usually only served to increase her curiosity about who he was and why he was ignoring her.

"Hey! Can I buy you a drink?"

Wade hid a surge of satisfaction and turned in faux surprise to the girls. He widened his eyes innocently. "Are you talking to me?"

The girl in the leather giggled and gave him a quick once over. He returned the favor and when his eyes once again met hers, there was frank interest in her gaze.

"Yes, I'm talking to you."

Wade turned side-on and leaned against the bar. The action pulled his Calvin Klein T-shirt tight across his chest, emphasizing the muscle tone beneath.

"What's your name?" he asked, his gaze never leaving leather girl's face.

"I'm Heather. And this is my friend, Naomi."

Wade dipped his head in acknowledgement. "Well, it's nice to meet you Heather and Naomi. I'm Trey."

Leather girl giggled again. "Trey. That's a nice name."

"Almost as nice as Heather," he quipped.

She blushed charmingly, but didn't drop her gaze. "So, do you want a drink?"

"Sure," he replied. "A rum and coke would be great."

"A rum and coke it is," she murmured and signaled to the barman.

The man scurried over. When Heather pulled out a gold American Express card, Wade knew why.

"My friend would like a rum and coke and get Naomi and I another bottle of Veuve Clicquot, please. We seem to have finished the last one."

"Of course, ma'am," the barman replied, reaching for the girls' dirty champagne glasses. "I'll bring you fresh ones," he tossed over his shoulder.

Wade raised a lazy eyebrow. "Fresh glasses? You must have been treating him right."

Heather shrugged insouciantly, like only the very rich can. "I do my bit to pay his rent."

Wade chuckled. "So, you're on the champagne. Would you like a little something extra to spice up your Saturday night?"

Both girls looked immediately interested. Heather shot him a smile. "Well, aren't you full of surprises?" She tossed him a sly look from beneath her lashes. "What did you have in mind?"

Wade reached into his pocket and pulled out a small plastic bag. "Just a couple of E's to get things happening. What do you say? Do you want one?"

He directed his question to Heather, but both girls eagerly held out their hands. They swallowed them dry without hesitation.

Not the first time they've done that, I bet... He kept the thought to himself.

What did he care if they took recreational drugs? Given their age and their access to ready cash, it was hardly surprising. Despite all the warnings on TV, no one took the risks seriously. Besides, the guaranteed buzz was worth any risk they might end the night in Emergency. He tossed an ecstasy tablet down his throat in full view of the girls. They giggled.

The drinks arrived and at Wade's suggestion, they moved away and found a secluded spot at a booth in the far corner of the room. Naomi reached over to refill her glass and sloshed half of it over the side. She giggled again and Heather joined in and then took the bottle from her. When Heather also sloshed the expensive champagne all over the place, the girls almost bent double with laughter.

They're already wasted... This probably isn't such a good idea after all.

The thought formed in his mind, but he struggled

to hold onto it. The E was already doing its job, along with is fourth rum and coke. He had a good buzz on, for sure and he was seated with two beautiful women, both looking for a good time. He might as well make the most of it.

"So, Trey!" Heather slurred. "What do you do for a living?"

He smiled and shrugged. "Who cares?"

Once again, the girls bent over with laughter. "You're so funny!" Heather gasped.

"Don't make me laugh so hard!" Naomi complained. "I'm going to pee my pants!"

This set both girls off again and Naomi slid across the leather seat and stood. "I need to go to the bathroom." She wobbled unsteadily on her feet.

"Do you want me to come with you?" Heather asked.

"No." Naomi hiccupped. "I'll be fine. Stay here and keep Trey company. We don't want him running off."

Heather giggled and slid closer to Trey. Her breast pushed against his arm and her bare thigh brushed against his Levis. His cock instantly hardened.

"Take all the time you need, Naomi. I'm not going anywhere." The last he said to Heather and she gave him a saucy smile and moved even closer. Another inch and she'd be in his lap. That suited him just fine.

He stretched his arms and let one fall across her shoulders. Pulling her in against him, he caught a whiff of her expensive perfume. It was rich and exotic and oh-so-erotic. His cock throbbed with need.

"You're a sexy little thing, aren't you?" he growled in her ear.

She giggled and pressed herself even closer. Her hand drifted to his crotch. Concealed under the table, she fondled him through the denim.

"You're not so bad yourself," she replied in a breathy little voice.

He shifted in his seat in order to get more comfortable and to allow her greater access to his cock. When she popped the button and undid his zip, he almost cried out in relief. Keeping up the pretense of normality, he picked up his glass and took a drink. All the while, her pretty little hand worked its magic.

"This isn't the first time you've done that," he murmured, taking another sip.

She gazed at him with eyes that were wide with innocence. "Are you complaining?"

"Not at all. I could tell the first moment I saw you that you were the one I wanted."

"And why was that?"

"You just had that air about you—one that screamed you wanted cock."

She smirked. "You're pretty confident, aren't you?"

"With reason."

"What about Naomi?"

He shrugged. "What about her?"

"She's a hot girl. Why did you pick me?"

"Yeah, she's hot, but you're hotter and I can tell you know just how to suck my cock."

Shock widened her eyes, but the smile remained on her lips.

Oh, yeah, she's interested all right. A few more drinks, another E and she'd be his.

"I don't feel so good. I'm going home."

Wade blinked and sat upright. At the same time, Heather removed her hand. Naomi stood beside their booth. It took him a moment to realize she'd spoken.

"Oh, I'm sorry you don't feel well," he managed.

"Are you sure?" Heather asked. "The night's only just beginning."

Naomi grimaced. "Yeah, I'm sure. I have a splitting headache. I can't bear to think what I'll feel like in the morning."

Heather made sympathetic noises, but when her hand stole once again inside his jeans, he knew she was glad her friend wouldn't be bothering them again that night.

"Do you need a ride somewhere?" he offered. He didn't have the least intention of driving her home, but they didn't need to know that.

"Oh, that's so sweet of you," Heather crooned. Her hand tightened around his cock.

Oblivious to all that was going on under the table, Naomi shook her head. "No, but thanks for the offer. I don't live too far away. I'll catch a cab."

"Are you sure?" Wade insisted. "Because I don't mind driving you. I haven't had that much to drink."

Naomi smiled, then winced and reached for her head. "I'm sure. I guess I'll catch you later,

Heather. Wade, it was nice to meet you. Maybe I'll see you around sometime."

Wade inclined his head in her direction and gave her his sexiest smile. "Maybe you will."

With that, Naomi turned away and Heather renewed her efforts on his cock. In the dimness, he reached out and fondled her breast, his fingers finding her nipple through the thin lace. He flicked at it with his finger and it pebbled beneath his attention. He smiled with satisfaction. Still, it wasn't enough.

His cock was throbbing so hard, it felt like he might come there and then. He wanted to feel her lips around him, bury himself in her wetness. His hand stole down across her thigh and slowly slid upwards. She moved, opening her legs to allow him greater access. Beneath the table, his hand shifted higher, up the length of silky smooth thigh. Higher still, until he found her center. Pushing aside her panties with his fingers, he slid one across her swollen flesh.

She gasped and tightened her hold on him. Her chest rose and fell with her breaths. With his gaze fixed on hers, he found her opening and thrust his fingers inside. This time, her gasp was audible and he leaned over and sealed it in with his mouth. His lips moved over hers and she opened her mouth and invited him in. His tongue slid in without hesitation and began to imitate the thrust of his fingers. She groaned and released his cock and her arms came up around his shoulders.

Dragging him toward her, she clung to his neck and kissed him like she was drowning and he was an oxygen tank. In a far distant part of his mind, he remained aware of his surroundings. They were in a public bar. They could hardly fuck each other here.

"Hey," he murmured and withdrew his hand.

She made a murmur of protest, but he ignored it and reached for her hands. Extricating them from around his neck, he gently set her aside.

She pouted. "What is it? Don't you want me?"

"Of course I do." He reached for her hand and mashed it against his erection. "Isn't that proof enough?"

He set her hand back in her lap and continued. "It's just that, I want to fuck you like there's no tomorrow and I can hardly do that here."

She looked around them and slowly nodded. "You're right." Her gaze came back to his. "How far away do you live?"

He smiled and shook his head. "Too far. But don't worry. I have a better plan."

She brightened. "You do?"

"Yes. Now, drink up and let's get out of here."

Leaning over her, he refilled her glass and watched as she emptied it in three swallows. He filled it again and she laughed. "What are you trying to do? Kill me?"

He laughed with her. "Of course not, silly. I just hate to see good champagne go to waste."

With a shrug, she finished the second glass. When it was empty, she shot him a triumphant grin. "Waste not, want not."

He grinned. "Exactly."

He reached into his pocket and pulled out the

small plastic bag. There were two tablets left in it. "Want another?" he asked, waggling the bag in her face.

She smiled. "Why not?"

He handed her an ecstasy tablet and took the other one for himself. Grinning madly at each other, like two naughty kids, he reached for her hand and together, they stumbled outside.

CHAPTER 2

The night was soft and balmy, but Wade barely noticed the warm spring breeze that gently lifted his hair. Tugging Heather by the hand, he led her down an alley that ran behind the bar. It was a place he knew well. This wasn't the first time he'd taken advantage of its many concealed places. She stumbled along behind him in her four-inch heels, laughing all the while. For her, this was a magnificent adventure.

He drew her deeper into the alley until he came to his favorite spot. Drawing her close, he pushed her up against the wall and immediately crowded her with his body. He placed his hands flat against the wall on either side of her head and kissed her again. Just the memory of her hand around his cock drove him wild. And then he remembered how she felt, how his fingers had slid in and out her opening. She wanted him as much as he wanted her and he couldn't wait to have her.

Opening his mouth, he pressed his tongue against her lips, demanding entry. She turned her head to one side and started to struggle against him.

"No! No, stop! I-I can't breathe."

"Hey, babe. It's all right. Just open your mouth. I want to see that pretty mouth wide open. Sucking on my cock. I'm so hard for you, I don't know how much longer I can wait. Come on, babe. Give it to me. You know you want to."

Heather's struggling increased and she managed to get her hands between their bodies. She pushed against him and when that had no effect, she began to pummel his chest.

"Please! Please, stop! I told you I can't breathe! I think I'm going to be sick!"

Wade cursed under his breath. *Great. Just what I need.* He released his hold on her just in time for her to turn her head and vomit all over the street. The acrid stench rose up to meet him, but he was drunk and high and pretty much beyond caring. The corset had loosened, exposing her breasts and once again, he grew hard.

She leaned against the wall, trying to catch her breath. "Do you have a handkerchief?" She asked.

He reached into the pocket of his jeans and pulled one out. "Here." He offered it to her.

She took it gratefully with a murmur of thanks and swiped it across her face. As soon as she was done, she offered it back to him, but he merely shook his head.

"Keep it." And with that, he put his hands on either side of her hips and drew her close.

Lowering his head, he went in for another kiss,

but this time, he went for her neck. She turned her head away.

"You've gotta be kidding!" she slurred. "How can you think of that now? All I want to do is go home and have a shower and maybe sleep this off."

Wade stared down at her in disbelief and slowly shook his head. "Oh, no you don't. You want this as much as me. A moment ago you were begging me for it! This doesn't stop until I say so."

Fear flashed through her eyes, but he was beyond caring. She had him so worked up, there was no way in hell he was going home until he'd gotten what she'd promised. Shoving her roughly against the wall, he jammed his leg between her thighs. She gave a little yelp, but he ignored it and bent his head and nuzzled her neck. She tensed, but he continued.

"Come on, babe. You know you want it. You were all over me back in there. You couldn't keep your hands off me.

"But-but that was before...before I was sick. Now I just want to go home."

She looked so forlorn, he almost gave in, but he'd already spent far too much time and effort on this one. He was damned if he was going home empty-handed.

"Shut up," he muttered, his voice rough.

Holding her against the wall with one hand, with the other, he popped the button on his jeans and unzipped his fly. Pulling out his cock, he reached between her legs and tore down her panties. They still smelled of her arousal.

"You say you don't want this, but your pussy says otherwise," he murmured.

In the next instant, he jammed his cock inside her and almost groaned in relief. She was warm and wet and slippery. She felt amazing.

With nothing more than his occasional grunt to break the silence, he fucked her until he was done. As he released her, she slid slowly to the ground. Her head, lulled to one side and he realized she was almost unconscious. He bent low and slapped her across the face in an effort to wake her up.

"How much did you have to drink, you little slut?"

She made a gurgling sound in her throat. Her eyes rolled back in her head and she slumped over.

He surged to his feet, panic flooding through him. "Fuck! Fuck! Fuck!"

What the hell was he going to do now?

The little slut passed out on him. What if she'd reacted to the E tablets. What if there was something in them that had set her off? He felt nothing more than the usual buzz, but what if there had been something else in hers? He couldn't let her die there, in the gutter.

With his mind racing a mile a minute, he did the only thing he could think of: he dialed his brother.

Trey Walker glanced out the window of his vintage red Mustang as he made his way slowly through the quiet Sydney streets. It was late, past one in the morning. There was hardly a soul about. He'd just come from the bed of one of his work colleagues, where he'd spent a very pleasant few hours. He knew better than to date his co-workers, but the truth was, he dated whoever he pleased. It didn't concern him that the relationship might turned sour and he would be forced to pass them in the corridors. After all, nobody broke up with Trey Walker. If anyone was going to do the breaking up, it would be him.

He thought of his comfortable king-size bed in his penthouse apartment overlooking Bondi Beach. He longed to lay his head down on his pillow get some rest. It had been a long week, with heavy court commitments and if Mary-Jane hadn't called him and begged him to come over, he probably would spend a quiet night in.

The sound of his phone ringing snagged his attention and he reached over and answered the call.

"Hey, Wade. You're calling late. What's up?"

"Trey! Thank God you're still awake! I need your help!"

Trey heard the urgency in his brother's voice and sighed inwardly. *What trouble had his brother got himself into now?*

"What's the matter, Wade?"

"Trey, you have to help me! You need to come fast!"

"What happened?"

"I can't tell you on the phone. Just get over here. Quick!"

Wade rattled off an unfamiliar address in an undesirable part of town and Trey pulled over long enough to enter it into his in car navigation system. Doing a U turn, he headed out into the quiet night. Arriving at his destination twenty minutes later, he drove past the alley and saw his brother standing over a girl. Parking the Mustang in an adjacent street and hoping like hell no one stole it, he climbed out and headed back. Upon spying him coming toward him, Wade's face flooded with relief.

"Trey! Thank God you're here!"

Trey sighed. "What is it, Wade? What's going on?"

Wade looked frightened. "I don't know! I met this girl in a bar. We had some drinks and got talking. She followed me outside. We started kissing and, you know, making out and then she kind of fainted. I don't know what happened. And now I can't get her to wake up. You've gotta help me!"

A surge of alarm went through Trey. "Help you, like hell. I need to help the girl!"

Hurrying toward figure slumped on the ground, he tugged out his phone at the same time. Dialing Triple zero, he waited for the call to connect.

"Police, fire or ambulance?"

"Ambulance! I need an ambulance!"

"What seems to be the problem?"

"I'm not sure. There's a girl. She... She's unconscious."

"Does she have a pulse?" the operator asked.

Trey knelt down on the side of the gutter and

felt for a pulse in the girl's neck. He was relieved when he found one. He spoke into the phone. "Yes, yes, she has a pulse."

"Okay, that's good. Is she breathing?"

Trey stared down at the woman on the ground and was relieved to see her chest rise and fall. He returned his attention to the phone. "Yes, she's still breathing."

"All right, then. That's a good sign. Stay with her. An ambulance is on its way."

With the immediate emergency now dealt with, Trey surged to his feet and turned on his brother.

"What the hell happened, Wade?"

Wade shrugged and stared at the ground. "I don't know. She seemed fine when we were inside."

"Well, she's certainly not fine now."

"Is the ambulance coming?" Wade asked.

"Yes. They're on their way."

Wade looked relieved. "Thank God! I didn't know what was happening! One moment we were both having a good time and the next she was on the ground."

Trey sent him a hard look. "Did you give her anything? The paramedics will want to know."

Wade shook his head. "No! Of course I didn't! What do you take me for?"

Unconvinced, Trey held his brother's gaze. Wade didn't flinch. Trey's shoulders slumped on a sigh. For all of their lives, he'd been rescuing Wade out of one bad situation after another. But they were no longer little kids getting into scrapes around the neighborhood. They were twenty-eight years old! When was Wade going to grow up?

The sound of sirens rent the still air and Trey sighed quietly in relief. At the same time, Wade's face filled with panic.

"I have to get out of here!"

Trey shook his head. "No way! You're staying right here. What if the paramedics have more questions? I don't even know who the hell she is. You're not going anywhere."

"Trey! You know how much I hate needles! I hate anything to do with hospitals! Ever since I had to visit Mom in there right up until the day she died... I can't stay, Trey! I just can't!"

Trey's hands clenched into fists as he fought hard to hold onto his temper. It was late and he was tired and he'd been in this position way too often of late.

"You're, you're not going anywhere, Wade. This is your mess. This has nothing to do with me!"

Wade slowly backed away from his brother, shaking his head. "I'm sorry Trey. I'm really sorry. I wish I could..." With that, his brother turned and ran.

Trey cursed aloud and thrust his hands into his hair. After all these years, he should be used to this by now. He'd lost count of the number of times he'd rescued his brother and lately, the incidences were becoming increasingly serious. Ever since Wade had fallen into the wrong crowd, his life had spiraled out of control. And now he had a girl who'd passed out in the street and God knows what the two of them had taken...

"Please! Please help me!"

The woman's panicked cry broke into his thoughts and he hurried over to her side. Cradling her head in his hands, he tried to reassure her.

"It's all right. The ambulance is on its way."

She blinked and opened her eyes and stared up at him in the dimness. A streetlight not far away cast his face in shadows, but still her eyes widened in recognition.

"*You!* Get away from me!" she cried, turning her back on him and huddling against the wall. "Help! Someone, please help!" she screamed, choking on tears.

At a loss, Trey stood and moved slightly away. No doubt she thought he was Wade. It was easy to mistake them, especially in the dark. After all, they were identical twins.

The Ties That Bind will be released on
28 June, 2018 and is available for pre-order
from your favorite digital retailer.

About the Author

Chris Taylor grew up on a farm in north-west New South Wales, Australia. She always had a thirst for stories and recalls writing her first book at the ripe old age of eight. Always a lover of romance and happily-ever-afters, a career in criminal law sparked her interest in intrigue and suspense. For Chris to be able to combine romance with suspense in her books is a dream come true.

Chris is married to Linden and is the mother of five children. If not behind her computer, you can find her doing the school run, taxiing children to swimming lessons, football, ballet and cricket. In her spare time, Chris loves to read her favorite authors who include Richard North Patterson, Sandra Brown, Kathleen E Woodiwiss and Jude Devereaux.

You can find out more about Chris and sign up for her newsletter at her website:

http://www.christaylorauthor.com.au